Better
in the
Mrning

Fern Ronay

Unlocking New Worlds

Better in the Morning
A Red Adept Publishing Book

Red Adept Publishing, LLC
104 Bugenfield Court
Garner, NC 27529
http://RedAdeptPublishing.com/

Print ISBN-13: 978-1-940215-64-8
Print ISBN-10: 1940215641

First Print Edition: April 2016

Cover and Formatting: Streetlight Graphics

For Howie

Chapter 1

"'OVERNIGHT PARKING. TEN DOLLARS AN hour.' That'll cost ya a pretty penny," Grandpa Sal said.

"'Intermix. Sale.' Look at that. They're havin' a big sale," Grandma Ant pointed out.

I sat between my grandparents in the back of a cab. It was impossible to go two blocks without one of them reading a sign aloud.

"'P.J. Clarkes.' I knew a P.J. years ago. Peter Joseph. The Scarpettas. Nice family. Owned a butcher shop."

I was squished, my knees high up as my feet rested on the hump in the middle.

"'Haru.' That's that sushi stuff you like, right, Veronica?" My grandmother patted my leg. "She enjoys her sushi, our Veronica. Gah bless her."

I studied the back of her head as she looked out the window. Her tight, white curls were sprayed in place.

"Why don't you try sushi, Antoinette?" my grandfather teased.

"Why don't you try it, Salvatore? Big shot. I'd like to see ya try that raw fish."

My grandfather laughed without making a noise, his chubby hands on his big belly as he cracked himself up. "With a little gravy, a little mozzarella, I might like it."

I smiled at the pronunciation. "Mootzadel," I whispered to myself. My non-Italian friends always laughed at how I said it.

"I'll believe that when I see it." My grandmother leaned past me to look over at my grandfather.

"'High-End Home Furnishings.'" My grandfather pointed. "That's where they try to sell ya a ten-dollar vase for a hundred dollars. They call it *high end*."

I laughed. I had bought a hundred-dollar vase there when I moved to the city.

"They got some beautiful stuff," Grandma Ant countered.

The cab stopped at a red light, and I sat up to stretch my back. My grandmother took that opportunity to push my long, brown hair to the side and rub my back. *The woman can't keep her hands off me.*

We were on our way to get cupcakes. I reminded myself that, technically, I was sleeping. And technically, I wouldn't really eat a cupcake. And technically, my grandparents were dead.

But it all felt real—the cupcake, the cab, my grandparents—and technically, that was all that mattered.

I looked up as the light turned green. *On our next visit, we'll be discussing the big news.*

"Right here," I told the taxi driver as we pulled in front of The Cupcake Shop on West Seventy-Second Street. We hopped out without paying the cabbie. That was how it worked there—the waiters and waitresses and taxi drivers on the other side never expected to get paid. Grandpa Sal would say that was why they called it Heaven.

As my grandmother and I surveyed the selection in the glass case, my grandfather tapped my shoulder. "They don't sell cannoli here? What kinda bakery is this?"

"Oh, um…" I looked up at the blackboard menu above the counter. "Nope. Sorry, Gramp. They have really good cupcakes though."

"Cupcakes? Who wants a cupcake?"

"Don't listen to him, Veronica," my grandmother said. "He's a pain in the coolie. What are you getting? I'm gonna have the red velvet. My friend Ruth was here with her grandson last week and said the red velvet is out of this world."

"I'll have the red velvet too," I said.

My grandmother ordered, and as we left with our cupcakes, she stopped at the condiment bar to grab a handful of sugar packets. Before I could say "Gram, seriously?" she shrugged. "What? For my coffee later on."

At restaurants, she used to take the leftover bread from the basket, wrap it in a napkin, and stuff it in her pocketbook. It mortified my mother and me, but she would say something about living through the Great Depression and 'going without' and 'It's a sin to let it go to waste.'

In front of the bakery, the three of us squeezed on a bench that I couldn't recall ever having seen there before. My grandfather bit into a cannoli that came from I don't know where. *Another reason they call it Heaven.*

The weather was perfect—a clear, crisp day, cool in the shade, warm in the sun.

I hope the weather is just like this tomorrow night.

"It'll be like this tomorrow night," Grandma Ant said. She was concentrating as she slowly pulled off the wrapper of her cupcake.

"I'm excited, but I don't want to say too much," I said. "I'm always afraid of jinxing things."

I thought I heard Grandpa Sal make a noise. A "Ha" or a "Huh." I turned to him as he furiously wiped cannoli powder off his sweater.

"Did you say something?"

"Me? No." He wiped faster.

I peeled the wrapper off my cupcake and took a big bite. I closed my eyes, enjoying the sun on my face as I worked my mouth around the perfect combination of cream cheese frosting and moist red cake.

"Look out!" my grandfather shouted.

I bolted up, eyes wide open. "What the fu—" I caught myself. "What?" I swiveled my head up and down the street and turned to look behind me toward the bakery, but I saw nothing amiss.

"That biker almost slammed into that car over there." My grandfather motioned to the street with a jut of his chin.

"Or ya could say the car almost slammed into that bike rider," my grandmother said.

"What? Stuff like that doesn't happen here." I looked around, still trying to find the biker and car in question.

"Nah, but ya know"—my grandfather held the cannoli wrapper in a tight ball in his fist—"close calls are always good reminders."

"Gotta brace yourself," Grandma Ant whispered.

"For what?" I asked.

"Ya know—this, that, the other thing. Life, Veronica. Life." Finished with her cupcake, she ran her pinky along each side of her mouth, making sure her orangey-red lipstick was still intact.

I looked back toward the street. Couples were holding hands as they walked. Young mothers pushed strollers.

"I don't want to hear that," I said. "Don't I brace myself enough? Aren't I nervous enough? Can't I enjoy this?" I let out a satisfying exhale. "Can't I enjoy this cupcake?" I sat back and took another bite. I chewed slowly when I felt my grandmother reach over and start smoothing my hair. I tried not to flinch or swat, but I did a sort of ducking motion instead. "Can you—can you—just please, Gram. Can I savor this in peace? Please."

"Oh, yeah, yeah, sweetheart, of course. You enjoy."

"You wanna have your cupcake and eat it too?" Grandpa Sal laughed. Grandma Ant laughed too.

I stifled an eye roll. "Yes."

"Good luck, my little *brasciole*," Grandpa said.

They know something. I can feel it, and I know I should ask them directly.

But I didn't ask. Instead, I did the only thing I knew how to do up to that point: I ignored that uncomfortable feeling and focused on my cupcake. *Cream cheese frosting is Heaven.*

Chapter 2

"Veronica, where does this one get filed?" my boss, Beverly, yelled, even though she was sitting less than twelve inches to my left.

Oh no. I should have known the answer to that because she had asked me to research it. But there we were, in the large conference room, with my yellow legal pad in front of me on the cold conference room table, sitting across from our new client. And I didn't know the answer. The reason I didn't know the answer was because I hadn't done the work. I had never researched it. But I couldn't say that. I thought of saying I didn't know the answer because I was too busy researching the ten other things Beverly had asked me to find. But I couldn't say that either because it wasn't even true. I hadn't researched any of it.

It was all Filamina March's fault... and Rosanna Zotto, the local newscaster... and HumanInterestStories.net for being so damned interesting and addictive. And me, I suppose. Yes, I was partially—or mostly—to blame for that moment. I was at a loss in front of our new client, and Beverly was about to explode.

"Veronica! Venue!" Beverly shouted. "Please. I think our new friend here would like to go back home to Queens sometime today." The glare from the sunlight beamed down through the conference room windows and reflected off the long mahogany table. I almost couldn't see Beverly's nostrils flaring.

What the hell do I say? Maybe I should make it look like I wrote it down somewhere in my yellow legal pad and I just can't find it. I bit my lip as I flipped furiously through the pages.

I could feel their eyes on me. Glancing up, I decided to tell the truth... well, not the *whole* truth, but the basic truth. "I don't know."

"What do you mean you *don't know?*"

Oh, frig.

Beverly rested her hands on the table and slowly lifted herself up from the chair. She shuffled out of the room without saying another word. Our new client, a middle-aged dog walker who was there to inquire about suing a cupcake truck that ran over his foot, didn't take his eyes off the "Basics of Personal Injury Law" brochure we gave all new clients.

I followed Beverly, or Grumpy Andy as I secretly referred to her. She looked like a female Andy Warhol with her stringy white hair and black turtlenecks, which she wore even on the warmest spring day. She was ten steps ahead of me, then twenty after I tripped over a box of paper near the printer and had to recollect myself. I straightened my suit jacket and dusted off a few paper particles.

I loved my suits, and I loved the long silver chain necklace I wore on this particular day that belonged to my Grandma Ant. Getting ready for work in the morning—selecting my outfit, jewelry, and shoes—was the best part of my day. Then it would pretty much go downhill from there. I pushed my hair back and readjusted my foot in my high heel. Looking put together and actually having it together are two completely different things. I was proof.

Exhibit A: Veronica Buccino, in her black pinstripe suit and towering black patent leather heels, certainly looks the part of the astute lawyer, but in fact, she has absolutely no friggin' idea what is going on. Ever.

Beverly was in her office pecking away on her keyboard when I arrived in the doorway.

Should I go in? Will she tell me to get the hell out? Probably. Maybe I should have brought my pen and pad. Kate would have remembered her pen and pad. But Kate would've actually done the research and had an answer rather than be in such a situation with Beverly. I had to give her that much even though she was a bitch.

Exhibit B: Kate Nogel—who, luckily for Veronica, is in absentia at the moment—is the other associate who works for Beverly. Unlike Buccino, Kate always has a friggin' idea as to what is going on. Always.

10

I went in and sat down quietly in one of the guest chairs with padded leather arms. The chairs in Beverly's office always looked comfortable, but I was never comfortable in her office.

I thought about saying I couldn't find the answer on venue, but that would imply I actually tried to find it. *Please don't ask me where I searched, or ask to see the links, or ask to see the actual history on my computer.* All she would have found were links to HumanInterestStories. net and Google searches for Filamina March. Honestly though, how could anyone have looked away from a story about a thirty-nine-year-old wife and mother from the picturesque suburb of Anton, New Jersey, whose arrogant plastic surgeon husband was going on trial soon for allegedly conspiring to kill her—on three separate occasions. Dr. March had been having an affair with a nurse from the office next door. The nurse was the one who had hired the three separate hit men. She was arrested after—

Beverly grunted. Her grunting didn't necessarily mean anything. She did that a lot. She also coughed incessantly, one of her other endearing habits. She was a smoker. When she wasn't grunting or sighing or breathing heavily, she was coughing.

I wondered why I let myself get so distracted. Maybe it was because the work we did was so boring, so tediously, hideously dull that I wanted to grab Beverly's fancy letter opener and stab myself in the eyes. *Right in the eyes, Beverly! You can't stop me. You've driven me to this. Now, look! Look at me, you—*

She grunted again and had a death grip on her mouse as she scrolled and clicked.

Okay, I won't stab myself in the eyes. I needed those eyes to read mind-numbing documents at my job for at least a little while longer— not much longer if my night went the way I thought it would, but a little bit longer.

I glanced around while she typed. Her office was so big, there was room for a credenza that took up at least five feet in length along the wall. A fake plant sat on one end, and a framed photo of a young girl in a soccer uniform was perched on the other. The girl was her niece, supposedly. The same picture had been in that frame since I started there almost five years ago.

Beverly's scrolling and clicking suddenly sped up.

Please don't ask me a question. I don't know why I even followed her in there, but I had to act as though I cared and actually wanted to do a good job and help out. That was what they paid me for. But after that night, it wouldn't matter anyway.

I'm going to marry John DelMonico. And then I'm going to quit. Hear that, Grumpy? I'm going to get married, maybe have a couple of cute kiddies and blow this taco stand. Ha! No more working on this dreary crap all day or living in fear of you. I will be free, free, freeeee—

"Schulster County!" Beverly shouted.

My heart thumped. "That's what I thought, but I wasn't a hundred percent sure so..." *Who am I kidding?*

"Schulster County," she repeated as she got up from her chair, hands on her desk for support. She coughed, grunted, and stomped past me. "I love doing your job, Veronica," she called over her shoulder as she marched back toward the conference room. "You know how happy that makes me?"

You know how happy it will make me when I give my two weeks' notice? You won't have to put up with me for much longer. I skipped a little as I followed behind her. *You're going to have to bark and cough in someone else's face, Grumpy Andy.*

Chapter 3

BEVERLY HAD ME RESEARCHING CASE law on default judgments until late that evening. But at five minutes past nine, I heard her grumbling and rumbling on her way to take a smoke break so I left the cases I'd printed out on her chair and made a run for it.

The reservation was for nine, and John was at least fifteen minutes early for everything. I thought about how one day, John would tell our kids, "Mommy was running late, and I began to wonder if it was the right time to pop the question. But when she finally arrived, I knew."

I blotted the sweat from my forehead and refreshed my lip gloss in the cab, then I looked down at my hands. I felt naked without my Grandma Ant's engagement ring—a small round stone, less than a half carat, set in a white-gold art deco setting. I usually wore it on my left middle finger.

But considering what I expected from John that night, I had taken it off so I had a clean canvas for a new ring.

When I finally got to Yoki Suru—our favorite sushi place near Union Square with the best tuna rolls and manju buns in town—I gave John's name to the hostess. She replied with a grin. "You must be Veronica."

She must be in on it. As I followed her through the dimly lit dining room with red-paneled walls and white tablecloths, my stomach flipped.

Crap! Am I going to be sick? No! Not tonight of all nights. Wait. No, that must be nerves.

No! That's excitement. Yes, I'm excited, not nervous. Holy shit, I need a cocktail.

I scanned the room and thought about how the other diners were strangers to us but were about to witness a special moment in our lives.

I wondered if John had asked my father. If he knew me at all, he would have ignored my father and asked my mother. Maybe he and my mother had even picked out the ring together.

I realized I was hunching my shoulders and clutching my tote bag tightly. My shoulders dropped, however, when we arrived at the table and I saw John, wearing a dark suit and talking on his phone. I took my seat and tried to make eye contact. Nothing.

I didn't know if I should open the menu. What if that was how he was doing it? With a "Will You Marry Me" sushi roll? I peeked at him from the corner of my eye as I opened the menu slowly. His dark skin, hair, and eyes all served as the perfect backdrop to his finely sculpted features. His straight nose and strong jaw looked as if Michelangelo had done the job himself.

I pretended to peruse the menu as I searched for other clues. The table was in a quiet corner, and there was no champagne or flowers anywhere.

"If they can cover it." John continued his phone conversation.

I never fully understood John's work chat. He used a lot of financial lingo I couldn't quite decipher. After all, I treated myself to a spa day when I made it through a semester of *Accounting for Lawyers* in law school.

John hung up. "You want a drink?"

"Yes. Pomegranate martini, please."

"You don't want to try something new?"

I realized I had a death grip on the menu. "It's my favorite." I released the menu and wiped my palms on my napkin.

"Okay. So... listen."

Oh, I'm listening.

"I'm getting transferred to London."

Huh?

I'd spent the night before last at John's place. The next morning while I was in the bathroom putting on my makeup before work, he stood in the doorway and said, "All right, listen. I just made reservations tomorrow night at Yoki Suru at nine." Then he looked me in the eye and said, "I want to talk to you about something. Okay?"

I'd thought it all made sense. He'd been acting strangely for weeks, taking phone calls in the other room and typing more and more of what I presumed were long emails on his phone. If I didn't know better, I would have thought he was cheating. But John was not the cheating kind. He was a lot of things—a workaholic, a sleep-deprived investment banker—but not a wanderer.

I had to catch my breath before I could talk. "Wait, what?"

"It's been in the works for a while. It's a move I feel I have to make to get where I need to be, to get to the next step in my career." He explained the situation very matter-of-factly as he bit into one of the complimentary edamame.

Where you need to be? Next step? You're already rich. "Oh. Wow. Okay. That makes sense." *No, it doesn't.* "Sorry," I continued. "I just need to take this in a minute. What does this mean for us?"

He sipped his water and opened his menu. "That's why I wanted to have a talk with you about it. In person."

He's proposing, but it means we're moving to London? Oh my God. Do I want to move to London?

"It's up to you if you want to come. I know you can't practice law there, but you could probably do something in consulting. And we wouldn't have to worry about rent for the first three months. We'll be in corporate housing. Then when we find a place to rent, we can split it."

"Up to me? What do you... what does that mean?" *Split the rent?*

"I mean, you know, up to you." He stared at me as if he were waiting for me to commend him on his great idea and how well he had thought it all out.

I looked away. *What about, "Veronica, I can't live without you. I'm moving to London, and you're coming with me because you're the love of my life?"*

Catch your breath. Do not say that.

"What about 'Veronica, I can't live without you. I'm moving to London, and you're coming with me because you're the love of my life'?"

Shit.

He smiled. "You're so funny, Veronica. You live in a dream world.

Who talks like that?" I clearly amused him with my silly talk. "You're like something right out of an old movie."

"I'm not trying to be funny. That's what any red-blooded American female would want, would expect. No one wants to hear, 'Hey, listen, come if you want. Up to you, ol' girl.'"

He shook his head and laughed harder. He returned to reading the menu and put his hand on my leg. "I know it's a lot to take in. Just think about it," he said as he perused the specials.

"Wait... so... you're not proposing?"

He looked up like a deer in headlights. "Proposing?"

"I honestly thought you were going to propose tonight."

That was when he let out a guffaw.

My throat tightened. I reached for my grandmother's ring with my thumb. *Fuck!*

I couldn't make eye contact with him. I studied the napkin on my lap. It wasn't just the London part. Or the "get a job in consulting" part. Or the "splitting the rent" suggestion. Or even the "up to you" part. But the idea that proposing to me was so absurd, so far from his mind, that he couldn't help but laugh? I'd never felt like such a fool.

I tried to catch my breath without appearing as though I was trying to catch my breath. I refolded my napkin three times.

Then, John did something that made it even worse, which I didn't think was possible. He placed his hand gently on my back. "Aw, babe," he whispered. "That's not—"

I held my hand up. "Please stop." I pushed him away and got up from the table. I ran out the door, into the street, and hailed a cab.

I barreled into my small studio apartment, not bothering to take off my heels before I dove onto the bed to cry into my pillow.

Wishful thinking, you idiot. How could you be so silly? So stupid?

I let it all out until my face and neck were hot and sticky, and I made a mental note to change my pillowcase.

When I finally rolled over, I automatically reached for my grandmother's ring again and realized I might as well put it back on.

I walked to my jewelry box and lifted the lid, then I lifted the tray to look beneath. I looked in my work tote bag, my smaller purse, my wallet, the inside pocket of my tote, the inside pocket of my purse, and the inside pocket of my wallet. I emptied the contents of my tote then shook it furiously upside down.

Fuck!

I searched every drawer of my desk, every drawer of my nightstand, my bathroom, and every drawer of my vanity.

Fuck!

I grabbed my wallet and keys and ran out the door, then caught a cab heading in the direction of the office. *Dear St. Anthony, please come around, something's been lost and something needs to be found.* Grandma Ant taught me that prayer.

It was past eleven, but the security desk was used to lawyers at Ellis & Blackmoore coming and going at all hours of the night. I raced to my office, and the motion sensor lights flicked on as I walked in. I scanned my desk, searched every drawer of my desk, the bookcase, the filing cabinet, the floors beneath my desk, and the area behind all of the wires. Then I raced to the ladies' room and searched every stall, the sink area, and the floors.

Fuck!

That was when I slid down the wall of the office bathroom in my fancy suit and cried. Again.

Chapter 4

"VERONICA! VERONICA! VERONICA BUCCINO!" BEVERLY usually gave me all of about one and a half seconds to respond to my name then called it again... and again... and again.

Do you call your husband's name over and over again? "Nathan! Nathan! Nathan!" I didn't actually say that.

"You're an hour late on the Hines motion. One hour. Time is money. How are you going to make that up? Want to write me a check? Make it certified."

This time before Beverly barged into my office, I didn't have to quickly shut the browser on HumanInterestStories.net. Instead, I was drafting an email to Jada, my eyes aching from only three hours of sleep the night before:

Subject line: My left hand is bare.

Message: He didn't propose, and just in case that wasn't bad enough, I lost my grandmother's ring. Cherry on top. I was going to call you, but I'm a mess. I can't meet for lunch because Beverly is a beast, but can I come over after work tonight?

At least I was typing when Beverly entered my office, so hopefully, it appeared as though I was working.

"Veronica Buccino." Beverly stood in front of my desk, breathing loudly and making other unattractive noises.

Beverly, did you honestly think I would finish researching and making your changes by eight a.m.? Not to mention the fact that you're going to change most of them back to what they were anyway. And we'll go back and forth this morning over a final product that we basically had finished. I really think this is a sick game you play in order to drive me crazy, and it's working.

I didn't actually say that. What I actually said was, "Uh… I'm almost done."

Beverly started snapping her fingers. "What does 'almost done' mean? You're already late, and now you're going to make me wait around for you? You don't think I want to go home sometime tonight?"

No, I don't think you do. I don't think you want to go home to Nathan. You're here when I arrive in the morning. You're here when I leave at night. Don't you ever go home to Nathan? Does Nathan really exist?

I didn't actually say that. What I actually said was, "I'm sorry. I need a little bit more time. I couldn't find the answers to the questions on insurance. I'm still looking."

"Stop looking. Print what you have and give it to Kate to find the answers. You should have come to me an hour ago. You could have started working on a new case already. There's only so much time in the day. Can't you feel it slipping away?"

Not really. Every minute here feels like an hour.

"Every hour is the chance to work on a new case. More cases, more money. You like money, don't you? You like getting paid?" As she left my office, she called over her shoulder, "Someone has to pay for those ridiculous shoes you wear."

How have I done this for almost five years? I had thought about switching firms. I had sent my résumé to headhunters, but the response was always the same: "Sorry, but the market is tough right now." Or my personal favorite, "If you'd gone to a top-ten law school, it'd be easier to get you interviews." *Oh, well, that's helpful.* And now, I was stuck working for Grumpy Andy so I could pay off the loans I had to take out to afford my non-top-ten law school. *Friggin' fantastic.*

I walked down the long hallway, past the secretarial cubes, toward Kate's office. Her door was shut as always. I knocked lightly then gently turned the knob. She gave me her usual blank expression and went back to her computer, clicking her mouse.

I explained what was needed for the Hines motion. She listened, I assumed. I couldn't be sure she was ever actually listening to me. She hardly ever made eye contact. I waited for a response as she stared at her computer screen, her blond-highlighted hair slicked back into a severe bun. *Why a bun, Kate? Every single day, a bun. Why? Let your hair down, literally.*

She finally said, "How much time could it take to research this one issue?" It sounded more like a statement.

I didn't think I was going to win Lawyer of the Year, but she had no right to sound so patronizing. Stone-Cold Kate Nogel was only one year ahead of me. When I started at the firm, I'd thought we might end up being friends. I had imagined Kate and I going to lunch and commiserating about Beverly. By the second day, I realized that was never going to happen.

While Beverly was indeed often cranky and always gruff, at least she had a personality. Kate, on the hand, was ice. But one thing she and Beverly did share was the uncanny ability to make me feel incredibly stupid.

Kate's comments, in particular, really stung. In meetings with Beverly, she had said things like, "Do you want to give *her* a deadline so we get this done on time?" "Do you want me to give *her* a template?" "Do you want me to review the complaint before *she* sends it to you?"

I wanted to scream, "I'm sitting right here!" But I never did.

While Kate clicked her mouse and tapped her keyboard, never taking her eyes off the screen, I opened the file in my lap and pretended to search for something.

Where did you grow up, Kate? How many brothers and sisters do you have? Do you have a boyfriend? Do you live with a roommate? I know you live on the west side because I heard you tell Beverly you were late once because the A and C trains were stalled. Will I ever get answers to these questions? These are things I'd really like to know. Don't you want to know about me and my boyfriend, who's moving to London and not proposing? Aren't you curious about me? About anyone? About anything?

"I don't know how to help you," she said, still staring at her computer. "This motion is not that complicated."

If it's not that complicated, then why can't you help me? I thought but didn't say.

She sighed as she moved her mouse and clicked. "Maybe you should take another look at the issue and really think about it, do some more research, then talk to Beverly."

Really think about it? That helps so much. Thank you, Kate.

She never finished a conversation with an "Okay?" or "Let's touch base later," or even "Goodbye." She would just go back to doing whatever it was she was doing, usually staring at her computer or crossing things off in the old-fashioned day planner she carried around the office all day.

What the hell are you always crossing off and jotting and circling?

I clumsily picked up the loose papers from the Hines file and walked out of her office, shutting the door gently behind me. I took the long route back to my office to avoid Beverly and slammed the file down on my desk.

Talk about a rock and a hard place. Kate wouldn't help me, and I couldn't ask Beverly because she'd told me to ask Kate. Approaching either of them again would result in nothing but disgust for my lack of understanding of the insurance issues.

Then the phone rang. "Veronica Buccino."

"Uh, hi, Ms. Buccino. My name is Trista Hines. I received something from your office... from you... saying that you are now representing Pat Stephens and if I don't pay $15,714.19 by today, there would be a motion filed and um..."

"Hi. I don't mean to cut you off, but if you have a lawyer, I can't be speaking with you. Have your lawyer call me."

"I don't have a lawyer."

I sighed. "Then yes, we will be filing a motion today"—*as soon as I figure out how to address the insurance issue*—"on behalf of Mr. Stephens as a result of the auto accident where he suffered physical injuries, unless you answer the complaint or unless you have the money?"

They never had the money unless they borrowed it. Usually, we would try to seize whatever assets the defendants had before they filed bankruptcy so that our clients could pay their medical bills.

Such uplifting work.

"No. I don't have the money. And I, I don't know how to answer that complaint, whatever that means..."

Is she crying? Oh, come on. How awkward is this? It's bad enough I feel dumb at my job. Do I also have to feel sorry too?

I got up and shut the door with my foot as I held the phone to my ear. "Mrs. Hines, I'm sorry. I really am."

"You don't have to call me *Mrs.* Hines." She was trying to catch her breath. "My husband left."

I sat back in my chair. "My boyfriend left—well, *is* leaving."

"Huh?" She seemed to stop crying.

"He's moving to London."

"Mine moved in with my hairstylist."

"Oh no. I'm sorry." *That really sucks. I bet the pickins of good colorists are slim in*—I picked up the file—*Millersville, New York, wherever that is.* "Did you find another salon?" *Did I really just ask that? I need to get off the phone with this woman right now and get back to work—filing the motion against her.*

"No. My sister does it for me now. Money is tight, you know, with him leaving and the kids and now this. Sorry to hear about your boyfriend. Do you think he has another... love in London?"

Yes. Money. "No. No, that's not it. How many kids do you have?" *Stop asking questions. Hang the hell up.*

"Two. A boy and a girl. Seven and five. They're smart too. I wish they weren't so smart. My son asked me this morning if his father is current—he even used the word 'current'—on his child support payments. I wanted to say, 'Not by a long shot. Your father is a deadbeat.'"

"What did you tell him?"

"I said 'Oh, well, the courts are working it out.' He knows though. And he knows his father's supporting Misty's two kids now too. I try to say 'He's your father. He hasn't forgotten about you.'"

"That's hard. I'm sorry."

"It's all right. But the thing is, the food truck is my only source of income."

Trista's Treats sounded like a solid business, one I would patronize if I were an office worker in Millersville. The file indicated Trista bought desserts, mainly cupcakes, from area bakeries at a bulk discount, picked them up in the morning, and sold them in office parks around lunch. Too bad that one day while Pat Stephens was visiting his cousin for lunch, Trista's Treats ran over his foot, costing him a visit to the ER and weekly physical therapy.

But what could I do? As Beverly would say, if you break our client's bones, you can say goodbye to the things you own. "Listen, Trista, I'm sorry. I wish there was something…"

I could hear her quietly blow her nose.

"And I have cancer."

Holy crap.

"I have breast cancer," she said, her voice hoarse.

I dropped my head in my hand. "I am so sorry" was all I could say.

"I'll be okay. I believe I will be. I have to be. My kids won't go live with him and sure as hell not with her. I'll be damned. It's stage one. So instead of paying for a lawyer to fight over child support, I've been paying the clinic. I had it all worked out. I had a budget. I have no payments on the truck, paid for it outright and then fixed it up with my sister. The business was booming… and then—" She didn't finish the sentence, but I knew the rest: my client's foot ended up under the wheel of her cupcake truck.

"I feel awful about Mr. Stephens," she continued, "and I'm sorry he has to go to physical therapy now. I learned my lesson and got insurance right after it happened. I'd buy all kinds of insurance if I could, like liability in case someone gets sick on a cupcake but, well, money is tight. But I will not file bankruptcy, and I will not stop working. I will do this. I was just wondering, maybe, can I pay Mr. Stephens in installments?"

I didn't have my grandmother's ring to fiddle with so I started twirling the phone cord. *A payment plan? Like a settlement agreement? Not Beverly's style.*

"I just need to keep the truck," she continued. "The business is going great. Honestly. It's just… other things came up, just when I thought I could have my cupcake and eat it too. Ha!"

I stopped twirling the phone cord.

Maybe it was the toll from almost five years of the Beverly-and-Kate treatment. Maybe it was my own breakup. Whatever the reason, the fact is that I did something so completely out of character, so brave and so risky, that I don't even think Jada, the person I knew with the least amount of fear, would have done it.

"Trista, I'm going to speak to my client and get back to you. Maybe we can work out a payment plan. Again, I'm really sorry. You're going to be okay."

"Thank you. I know. Well, I hope so."

I hung up. *Speak to my client? Who the hell do I think I am? A real lawyer? I'm Beverly's minion. What am I doing? How is this going to work?*

Everything—and I mean everything—went through Beverly. Even Kate had never dealt with the clients directly. I'd met clients in person, and I'd met the client in question, the limping Pat Stephens, briefly the day before, but I hadn't exactly made the best impression.

Should I just call him? No, I can't do that. Beverly will find out. But what will happen to Trista? She will definitely lose the cupcake truck and possibly her other car if she has one, and her house too. But Beverly's way can't be the only way. Still, if I go directly to the client, and we actually do this settlement, and Beverly finds out, I'll surely get fired—but that is—only if Beverly finds out.

There was a knock on my door. My heart sank even though Beverly never knocked and Kate never visited.

Luckily, it was Margaret, our group's secretary. "Hon, John called while you were on the other line."

Of course he did. He had been calling and texting since the night before. And I hadn't been calling back or responding. *One thing at a time.*

I hung my head in my hands and rubbed my sore eyes. Then, I called Pat Stephens.

"Hey there, Miss Veronica," he said after I identified myself.

It was a quick conversation, but he was rather receptive to the idea of a settlement agreement with a payment plan. "What would I do with a cupcake truck anyway?"

I didn't point out that he wouldn't actually end up with the cupcake truck in his driveway, but that it would get sold at auction, and he would get whatever it was worth, which most likely wasn't even close to the amount he'd originally sued for. Still, all he wanted, as he'd pointed out, was enough to cover his physical therapy. So I just said, "Cool!" *So professional.*

I hung up the phone and smiled for the first time that day. *Ha! Fuck you, Beverly. And fuck you too, Kate. You're not going to scare poor Trista Hines like you scare me. She has enough to deal with.*

I gave the Hines motion to Beverly to review as she'd asked me to do. Then when she asked me to file it so we could begin the process of repossessing Trista's assets for Mr. Stephens, I did the complete opposite. I stuck it in the bottom drawer of my desk. I called Trista and said, "Deal. My client wants to work it out."

We handled hundreds, maybe thousands, of personal injury cases. Beverly just happened to have very little to do that day, a slow Friday. That was why she'd been fixating on Trista Hines's case. Normally, we were spitting out legal filings as though we were a factory. *Is she going to remember the Stephens v. Hines case a week from now? Not a chance.*

As I stepped out in front of Jada's apartment building, I noticed a penny on her stoop, a shiny penny. I left it, of course. I never picked them up.

I took the elevator up to her floor. She was waiting for me at the end of the hallway, dressed in oversized gray sweats, already holding a glass of wine, her long, brown hair in a sloppy ponytail at the top of her head. "What the fuck is going on?" she shouted down the narrow, dimly lit hallway.

I walked past her, through the door into her apartment, ready to collapse on the couch, cry it out, and tell her everything that had occurred in the past twenty-four hours. Then it occurred to me that her boyfriend might be over. "Is Mark here?"

She assured me she was alone, and I sank into her big beige sofa, where I started from the beginning while she got more wine from the refrigerator. Unlike my refrigerator, which was dotted with magnets like Betty Boop as Marilyn Monroe, Jada had only one. It said, "Fucks to be given today: zero."

"Wait. London?" she asked. "You don't just decide to move to London like that. He must have been talking about this with work for at least a couple of months, right? He never gave you any clue?"

I shook my head. I knew Jada wasn't trying to make me feel worse, but she did—only because she was one hundred percent right.

John and I had been dating for two years. I would have thought he'd have talked to me about moving to another country long before it was definite. I would have thought he'd have filled me in, gotten my perspective, gotten my opinion, asked how I felt, all before it became final. That was what couples did. *But not us, I guess.*

Jada sat down on the coffee table in front of me and uncorked a bottle of pinot grigio. "Listen, I know it's so fresh—too soon to be saying this—but you'll get over him. It'll get better."

"Get over him? Are we even broken up?" I sat up. "I mean, it just happened last night. I haven't picked up his calls or replied to his texts because... I don't know. Maybe he'll go out and buy a ring, and we'll be engaged by Monday... But would I move to London? London?"

"London's nice," she said. "But yeah, it's a lot to absorb. It just happened. You've got to soak in it a bit."

"I'm soaking." I looked down and played with the fringe on one of Jada's decorative pillows. "On the way in here, I saw a penny."

"Who are the pennies again? Grandma?" She poured a glass of wine and handed it to me.

"Both Grandma and Grandpa. It started with Grandpa. He left them first because he died first, but it's both of them now." I immediately wished I hadn't said anything about the penny. I knew Jada wasn't a believer, and the last thing I felt like doing at that moment was explaining, or even worse, defending.

"How'd that start again?"

"It's silly. It's—" I was saved by the bell when my phone started ringing.

It was John. I didn't pick up.

Jada and I stared at the phone, and then she bent forward and filled my wine glass to the top. "I can't believe you went to work today. You should take some time off. You can't deal with Beverly and Kate right now."

"Oh God, work." I sank deeper into the sofa as I reached for my grandmother's ring to twirl around my finger. Habit. "I got this call today." I told Jada about Trista.

"You are so fucking going to get canned." Jada was in my face. I could see flecks of old mascara on her cheeks. "Are you nuts? Beverly will definitely find out."

"She might not. We have a million cases." I gulped my wine. "Don't stress me out any more than I am."

"Sorry." Jada backed away.

We sat in silence for a while, sipping our wine.

"Isn't it amazing, all that can happen in twenty-four hours?" I asked. "Yesterday, I thought I'd be getting engaged and eventually quitting my job, and now I'm not getting engaged and really can't afford to be risking my job. But this woman, oh my God, this poor woman."

"You're a good egg, Veronica Buccino."

"Thanks. But I want to be a married egg. And I want to fly the Beverly coop. I'm cooped up there. Do chickens fly? Am I a chicken egg?"

"I don't know. Listen. I have to ask this. I know Beverly and Kate suck, but are you serious when you keep saying you don't want to work at all? I mean, why would someone so smart, a lawyer, not want to work? Why'd you go to law school?"

"I was young and stupid. I needed the money. I thought being a lawyer would be a ticket to freedom, money, and happiness. I was wrong."

Jada laughed quietly.

"It's not like I'm nineteen and not studying because I'm banking on marrying rich," I continued. "I did the studying. I did the hard work. I did it all. And you know what? It sucks. I'm done. Ready for the next chapter. No more stress. No more Beverly. No more dull legal work. I just want to get married and read HumanInterestStories.net all day."

Jada sipped her wine. I had an inkling she felt the same way, but she would never admit it. Maybe she didn't want to read news websites all day, but she definitely didn't want to be doing what she was doing. I knew that much.

We had met on our first day of law school at Fordham and now worked at separate law firms, oddly enough, in the same building in Midtown. Back in law school, our lives were pretty much dominated by a study group during the week and a bevy of dive bars on the weekends. Now, our lives were pretty much dominated by work—during the week and on weekends. At least we were only a few floors away from each other and able to meet on a moment's notice at the Starbucks downstairs. I usually vented about Beverly or Kate, and she vented about whoever was on her nerves that day, which could range from Mark, to her family, to her boss, to her coworkers, to the salad guy who had put white button mushrooms in her salad when she'd asked for portobello.

I checked my phone. John hadn't left a voicemail.

"You know, for a while, I've had this feeling—this weird feeling—that something was going to change, something was going to happen. Something big." I sighed. "Well, I was right. Something big happened."

"Aren't you the one who always says everything happens for a reason? So, maybe there's a reason. A good reason."

"I know." *No, I don't.*

"Hey, think about the penny. Your grandparents are all around you. They're going to make sure you're okay."

"I know." I appreciated her effort.

Jada was my best friend. I was an only child, so I didn't know what it felt like to have siblings, but she felt like my sister. We even looked alike. We were both one-hundred-percent Italian, five foot three with brown eyes and long, brown hair. We were mistaken for sisters a lot. I could tell Jada anything, and I knew she would always tell me the truth.

"What do I do now?" I asked her.

"Make it final," Jada said. "That's what you have to do now. I'm sorry, Veronica, but I think it's over. London? Just like that? Come on. Seriously. Come the fuck on."

And sometimes, the truth hurt.

I swallowed hard to push down the lump that had formed in my throat.

"Where's Mark?" I asked.

"Working."

While she was so confident, and so very blunt, about what I needed to do regarding my relationship, I often wished she would take her own advice. Jada had been dating Mark Marlone for two years and, for two years, had been unsure about whether she was in love with him.

"He's working a lot again? Poor Mark. I think he works more than the both of us combined, which I didn't think was possible."

"Yeah, but we're going to Florida for the weekend after Easter," Jada said.

She was letting me have the stage tonight. Top billing in the "Relationships Shouldn't Be This Difficult" show. I took it.

I also took her blunt advice. I knew I had to call John back. I knew I had to make it final.

But first, I had to finish my wine. And get a good night's sleep. I would call him the next day. Wasn't everything clearer after a good night's sleep? Yes, it was. I had always wondered why that was true, but it was.

Unfortunately, I didn't get a good night's sleep. After another night of tossing and turning, I splashed my face with ice-cold water and went to work with a pounding headache and sore eyes.

I knew the first thing I had to do that morning, aside from calling John, was deal with the Trista Hines matter.

I started drafting an email to the client.

Dear Pat,

Pat:

Hi Pat!

No. No exclamation points. What am I thinking?

Oddly enough, I was a fifth-year associate, and I'd never written an email to a client before. Since everything went through Beverly, she did all of the emailings and the phone calls. Kate and I just did the grunt work. I'd also never drafted a settlement agreement before. Luckily, Jada had and was going to give me a template to use. I couldn't ask Beverly to review it or approve it, but the client and Trista were the only ones who had to sign. *So screw you, Beverly.*

"Veronica!"

Oh crap.

Beverly was in my doorway, sweating and antsy. It was seven thirty on a Saturday morning. *Does she live here? Doesn't she ever want to be at home with Nathan?*

"Meeting in my office at eight. We got about twenty new referrals late yesterday."

"Okay." *Please don't look at my computer screen. Please don't say, "Let me see your history. How many times have you been on HumanInterestStories. net today?" She's done that before. I had to show her. Did I have a choice?*

"What are you working on now?"

"Um, the Soto case."

"The interrogatories?"

"Yes."

"Did Kate review it yet?"

"Not yet. I'm going to give it to her as soon as I'm done." *Or as soon as I'm done working with our client to settle a case that I pray you'll never find out about.*

She suddenly became interested in something outside my office window. She trod closer and closer. Her orthopedic shoes squished with every step.

Please don't look at my computer screen.

"What the hell are they protesting now?" she asked.

"I think it's to free Tibet."

"Freaks. Nathan gives every freak on the corner a dollar bill. I can't walk down the street with him anymore and watch him give our money away. Drives me crazy." She turned back around and looked at my screen for a split second then stomped out the door. "Eight o'clock! In my office!" she called over her shoulder.

After the meeting with Beverly and Kate, I finished the email to Pat, laying out all of the terms of the agreement.

Then, I did the thing I'd been avoiding. I sent a text to John. —Hey. Are you up?—

It was the first contact I'd made with him since the dinner debacle two nights prior. I knew he was up. It was only nine, and he was up at six every day of the week.

I put my phone aside, took a deep breath, and was about to take a HumanInterestStories.net break when my phone rang.

"Hey." John sounded amused. *What the hell is he so happy about?*

"Hi." I took another deep breath. *There's not going to be any air left in this office soon.* "Listen, about your offer, you know, it being 'up to me,' well… I can't. I just can't." I cleared my throat. "Thanks but no thanks."

Take that. I sat up straight, gripping the phone cord.

"I kind of figured that was your answer, considering how you left it and, you know, how you left."

I sank back down in my chair and let go of the phone cord as my entire body tingled in shame at the flashback of running out of Yoki Suru.

"Listen," he said. "I'm almost finished packing, and I have a few things of yours."

Packing already?

He continued. "A pair of shoes, a sweatshirt, a ring, if you want to come pick them up. I'll be here all day, getting stuff ready to be shipped."

The ring! Yes! Two nights before the non-proposal when I stayed over at his place, I must have put it in "my drawer" in the bathroom after he told me about the dinner reservations for the next night and needing to "talk about something." Oh, thank you, St. Anthony!

"Leave everything with your doorman." I tried to sound unaffected. "I'll pick it all up in a few hours as soon as I can leave here. Put the ring in an envelope. I trust Felix, but put it in an envelope anyway. Please. Thank you."

I hoped my cool demeanor would sting, asking him to leave my things at the front desk rather than going up to his apartment to see him to retrieve it all.

He sighed with an "Okay" that sounded sad enough to give me some satisfaction.

By the time I got out of work and went to John's to pick up my stuff, it was already dark out. The day had succumbed to an I'll-never-get-a-cab-in-this-rain kind of night.

Taxi after taxi passed me. I walked up another block and finally saw a cab pull over and turn its light on, but a blond woman beat me to it. I don't know what made me do it, but I did something I'd only heard of other people doing.

"Excuse me," I called out. "Can I ask where you're headed?"

"Sixty-Ninth and Broadway." She was tall and thin, wearing a shiny black trench coat with a belt. Her blond hair was highlighted to perfection and slicked back into a low ponytail. She was carrying a cake box.

"I'm going to Seventy-Second and West End. Do you mind if we share?"

"Sure!" she yelled over the rain that was getting heavier and louder. She motioned to me as if to say, "Come on in."

After thirty blocks, two avenues and two exclamations of "I'm sorry. I can't believe I'm pouring my heart out like this," the blond woman knew that John and I had been dating for two years, that I was twenty-nine, that I'd never been to London, and that as appealing as the thought of quitting and moving to London with him was, I needed more than a "Come if you want. It's up to you."

That didn't leave much time to hear about her, but I learned she lived in my neighborhood and was on her way to a friend's for dinner. I also learned she had another friend who'd dated a guy for five years before moving to Santa Fe with him. Then when the friend turned thirty-six, her boyfriend broke up with her and married a twenty-five-year-old yoga instructor/pottery maker.

When the cab arrived at her stop, she said, "Good luck," as she shifted the cake box to her left hand and opened the door. Before she shut it, she leaned in from the rain, looked me in the eye and said, "You're doing the right thing."

When Felix, the doorman, handed the shopping bag to me, I immediately grabbed the envelope and tore it in half only to see a flash of silver fall out. I fished it out from the bottom of the bag. It was a spoon ring I had purchased at a store in Soho. I loved that ring, but it wasn't *the* ring. My heart fell.

I rested the bag on the floor and kneeled down, making sure to check every inch of it. Nothing. I put my head in my hands.

"Are you all right there, Veronica?"

I stood. "Was there anything else, Felix? Another envelope maybe?"

He shook his head as he scanned his desk. "No, no, that's all John gave me. Want me to call him?"

"No, it's okay. Is he home?"

Felix buzzed me through the glass doors to the elevators.

John and I would have to meet face-to-face. I wanted to retrieve my grandmother's ring, and I also didn't want my exit from Yoki Suru to be the way he remembered me.

"Hey," was all he said when he answered the door.

"Thanks for leaving these." I lifted the bag and put it down in the foyer. "Mind if I do a double check of 'my drawer' in the bathroom?"

"Sure." He had clearly just gotten out of the shower. His hair was wet, and I saw beads of water on the back of his neck as he let me in and shut the door. I wanted to hug him and kiss him and smell the scent of his aftershave.

"And if you find anything else of mine, just leave it with Felix," I said.

"Okay." He walked past me, down the long hallway into his living room.

I followed and made a left to the bathroom. I frantically opened and re-opened every drawer. Nothing.

I knew it couldn't be anywhere else. I had my designated drawer, though sometimes it overflowed to another drawer, but that was it.

Fuck.

I went back to the living room, where he was taping a moving box shut. All of the artwork was off the walls. His fancy rug that he'd bought in Turkey was gone. There were several other boxes lined up in such an orderly fashion that it looked like a sample sale or a really high-end yard sale. Leave it to John to transform the packing process into a well-oiled machine.

I glanced down at one of the open boxes along the wall. It was filled with expensive shoe boxes, neatly stacked. In another one, I saw a Rolex watch case.

"You're shipping your watch?"

"No. I'm going to wear it. That's just the case." He was focused on the stack of books he was organizing. He read each cover then placed it to either the left or right side of the box in front of him.

I remembered when he bought me a watch. It was a year into our relationship. I had been wearing my old one from law school with all its nicks and scratches. I still liked wearing a watch. I was old-fashioned that way. I'd been planning to buy myself a new one, particularly after John commented, "Why do you still wear that beat-up thing? You're a lawyer now. Get yourself a nice watch."

"I know." I stared at it. "I haven't found one I liked yet."

"And some of that jewelry you wear is loud. You wear that to the office?"

"Hold it. All of the jewelry is my grandmother's. Off the table. Not up for discussion."

"Well, you need a new watch."

"Yes. I know."

Not long after that, we were cooking dinner in his apartment when he asked me to get an onion from the crisper. I opened the crisper and found a Gucci box inside.

"What do you keep in that Gucci box in your crisper?" I asked as I shut the refrigerator door and placed the onion on the counter.

John stopped chopping. He turned toward me and looked me in the eye. "Veronica, honestly?" He smirked. "Why don't you open it?"

Lightbulb. "Oh, okay." I opened it. It was a gold Gucci watch. For me.

Even though it wasn't what I would have picked for myself, I appreciated it and tried to wear it often. But not every day. Not like my grandmother's ring. I found it hard to swallow as my throat constricted at the thought of the ring. I consciously shifted my focus back to John as he continued to organize his reading material.

I hadn't told him I'd lost it. I was hoping he wouldn't notice I wasn't wearing it. I didn't want to hear what a "Hurricane Veronica" I was—

always tripping, falling, and misplacing things. He was right about that. I just didn't want to hear it at the moment.

"So, do you have that much more to do?" I asked as I watched John go through another stack of books. Lee Iacocca. Jack Welch. Some finance textbooks from his MBA days at Columbia before we met.

"The movers are coming Friday, and they're going to pack up the rest of my stuff, all the kitchen stuff, bathroom, pantry. I just have to figure out what I want to keep."

I watched his triceps flex each time he flipped through a book. He looked great in suits but just as handsome in a white T-shirt, jeans, and barefoot.

John was exactly the type of man I'd dreamed my husband would be when I used to play "bride" at my grandparents' house. At seven years old, I would march down my grandparents' stairs with my mother's old veil on my head, holding a chipped porcelain flower figurine that my grandmother had kept in the bathroom. My grandfather would play the role of celebrant. He would never get up from his recliner, but he would put the footrest down and sit up straight, pretending to read from the Bible.

Whenever it came time to announce the new Mr. and Mrs. Whomever, my grandfather would always come up with a different name. They were always Italian. *Mr. and Mrs. Marino. Mr. and Mrs. Rizzo. Mr. and Mrs. Vicidomini.*

"I can't believe you're leaving already," I said.

"Well, it's been in the works for a while." That made my throat constrict a little too. *A while?*

He had moved on to a box of wine glasses and reached for the roll of bubble wrap.

I wonder if he'll go to any wine-tasting events in London. We'd met two years earlier at a charity wine-tasting event. John had been in line to taste some sort of Australian pinot noir, and I had stood in line behind him with a napkin full of mini spinach quiche.

"Did you know they had wineries in Australia?" He turned around and smiled at me.

I had a mouthful of quiche and couldn't answer him, so I shook my head.

"I thought it was all Vegemite and koala bears there," he said.

I tried to laugh, but my mouth was too stuffed. I suddenly became aware of my napkin full of even more quiche and held up my hand to offer him one.

"Nah, I'm good. Gotta keep the palate clean." He winked.

What guy winks? No, rather, *who winks and doesn't make it look sleazy?* John.

"I'm Veronica." Finally able to talk, I reached to shake his hand.

I could tell from his handshake that he had nice hands. I also got a peek at them when he scratched his neck. *Yup, nice ones.* Thick fingers, but not too thick. Veiny, but not too bulging. Perfect, masculine hands. The kind I would like brushing up my lower back as I walked into a restaurant or stepped into the back of a cab.

We talked our way through five different Australian wines and a few from New Zealand. When Jada came over to inform me that everyone was going to regroup at a champagne bar, I politely asked her to get lost. She obliged. She was a good friend.

Eventually, John and I left together and found ourselves sharing falafel at the hole-in-the-wall next door. It had definitely been the first and last time John had ever set foot in such a place. I must have suggested it, though I couldn't remember much after the fourth Australian wine except that I couldn't wait for our first real date.

"Are you going to miss me?" I blurted out now as I picked at a piece of duct tape on a box in front of me. *Did I really just ask that?*

He raised his head and, for a second, I thought he looked sad. "Veronica, I told you that you could come, that you *should* come. I actually thought you'd be happy, excited, to quit the job you hate. But it wasn't good enough for you. You had to storm out of the restaurant like a child."

"Wasn't good enough? You said it's 'up to you.' I don't want to hear it's 'up to you.'" My voice was louder than I wanted it to be.

He walked away from the box of books and came toward me. He reached out to hug me, but I backed away. *I don't want your pity! Again. Say the right thing!* I headed for the door, hoping to leave before he saw me crying. *Oh no, not another tearful exit.*

"You're going to regret this, John. You're going to seriously regret this," I blubbered. "You will never, nev-er, find another girl like me."

Tears flowed. *Get out of here now, you idiot. This can't be the way he remembers you!*

Then, in true "Hurricane Veronica" form, I tripped over the wire of a lamp that was on the floor in the hallway.

Ouch. My knee took the brunt of that. That'll be attractive. Fuck.

"Are you all right?" John was behind me, but I didn't look back.

And now my nose was running. A lot. *This was not the look I was going for. And definitely not the exit I was planning.*

I opened the door and limped as quickly as I could to the elevator with my hand under my dripping nose. When I got to the lobby, I couldn't make eye contact with Felix. I hurried to the corner and hailed a cab. I was halfway home before I realized I'd left the bag with my stuff.

Of course. Cheeri-fucking-o.

Chapter 5

I LOVE THIS DRESS I'M wearing. I don't actually own this dress, but it's adorable. It was white with red polka dots, a thick red belt, and a full A-line skirt. And I had on the cutest red kitten heels to match. I never wore anything lower than three-inch heels, but I liked these, and they were easier to vacuum in than what I normally wore.

The vacuum I was pushing was heavy. But I couldn't use both hands because I was holding a martini in the other.

"Where are we?" I asked my grandparents, who were sitting, arms crossed, on the couch in front of me. I had to holler over the roar of the vacuum.

Grandpa Sal shrugged. "Some house," he called out with his hands cupped over his mouth like a megaphone. "Nineteen fifty-five."

1955. Hmm.

It was a small house. The living room had long yellow curtains. The couch was beige, and the lamps had fringe in the same color yellow as the curtains. That was another great thing about my dreams, or visits, or Heaven, or whatever they wanted to call it. We could be anywhere.

The way my grandparents had explained it was when a person died, he passed to the "other side," but it wasn't actually a physical place. Our souls continued to exist, but just on another plane, in another place, a place called the "other side." And us living souls could actually still communicate with our loved ones who had passed over, but when we were awake, that hardly ever happened. We were too guarded and distracted when we were wide awake, walking around, living our lives. The best "visits" and communications happened when we were asleep, when our hearts and minds were more open and receptive to "meeting," even if we didn't remember the meeting when we were awake. And together on that different frequency, on a different plane that was not a physical place, we could be anywhere, any time in history.

"Oops!" I spilled a little bit of my martini on the carpet.

Grandpa laughed. Grandma shook her head.

I couldn't find the off switch on the vacuum. "Is it in the front?" I whispered to myself and tripped over the cord. Another spill.

I was about to yell "How do you turn this thing off?" when I noticed Grandma Ant standing behind me. She pressed some lever with her foot before sitting back down.

"So, this"—Grandpa Sal made a hand motion as if he were slowly twirling invisible pizza dough with one hand—"This is what ya want?"

I took a sip of my martini then grabbed the vacuum handle and swooshed the quiet vacuum and my hips to the left. "Yes!" Swooshed to the right. "Yes, it is."

"Ya'd rather do this than be a lawyer?" Grandpa Sal asked.

Swoosh left. Sip martini. Swoosh right. "That is correct."

"And what if your husband leaves you? What do you do then?"

I stood up straight. "He won't. I'm not going to marry an idiot like my father."

I searched for a reaction, but their faces betrayed nothing.

I looked down at what I was wearing and ran a hand over my pretty dress. I noticed Grandma's ring, even here, was gone.

I'd been through every drawer in my apartment and in my office, but I still couldn't figure out what I'd done with it. It had to be around somewhere. I felt naked without it. I felt awful that I'd misplaced it, let alone that it was all for nothing.

"And this is what you want to do all day?" he asked.

I went back to swooshing. "Yes." I giggled.

I caught Grandma Ant pinching the bridge of her nose.

"What's so great about this?" he asked.

I paused mid-swoosh. "I realize we're in the nineteen fifties here, probably because I'm always saying, 'Why couldn't I have been born fifty years earlier?' So, thank you for this fun jaunt. But I could do this in the present day. Why not? It's a free country." I grabbed the vacuum cleaner handle and pushed hard. Swoosh. Sip.

"I hate to repeat myself, ya know, but what's so great about this?" Grandpa Sal asked again.

Ugh. He doesn't get it after all. I grabbed one of the heavy dining room chairs and dragged it into the living room. "Let's see. Well, for starters, no one is yelling at me. There's that. No one is making me read hideously boring documents. No one is telling me to 'really think about it.' Oh, and no one on the other end of the telephone is begging me to please not have my client seize their only source of income and force them into bankruptcy. Should I go on?"

I straightened my back against the stiff chair and continued. "I don't know if you see what I go through on a daily basis, but—"

"Oh, we see. We see everything, my little *brasciole,*" Grandpa Sal said.

I cleared my throat. "What do you mean by *everything*?"

"Well, we know you don't vacuum." Grandpa Sal laughed. He looked like a happy Buddha statue with his big belly and smiling face.

Grandma Ant piped up. "Let's see. How do we explain? We see the things we want to see, the important things. We don't see the private things. We don't care about that stuff. Believe me, honey."

Thank God. Not that I'm some sort of floozy, but no one wants to think their dead loved ones have seen all of the drunken hookups of their 20s. Mortifying.

"Can you see the future? Do you think I'm going to get fired for helping this Trista woman?"

Grandma said, "We can see things as if we're a fly on the wall. But we can't see the future like a crystal ball."

"That's too bad." I took off my kitten heels. They were starting to pinch.

So I guess they couldn't tell me if John would regret not proposing once he got to London. But it didn't even matter at that point. He had made his feelings clear. It was over.

I took a deep breath, hoping to loosen the sudden tightness in my chest.

"Let's talk about the fella, John," Grandma Ant announced.

"What's there to say?"

They watched me as I traced and retraced a small half circle with my right foot in the thick carpet.

"All right, one thing at a time," she said. "Let's talk some more about your job."

"Do we have to?"

"Oh, *Madone*, then we might as well go back to sitting here in silence while you vacuum," Grandpa Sal said. "Maybe you can dust a little too. Bake a pie while you're at it."

I scrunched my nose. "Nah."

"Got over that fast," he said under his breath.

"Ya know what the next step is—" Grandma Ant continued as if I'd said yes, I wanted to talk about my job.

"Listen, I've looked for other jobs," I interrupted, "and yeah, I'd be around different people, but they'd probably be grumpy too. Worst of all, I'd still be lawyering. Day in, day out, in an office, in front of a computer, trying to decipher the most uninteresting crap. As far as jobs outside of law, well, you know, I'm not a trust fund kid. I'd love to do something different, but I have bills to pay, school loans, rent." I pushed one of the kitten heels with my toe. "It's a vicious circle."

The vicious circle actually began a long time ago. I became a lawyer because when a girl grows up in a you-can-do-anything-boys-can-do generation and in a town considered to be "working class" with teachers who declare you to be "really smart," you're brainwashed into becoming a doctor or a lawyer. It was as simple as that. I sucked at math and science, so I became a lawyer.

"Veronica, what I'm hearing... and seeing, now correct me if I'm wrong, is that law is not your *passion*," Grandma Ant said, holding out her hands like she was serving something on an invisible tray.

I stared at her. *Is she serious? I could say something sarcastic right now, something absolutely hilarious. All three of us would probably laugh.* But I didn't. Anyone who lived through the Great Depression, who put the extra sugar and bread from a restaurant in her pocketbook, wasn't exactly concerned about finding her "passion." I appreciated her effort. The least I could do was play along. "It's not," I said.

"So you have to find your passion," my grandmother said. "That's the first thing. Being a housewife is not a passion."

If I'd been born in the thirties or forties, no one would have batted an eyelash if I wanted to be a housewife, but just because I was unlucky enough to be born a few decades later, I was expected to wave the proverbial "girl power" flag and endure a stressful career. *How unfair.*

Now I am working around the clock at a job where I have to decipher the most mind-numbing documents known to man all day and dream of not working. I'd call that more powerless than girl power.

"Then my passion is being a stay-at-home mother." I gave her a look that said, "Are you going to argue with that?"

She ignored it and continued. "But there is one way to find out what your passion is. Ya ask yourself this one question. Ya ask, 'If you didn't have to work...'" she spoke slowly.

I like where this is going.

"If ya had all the money and time in the world, how—how exactly— would you spend your days?"

"Easy," I said.

"She'd eat bonbons all day," Grandpa called out.

"No."

"I mean cupcakes. Ya like those cupcakes at that place."

"No! I'd be on HumanInterestStories.net all day."

"Well, there ya go." Gram said, as if we'd just solved all of my problems. "You should be doing something like that."

How anticlimactic. "If only it were that easy," I said. "Honestly, Gram, I know you're trying to help me, but that's just not realistic. Believe me, I've thought about this. I think about this all the time, actually. There's only one way out. I had a plan, and now my plan has gone to sh-crap."

It might not be the most feminist plan, but it's my life. It's the perfect plan for me. I could spend my days doing exactly what I wanted: reading and engaging in subject matter that actually interests me. And eliminate the stress in my life. And be married to the man I love. It would have worked out so perfectly with John if it, well, had worked out.

"What'd ya say about realistic?" Grandpa Sal said under his breath as he put his arm around the back of the couch.

He doesn't understand. Grandpa Sal was a barber his whole life. He had to work to help his family and couldn't go to high school. He started apprenticing for a barber at age thirteen. For fifty years, aside from his time in the war, he gave haircuts and shaves and basically talked all day—sports, politics, if you could have only one dessert for the rest of your life, would it be a cannoli or a tartufo? Of course, he didn't understand. It sounded like a pretty fun way to spend each day to me.

"Don't you think there should be more housewives?" I turned to the dining room table and wiped my hand across the top. "It's a lost art. Didn't you love being a housewife, Gram?"

"I worked! I worked as a secretary for Havish Printing Company for fifty-three years!"

"Oh, yeah. I forgot."

"And I still did the cleaning and the cooking and the wash." She said each of those with a slice through the air. The cleaning. Slice. The cooking. Slice. The wash. Slice.

"Okay, I get it, Gram. But you never had to work like I work. It's different now. And you liked your job. You were the fastest typist in North America."

That was my grandfather's joke. My grandmother didn't go to high school either. She had to quit school to help at her parents' bakery, but a neighbor had a typewriter and taught her to type. She was so good at it that she got a job at a printing company after my grandparents got married. She'd always boasted that she typed eighty-eight words per minute.

My grandfather would say, "An hour?" And then, "Oh, that's right. You're the fastest 'typer' in the Northeast," or in North America or Newark. He switched it up. She would ignore him and swat the air in his direction as if she were swatting a pesky fly.

"What if you could switch jobs with that pretty Italian gal?" Grandma Ant asked excitedly. "That newscaster, Rosanna Zotto?"

"She does have the best job," I said. "Still, that all sounds very nice in theory, but I'm just going to quit the firm and go work in news? You see everything, right? Can you see that I have bills to pay? Can you see that I'm stuck?"

"I don't see shackles on ya anywhere," Grandpa Sal said.

"They're invisible. But believe me, they have names. Sallie Mae is around my wrists, and Bloomingdales Credit Department is on my feet. I mean that almost literally. On my feet every day. Three inches or higher."

Grandma Ant shifted around until, pointing her finger, she yelled, "What about the biggest one? The one named Veronica!"

Grandpa Sal turned sharply toward her as if something suddenly caught his eye, and grinned.

Gram was clearly proud of herself for that one. She cocked her head and stared at me. "Baby steps, Veronica. You have to stop thinking you're stuck and do some things you're afraid of. Ya hear me?"

"Okay," I said. *Maybe I should just shut up and listen. My own plans that I was once so confident about haven't exactly panned out.* "How would I go about this? Logistically, I mean."

"Rome wasn't built in a day," Grandma Ant said. "But you start by, let's say, taking a news reporting class. Look on your computer."

"Okay." I exhaled. I stared down at my toes, making an impression in the thick yellow carpeting.

"We're going to make a deal," Grandma said. "If you do that, we'll tell you where the ring is."

My mouth dropped.

"We see everything." Grandpa Sal laughed.

"I cannot believe we have spent this entire visit talking about work. I cannot believe this wasn't the first thing we discussed. I have been sick over it!"

Grandma Ant shook her head. "It's fine, Veronica. Don't worry about it. Really. It's in a… safe place. But listen, the first thing you have to do is take this news class. Deal?"

"What the hell—heck—does one have to do with the other?" I stood up. "I've been stressing about this ring on top of everything else. Please! Just tell me where it is."

"We will do no such thing," Grandma said. "Sit back down."

I slowly lowered myself onto the dining room chair, digesting what had just been revealed.

"Deal?" Grandma asked.

I sighed. "Deal."

"A little more oomph, Veronica," she said. "Ya get points for enthusiasm in this game, ya know."

I stifled an eye roll and showed my teeth in an exaggerated display of excitement.

Sure. Why not? I'll take a class. Use up all my spare time.

"Don't you think a news reporting class would be fun?" Grandpa asked. "You can talk to other people face-to-face about all that stuff you're always reading on that website. And you can pretend you're Rosanna."

I had to laugh at this. "Yeah," I conceded. "I guess I should do something outside of work. Something fun."

"Atta girl. So get started on this first assignment." Grandpa Sal clapped his hands once. "The first of two."

"Two? What's the other assignment?"

"You'll see."

"When?"

"When the time is right."

"Are you serious?"

"As a heart attack."

He died of a heart attack. I didn't think that was funny. He found it hilarious.

Chapter 6

THE WROUGHT IRON CHAIR WAS cold against my thighs as Jada and I sat across from each other at one of the bistro sets lined up along Bryant Park. It was our usual lunch spot on warm days.

"Okay, so it's final." Jada chomped on a cucumber from her takeaway salad. "Does your mom know that you're, you know, technically broken up?"

"Not yet. I still can't believe it myself," I said. "My mom will be easy. It's my dad that I'm not looking forward to informing." I moved my fork around in my salad. "I have to go to my Aunt Marie's next week for a family party. I'll call her before I get there and tell her to tell my father and everyone else so no one asks where John is."

"Good plan. Put everyone on high alert," Jada said. "I'll tell Lauren and our other friends. Have you made it F-B-O?"

"What's that?"

"Facebook Official."

"Oh. I don't have my relationship status on Facebook. John's not on it so I didn't do that 'In a relationship with so-and-so' thing. Believe me, I wish he were on Facebook because then I would actually check it every day and stalk him. I never check Facebook. Or Instagram. Or any of that stuff."

"I check it at least twenty times a day," Jada said matter-of-factly.

"Twenty times a day?"

"At least. I have to make sure the mean girls from high school are still saddled with ten kids each and never leave home. It makes me happy."

Somehow, I couldn't picture anyone being mean to Jada, or her taking it.

"So, how do you think your dad will react?" she asked. "He might have a breakdown."

"I know." I sighed.

My father left when I was six years old. John said on more than one occasion that I came from a "broken home." I thought that was quite retro and a little tacky, but I never said anything. I reasoned that was his way of being kind, using it as a euphemism. He had a "nuclear family" and was proud that his parents had been married for so long.

My father had had an early mid-life crisis that took the form of a car he couldn't afford and an affair with a waitress at Bella Notte, the restaurant he'd owned from the time he was twenty-five years old. It was a typical inexpensive Italian place with wood-paneled walls, framed posters of Capri and Florence, and those faux leather banquet chairs with metal legs.

The waitress—who I called The Perm for obvious reasons— eventually became my stepmother. Her real name was Carla, but I never called her that. Of course, I never called her The Perm either, not to her face anyway. Come to think of it, I never called her anything. I only saw them at occasional family parties and on holidays. I did once ask The Perm where she got her hair done because the curiosity was killing me. I couldn't imagine what salon still permed people's hair. Turns out, she did it herself. That was believable. She said my father would "carry on" about the smell every time she did it, which was also believable.

My father was a big fan of John's. Jada was right—he might take it hard.

I had to change the subject. "What are you and Mark up to this weekend?"

"Nothing." She stabbed her salad.

"Have you been following the Filamina March case?" I tried a new topic.

Through a mouthful of lettuce, Jada said, "Are you kidding me?"

She was not a fan of HumanInterestStories.net, and she was definitely not on the forum with a handle like RosannaZotto2.0 like me.

"Rosanna is going to interview Filamina," I said. "I can't wait."

"What's the story again? Her husband tried to kill her?"

"Well, conspired to. He's a plastic surgeon and was having an affair with a nurse, and the nurse supposedly tried to have her killed three times. Three times! Filamina thought it was strange when she heard a gunshot outside her house one night, and another night, and another night. They weren't exactly marksmen. Then, the nurse tried to hire a fourth person to finally finish the job when she was caught. She ultimately struck a plea deal. Twenty-five years instead of life if she testified against Dr. March. She says he was in on it. And he's so damn arrogant. He said Filamina would be dead if he were in on it because he succeeds in everything he does."

"Of course he was in on it," Jada said, popping open the top on her Snapple.

"So, Rosanna is going to interview Filamina, and I'm dying to see it because she's still married to him and standing by him one hundred percent. Could you imagine? Even after a grand jury indicted him, she's not wavering. She filed for divorce after it was revealed he'd been having an affair but then dropped it. How could she forgive him? Who would stay with a cheater? I have fifty million questions." I sipped my water. "Rosanna has the best job."

"When do you have time to go on these websites?"

"When do you have time to go on Facebook?"

"True." Jada laughed.

"Have you ever thought of taking a class at MediaHouse?"

"What's that?"

"It's downtown," I said. "They have classes. I think I might take a news reporting class."

Earlier that morning, I had marched into the office, slammed my tote bag down next to my chair, and Googled "news reporting class New York." I spent the rest of the morning researching a class, in between answering calls from Beverly and procrastinating doing my real work. I finally had it narrowed down to one and was ready to hit "Purchase Class" when Beverly barged into my office and threw a case file on my desk. I kept the window open all morning, waiting for the courage to hit the "Purchase" button.

Jada stopped chewing. "Did you say a news reporting class? Why? For what?"

My jaw clenched a little. "Why not?"

"Okay," Jada said slowly. "Don't you have enough on your plate at the moment?"

"Maybe it'll get my mind off things."

"What would make you even think of that?"

"I don't know. I was looking into it this morning, and I want to do it. I think it will be fun. I want to try something different."

"Interesting."

Interesting? That's all she's got? Can't she cheer me on a little? Would that kill her?

Before I could say anything else on that subject, Jada said, "Hey, I saw a penny in the work elevator when I came down here. I thought that was a weird place for a penny. I thought of you."

I forced a smile.

"I don't get it though," she said. "Like, your grandparents are literally the pennies? Does that mean I can come back as a two-dollar bill if I want?"

No, they are not literally the pennies. The truth was my grandfather used to save Indian head pennies and give them to my mother. After he died, she started finding pennies, regular pennies, all over the place, but mostly in odd places—like in drawers where there was never loose change, or behind the TV stand when she was cleaning. It made her start thinking, and one day when she was alone in the car, she spoke to him out loud. She said, "If it's you, send me three shiny pennies, and I'll believe." And the next day, at the deli counter where she would get her morning coffee, were three shiny pennies.

"No, it's just their sign for me," I said.

I planned to end that subject right there, but she still looked confused so I continued. "It's their way of communicating without a human body. Energy doesn't die. They can use their energy to send us signs. And I think the signs mean, 'We're here. We're with you. You're not alone.'"

"Ah, okay. I think I get it. So maybe after all that's happened, they're here to kind of say, 'Hey, this shit shall pass.'"

"I think the saying is 'This too shall pass' but yeah."

"So why don't you pick them up and save them? Like, here's Granny in a jar. She's up to ninety-eight dollars and forty-three cents!"

"Because I'm not the only person who believes in this. What if it was meant for someone else or for you? I'm sure your grandparents are watching over you."

Jada contemplated this. "I don't know. My mom's parents died before I was born. I never knew them."

Doesn't matter.

"So these are your mom's parents, right?" Jada asked.

"Yeah."

"That's right. Your dad's parents never leave Florida."

"Not in twenty years." My father's parents were still alive but they had moved to a "senior living development" in Tampa when I was nine and never left. Literally, they hadn't left Florida in twenty years. They missed my law school graduation. My Aunt Marie had said, "Too bad Grandma and Grandpa can't be here to see this," as if they were dead. I always found this funny, but not as funny as Jada did.

When we got up from the chairs to head back to the office, Jada said, "Let me know if you want to drown your sorrows in wine tonight. I've restocked since your last visit."

"Thanks." I dumped my mostly uneaten salad in the garbage. "I think what I really need is another good night's sleep. I've been running on adrenaline and fear for days. I guess the finality of John helped me sleep like a baby last night. I need to wake up again like I did this morning."

"Boring."

"Drink with Mark," I said.

"Boring," Jada said, and although it was a little mean, we both laughed.

When I walked into my Aunt Marie's house a week later, the first person I saw was The Perm. She was standing over my aunt's kitchen table, rolling thin slices of salami for the antipasto platter. She wore skinny black pants and a leopard shirt cinched with a gold belt.

"Hi there," she said when I came through the back door into the kitchen. She gave a little wave but didn't attempt to kiss me on the cheek. She still didn't know how to greet me even after twenty-three years.

And I still didn't know how to greet her either. I waved back. "How are you?"

"Oh, I'm good. Really good." She beamed. "Ya want to pick a little?" she asked, pointing with her hot-pink acrylic nail to the dish in front of her.

"No, thanks. Is my father here?" I wanted to get it over with. If Aunt Marie had done her job, I knew he knew about John, but I was still anticipating a conversation.

"Yeah, he's in the living room," she said.

"Oh! I brought a cheesecake," I said, remembering the white bakery box in my hand. "Where should I put it?" I couldn't see an inch of counter space.

"I love cheesecake, especially from anywhere in New York City. Let me take that from you. I'll ask Marie where she wants me to put it for now. I like your blouse. Pretty color."

The Perm once described a skirt I was wearing as "very classy." She also referred to law school as "going back to college." "How do you like being back at college?" she would ask.

I would respond, "It's graduate school, not college."

She also couldn't understand why I didn't have a car in the city. She drove two blocks to her nail salon and to the supermarket. And when I had to work over Thanksgiving weekend last year, she'd asked genuinely, "Can they do that?" *Uh, yes, they can.*

"Thanks." I handed her the cheesecake box and headed into the living room.

I was immediately struck with the stink of cigar smoke. I waved the air in front of me and saw my father sitting on one of the two recliners in the living room, a short cigar between his teeth, one of a dozen that "a very prominent customer" had given him. He clearly hadn't brought one for Uncle Al, Aunt Marie's husband, who was sitting next to him in the other recliner, cigar-less.

I kissed Uncle Al first. "Hi."

I waved the smoke out of the air again before I kissed my father hello.

I turned back to Uncle Al. "Are Paul and Kara coming?" My cousin Paul had twins—a boy and girl—Jake and Hadley. They were five years old and adorable. It had always amazed me that I-want-five-kids John— yes, he would say he wanted five kids, yet marriage was still not on his radar—had never played with them, and they'd never warmed up to him in return. I, on the other hand, couldn't get enough of them, especially Hadley, in particular. We'd bonded while playing "school" and "hair salon."

"They're on their way," Uncle Al said. "You look great, Veronica. I hope they're not working you too hard at that law firm."

"Aw, I'm all right," I said. "Where's Christopher?"

"He taped something about the Jets on that NFL network, and now he's watching it over and over again in the basement." Uncle Al laughed.

"Of course he is. I'll be down there." I was hoping to hide out in the basement with my cousin until the rest of the guests arrived. Then, Aunt Marie would call us upstairs and tell us to grab a paper plate and get in line for the buffet in her dining room. That way, I could avoid, or at least delay, having to answer probing questions about John from my father.

"I haven't seen you in how long? Don't go downstairs and hibernate. What's going on?" asked my father. *Here we go.*

I sighed loudly as I sat down.

"How's work?"

"The same. It's okay."

"You know who came into Bella last week? Frank Fabiano. His son's a lawyer. He works for some big firm in Newark."

I nodded. I had no idea who Frank Fabiano was. The name sounded familiar. I thought I'd seen it on lawn signs asking people to vote for him for the Board of Education. I couldn't remember, and I didn't care that much. I started to feel for my grandmother's ring but then remembered.

My father went on about what Frank Fabiano ordered at Bella Notte and how much he loved the veal parmigiana. Uncle Al got up and went into the kitchen. I wished I could follow him.

"...said he can't wait to bring his wife back. He said she'd go crazy over the veal."

"That's great."

He sat up and rested the cigar in the ashtray next to the recliner. "So Marie says you're not seeing John anymore."

"That's right."

"I always liked him. Italian, good lookin' guy, smart guy, knew his stuff." He stared at me.

Yes, please go on and rattle off all the things you liked about him. I recalled the first time they met. It was at Bella Notte during Christopher's college graduation party. My father had worn a white suit, black shirt, and black-and-white tie. John jokingly complimented my father's channeling of Frank Sinatra, and I watched as my father's ego inflated by the comparison. He laughed loudly and patted John hard on the back. "Extra antipasto for my new friend here," he called to the waiter. After that, whenever we saw my father, he would ask John for stock tips, where he bought his suits, why he chose a black Jaguar convertible instead of a red one. It should have all been repulsive to me, but I had secretly liked that my father was so in awe of my boyfriend.

But now, I was repulsed. I was relieved to see several more family members arrive through the kitchen. "Paul and Kara are here." I stood to walk toward them.

"Wait a minute. Now tell me, is it really over with John? This is it?"

"What do you mean? Yes, it's over. He's moving to London."

"For how long? Did you talk about, ya know, a long-distance thing?"

I stared him straight in the eye. "No."

"You didn't think of joining him across the pond there? Sure, they're not gonna have Italian bread like they got here, but—"

"Are you kidding me?" I screamed.

"Hey, hey, hey." He held his hands up as if in surrender.

It was too late. It hadn't taken much, but the right buttons were pushed, the nerve hit. "What do you think? I should move to London, leave everything, and hope he marries me? We'd probably get married and have a kid, and then he'd leave me six years later for one of his employees with bad hair!"

At that point, the house was silent. I didn't need to see what was happening in the kitchen to know that everyone had stopped in their tracks. My father stared at me wide-eyed.

I picked up my bag and would have given anything to leave through the front door, but it was Aunt Marie's house, and no one ever entered or exited through the front door. So I had to bear all of the stunned faces in the kitchen in order to get out of there.

"Hey," I mumbled to Kara and Paul with my head down. "I have to go."

I hurried through the short maze of tables and chairs and platters of food everywhere. I didn't take note of where The Perm was, and I certainly didn't make eye contact with her or anyone else.

I fiddled with the screen door, walked out into the fresh air, and ran to my rental car. After I turned the key, I screamed into my hands. As I drove back into the city, I didn't listen to the radio but kept reliving the conversation in my head, making new points—"And furthermore, I'm your daughter. How about a 'You're too good for him anyway'? Isn't that what you're supposed to say?"—all the way through the Lincoln Tunnel.

When I got back to my apartment after dropping off the car, I put on sweatpants, poured a glass of wine, ordered food since I didn't eat at my Aunt Marie's, and tried to watch a documentary on Sophia Loren.

Normally, this would have been a perfect way to spend an evening, but my mind was swirling. I thought about all that had happened in the past week. I thought about John, wondering how the packing went, wondering when I would hear from him again. I thought about work and Trista. I thought about the fight I'd just had with my father. And I thought about my mother. I'd called her earlier in the week.

Don had answered. "Hi, honey. Your mom is coming to the phone. Let me know if you need a refill on your pill."

Don was a pharmacist, which was how he'd met my mother. They'd always chatted when she picked up her allergy medication. He was a widower with two children of his own. He and my mom were content living separately, but they had a sweet and lasting courtship. At my law school graduation, I had seen through the corner of my eye that Don was wiping tears away when my mother handed me a bouquet of roses. I'd also noticed that my father handed my contracts professor a catering menu for Bella Notte.

After I'd explained the John situation to my mother, I said, "I'm fine. I'm okay with it." *Not entirely true, but why worry her?*

She'd replied, "I'm so sorry, sweetheart. But as long as you're okay with it. As long as you're happy."

And that was the difference between my mother and father.

Chapter 7

WHEN I WOKE UP THE next morning and heard Rosanna Zotto say that the crosstown shuttle was out of service, I walked to the office. It was a beautiful spring morning, bright and warm, an open-toe-shoe day. Still, no matter what mode I used to get to the office each day, the closer I got, the more I felt that pang, that stab of dread, that thought that I should just walk to the port authority to hop a Greyhound to California and start a new life.

I stalled by stopping at Starbucks. As I waited in line, I wondered how things were going for John in London. It had been over a month—seven weeks and two days, to be exact—since I ran out of his apartment with snot bubbles coming out of my nose and a new bruise on my knee. I wondered what his place in London was like, if all his stuff had arrived safely, if he liked his new office, if he was getting used to the exchange rate, if he'd found any favorite restaurants yet, if he missed me. We hadn't spoken.

I grabbed my latte, took a long sip, and headed upstairs.

As I rode in the elevator, I texted Jada and our friend Lauren, who was our "triplet," the other friend in our little trio: —I have my first news reporting class tonight. Wish me luck.—

Lauren replied right away: —Good luck! I bet you're going to love it.—

Jada never replied.

I shut my office door with my heel, dumped my tote by my desk, shimmied my mouse around, and stalled some more. Instead of responding to work emails, I checked things I was actually interested in on HumanInterestStories.net. "Excerpt from new Jackie Kennedy biography." *Interesting. To be read.* "100-year-old woman reconnects with 81-year-old daughter she gave up for adoption." *Wow. To be read.* "The lost Princess Diana tapes." *Oh. Must read.*

"Breaking news in the Dr. March case." The trial had been postponed. Apparently, this wasn't the first time the mistress nurse, Sally Ann Fenway, tried to get someone offed.

What? Wait. She has tried to have someone else besides Filamina March killed before? How and when did this new evidence come in? How did the prosecutors not know about this sooner? But who cares? This is postponing the trial? This doesn't mean Dr. March is innocent. It just means Sally Ann is crazier than originally thought. Why wasn't she already locked up? He could still have been in cahoots with her. She said he gave her forty thousand dollars to find the hitmen. And according to this article, Dr. March apparently referred to Filamina's old emails to Sally Ann as "disgusting" and said there was no brilliant plastic surgeon—not even him—who could fix what two kids and ten years of marriage had destroyed. Wow, he is the disgusting one. How could she support him? After all this humiliation? It makes no sense. He's a cheater. He's emotionally cruel. And he may be a conspirator to murder. Those aren't deal breakers? Come the fuck on!

I started typing furiously. These were all questions I needed to explore with the other commenters at HumanInterestStories.net, then I heard a familiar refrain.

"Veronica!"

Margaret appeared in my doorway, and I quickly scattered to grab a pen and pad. "She's calling for you, dear."

"I hear her. Thanks, Margaret." *Breathe. As long as this isn't about Trista—and what are the chances of that? It's been over a month—it'll be okay.*

"May the force be with you," Margaret said.

We both laughed until I dropped my pen then whacked my hip on the edge of my desk as I was getting up. I winced, rubbed my hip, and walked out of my office.

"Veronica!"

And then to add insult to injury, as if Monday mornings weren't bad enough, my life at Ellis & Blackmoore continued as normal. Kate slammed the door in my face then claimed, after I let myself in, "I didn't know you were called into this meeting as well." *Really? You didn't hear Beverly screaming my name?* Beverly asked if I'd given the Bailey motion to Kate to review. *Oops. No, I was on the Internet, reading more riveting stuff.* Beverly caught me rubbing my hip where I slammed it into the desk. "What the hell is wrong with your leg there?"

"Nothing." And we went back to discussing work.

Right before Beverly asked me about the status of another case, I had composed a list of questions in my head that I planned to finish typing out as soon as I returned to my office. Unfortunately, they weren't related to my actual job. *Why wasn't Sally Ann charged with attempted murder before? Who found this new witness that says she tried to kill someone before? I'm assuming the defense found someone to make these claims? And again, who cares? So, she's crazy? It doesn't mean Dr. March isn't also crazy and planned the hits with her? Right?*

"Veronica!"

That was when, flustered, I pretended to search through the blank pad in front of me for the answer and was met with a sigh and a "Let's concentrate," from Kate.

I imagined grabbing the three-hole punch off of Beverly's desk and smashing it over her head. And then, because if Kate weren't around, I'd have to do all her work, I imagined smashing it over my own head. Poor Beverly would be left with no underlings to torture. *Ha!*

I started laughing to myself, and Beverly wanted to know what the hell was so damn funny. My heart skipped. "Nothing," I murmured.

Silence.

I just imagined smashing in my head with your hole puncher to put me out of my misery.

I didn't actually say that. I just squirmed and bit my lip.

Beverly ended the meeting with, "All right, enough with this powwow."

Powwow? Yeah, that's exactly what it feels like. Why aren't we sitting on the floor in lotus position?

"Back to work," she said.

One minute after I returned to my office, the phone rang.

"Veronica? Hi. It's Trista Hines. Thank you for the contract you sent. I know it's been a few weeks. I'm just going over it with my sister now, and I know I agreed to pay three fifty a month, but I don't know if I'm going to be able to swing that after all."

Do not sigh into the phone. She's going through a hard time. Stifle the sigh. Make this work. It had taken a few weeks to work out the exact terms of the settlement agreement and to wait for Trista to finish a week-long stay at a clinic and to wait for my client Pat Stephens to return from a trip to Ireland that he'd won in a bar raffle. But luckily, Beverly had forgotten about the case as I predicted.

"Okay, why don't you work on your budget, really firm it up, and when you know exactly what you can pay, I will go back to my client. We can adjust the agreement, but I don't know if he's going to take much less than—"

"I can afford two hundred. My sister and I are working on our budget right now. I know what I agreed to, but I think I just kind of blurted out that number. I was so grateful for your help, ya know? And it's been such a hard time. I—I—I don't know." She sighed.

"It's okay. Trista, listen. Two hundred. I'll let my client know. I'll let you know what he says. How do you feel?"

"Better. Tired. But I feel better. Thanks."

I hung up, called Pat Stephens, and before getting back to the Bailey motion, checked HumanInterestStories.net. Beverly had her cigarette breaks, and I had mine.

It is 5:54 p.m. I need to leave by 6:40p.m.at the latest, or I will be late, and I don't want to be late for the first day of class. If I can avoid Beverly and Kate for the next forty-five minutes, I can make a clean getaway. Let me shut my door.

It is now 5:57 p.m. My door slowly opened. *Oh crap, please don't be Beverly.* It wouldn't be Kate. She never came to my office. It was Margaret. *Thank you, God.*

"Sorry to bother you, hon. We're doing an office pool for the Mega Millions. It's up to five hundred million! You want in?"

"Oh, yeah, sign me up." I reached for my wallet. I never played the lottery, but Margaret was so sweet, so I always chipped in if she asked. "Is Beverly playing? Or Kate?"

She shook her head. "I never ask them."

We shared a conspiratorial smirk. The thought of me, along with all of the secretaries and mailroom staff, calling out rich and leaving Beverly and Kate alone to continue working made me giddy.

It is 6:03 p.m. My phone rang. Beverly's line. I didn't pick up but ran to the bathroom instead.

It is 6:05 p.m. I washed my hands. *What am I doing? She's going to find me and ask where I was. I'll say I was in the bathroom, and she'll say she was calling to tell me to do something. Hopefully, I'll finish whatever it is before 6:40. So what am I doing wasting time in the bathroom?*

It is 6:08 p.m. I sat back down at my desk and noticed there was no voicemail. I tiptoed to Beverly's office and saw she wasn't there. *Maybe I'll leave now and send an email that I left because I wasn't feeling well.*

It is 6:09 p.m. Time to bolt. I grabbed my tote bag, turned around, and saw Beverly, sweating at the brow.

"Where are you going?"

"I was going to send you an email when I got home." I gently touched my forehead. "I'm not feeling well."

"I need you to do something."

I placed my tote bag down and reached for the piece of paper she was holding out.

"I need filing statuses on all of these." She marched out.

"Okay." I glanced at the five defendant names on the list. Crawford, Robinson, Lavelle, Jensen, and Hines.

Hines? Shit. No. Really? How do I tell her there is no status for Hines because I'm settling it behind your back?

I got to work on the other four. I think I worked faster in those eleven minutes than I had in the past five years.

If I hand this to her, she'll look at it and ask where Hines is. Maybe I will leave it on her desk while she's in the bathroom or taking a smoke break and make a run for it. But what if she doesn't do those things until 6:45? And anyway, she'll still notice at some point that Hines is missing. Maybe I'll shred this paper and send an email instead with the statuses of the other four. If she says there were five on the sheet of paper she gave me, I'll say there were only four. Yes, that's a plan.

At 6:21 p.m., I walked past Beverly's office as though I were headed for the printer or the bathroom. I noticed she wasn't in there, so I sprinted back to my office, grabbed the paper with the defendant names, ran to the mailroom, and threw it in the shredder.

But it didn't immediately chew the paper up.

I hit the button on the side.

"Where's Veronica?" I heard Beverly call.

Shit.

I hit the button on the front of the shredder.

"Veronica!"

Then I hit the side button again. Finally, the paper shimmied down and into the teeth of the shredder.

I ran back to my office the long way so I wouldn't pass Beverly's office, hit send on the email, grabbed my tote bag, and hurried to the elevator, out of breath.

"Veronica!" Beverly was coming out of the bathroom.

I spun around. "I sent you an email with all the statuses. I'm really not feeling well." I touched my forehead again.

She strode away, sighing loudly as if I were leaving in the middle of the day to get my nails done. "Fine."

I stepped into the elevator.

"All of them?" I heard her call back to me.

I hit Close Door.

After all that, I actually arrived early to class. It was held in a pre-war office building on Fifth Avenue between Twenty-First and Twenty-Second. The class was on the third floor, and there was no elevator. Just when I thought I'd gathered myself in the cab on the way there after the great escape from Beverly and the filing statuses, I found myself sweating and huffing again as I opened the door to class. *Am I nervous? Of course I'm nervous. I'm always nervous. Why should it stop me now?*

One other student was already there. She had a short pixie cut and was wearing thick, black-rimmed glasses. We exchanged a friendly smile as I sat down on the other end of the long table.

What a difference from the offices of Ellis & Blackmoore with their high ceilings and mahogany everything. There, the hardwood floor was beaten and cracked in some places. It creaked and was dusty. In one corner was an easel, and in the other was a large television with a built-in VHS player atop a metal TV stand with wheels.

I glanced at my phone, trying to alleviate the awkward silence by scrolling.

"Hi, I'm Asa," the dark-haired young woman said.

"Veronica."

"Is this your first class with MediaHouse?"

"Yeah," I said. "I'd never heard of them until I looked for this kind of class online. How about you?"

"I've taken a bunch of other classes, mostly writing classes. But I wanted to take this because I work for an international human rights organization, and I'm going to start giving interviews to TV stations all over the world, so I thought this would help. What do you do?"

"I'm a lawyer," I said.

"Wow, really? What made you take this class?"

I shrugged. "Just trying something different."

"A lot of people in news are lawyers."

"Really?"

"Yeah, isn't Charlie Rose a lawyer? And Bob Woodruff from ABC? And Jerry Springer and Geraldo Rivera are lawyers, aren't they?" she asked.

Perhaps this isn't so silly. Who would have thought being compared to Jerry Springer could be so encouraging? "Today, on the Veronica Buccino Show, Who's Your Daddy? Fraternal twins with different fathers!" *Well, sounds more fun than working for Beverly.*

"Hi! I'm Dave." The teacher walked in, moving quickly, putting his messenger bag down at the head of the table, and wasting no time moving the TV to the front of the room. He was tall with floppy blond hair and a boyish face. "There are going to be two more of you, I believe."

The other two students, both women, arrived then. One was tall and thin with long blond hair and carried an oversized black nylon bag with a drawing of the Earth dripping blood. *Bizarre. Get poor Earth a bandage.* The other was short, perhaps shorter than me, with brown hair and a nose ring.

"And here you are. Hi! I'm Dave," he called out.

As Dave started class, he explained that by the end, we would have two segments for our "demo reel" and shouldn't feel reluctant to send it to media outlets. The old way of having to move to the middle of nowhere to get experience as a news reporter had been somewhat diminished since the advent of the Internet. There was, in his words, "so much more media now." He, for example, worked for NewYork3News.com, an online news site, reporting on all things—good and bad—happening in New York, Connecticut, and the great state of New Jersey. I'd never heard of it but made a mental note to look it up after class.

Then he said something that made my stomach flip. "And we hire new reporters all the time—out of school, just starting out, changing careers. We can do that because our segments are never live, so we can really train people. You mess up? No harm. Do it again. And we cover local stories, but compared to your local evening news, we cover a lot more events and do more in-depth interviews. Compared with the two minutes you might see for a story on the eleven o'clock news, we do four- and five-minute stories. Sometimes, up to ten minutes. It's like television, but it's different. And *I* think—call me biased—better. And that's why there are a ton of other online news outlets out there, popping up every day, doing the same thing—or trying to do the same thing. I think we're the best, naturally, but if that's what you want, a job at an online shop, you're in the right place. I've already gotten two former students hired at other outlets. None at NY3N—yet—but two other places that I have to say are pretty decent."

Holy crap, this could turn into something? Like another job? I wished I hadn't heard that. I wished I was still thinking of this class as something to do for fun, something different to try, not something that could actually lead to an opportunity because then it was Choke City.

And there goes my anxiety again. Heart pounding. Throat dry. Try to stay calm. Try. Just try, dammit! I glanced at the other ladies. They all seemed to be listening attentively, unaffected by the news.

"Now, I'd like each of you to come up here, stand where I'm standing, and hold this microphone just to get used to the feel." He pulled a mic out of his back pocket. It was about a foot long and said NY3 in red letters. "And tell me about yourself. Who'd like to go first?"

I reflexively reached for my grandmother's ring. *Frig.* Seven weeks, and I was still forgetting. To say my heart was racing would be like saying Beverly was sometimes abrasive or I kind of wanted John to propose. *Who do I think I am taking this class? I know I'm a lawyer, but most lawyers don't actually do any public speaking. I only had to do it once in law school for the final exam for Trial Practice.*

That was actually when the ring thing had started. In my second year of law school, I had a Trial Practice presentation and was crippled with fear just thinking about it.

"I want you to do something," my mother said. "Wear Grandma's ring and touch it when you feel nervous."

I did, and it worked. I made it through without my voice shaking, my hands trembling, or me fainting. I'd been wearing it ever since— well, until recent events—and I touched it often, usually during work.

Is it hot in here? I pretended to brush my hair back with my hand, but I was really wiping away the beads of sweat that were forming on my forehead. *Don't make eye contact. If I learned anything in law school, it's don't make eye contact if you don't want to be called on.*

"How about you?" Dave was pointing at me.

Fuck.

"Sorry to point. I won't know all of your names until you get up here and introduce yourselves. So come on down. The floor is yours."

I'm going to vomit. Truly. I might actually vomit. I'm just going to leave. What am I doing here? I'll just continue to be a lawyer. It's nice and boring and secure, and the pay is good.

"You can do it. You're a lawyer," Asa said, smiling.

I smiled back. *Hey, yeah, that's right. I might not find it fulfilling, but I've suffered through the LSAT and law school and the bar exam and long hours at the firm. I should wear it like a badge of honor. It gives me some credence if nothing else.*

I walked toward Dave, ready to regale the group with the life of a lawyer and make them think it was as glamorous as it looked on TV. But just as I was about to take the microphone, my heel got caught in one of the cracks in the floor. My body was moving forward, but my right foot was stuck, which thrust me into a lunging motion. There was nothing to grab to regain my balance... except Dave's pants.

It all happened so quickly: my right heel getting stuck, my right hand reaching for the microphone but missing, my fingers catching the top of his jeans and his belt, my palm brushing against the denim. *Shit!*

My left heel stomped to the ground, and I managed to steady myself. From the corner of my eye, I saw Dave adjust his pants. Luckily, I hadn't pulled them down. I heard murmurs of "Oh!" "Oh my God!" "Are you okay?" My entire body radiated with panic.

I have two choices: run or recover. I eyed the door. I swallowed hard to push down the lump in my throat.

Then, carefully avoiding eye contact with Dave, I straightened up and reached for the microphone. *Just do it. If worse comes to worst, you can drop this class. You never have to see these people again.*

"That's right. I'm a lawyer... and that's probably a good thing since I suspect Dave might file a sexual harassment complaint against me soon."

They all laughed. I glanced at Dave. He shook his head as if to say, "Nah. All good."

"Well, I'm Veronica." My voice shook, but it steadied the more I spoke. I covered growing up in New Jersey, my father's restaurant, my college years, going to law school, and living in the city. By the time I got to life at the firm and why I was there, I thought Dave was going to take a cane and pull me by the neck.

"Excellent." He clapped his hands once. "Good job. You started at the beginning and led up to where you are now. Good storytelling. All right, who's next?"

I sat down and returned the favor of laughing and nodding in all the right places as we encouraged Asa, then Jo, and finally Elena. They all told their stories well, I thought. I enjoyed hearing about all of their lives. At the end of class, Dave—who I could have sworn kept pulling up his jeans—gave us an assignment for the next week: present a news story of interest to you, who you would like to interview, and what you would ask them. It could be anything at all. It just had to be local. Whatever we were interested in.

Easy.

The next morning, I sat in my office not working on work but on my new homework assignment. I'd just scribbled "Questions for Filamina March's maid of honor" at the top of a yellow legal pad when the phone rang.

"Hi, Veronica. This is Pat Stephens. So, I got the new settlement agreement with the new amount, and I'm okay with it. My physical therapist just wants to get paid. Let's do this."

"Great," I said. "Just fax over the signature pages, and we should be all set."

I couldn't remember ever having received a fax at the firm, but Pat did not have access to a scanner, nor was he comfortable using the electronic signature feature. He eventually asked "Can't I just fax it to you from the office supply store down the street?"

I hung up, satisfied the case was finally getting squared away until I realized the fax number Pat had was probably the one that went directly to Beverly's email. *Oh no!* He'd never signed the first draft because I told him to delete it after Trista asked to lower the terms. So, this was the first time he was faxing anything to our office. I quickly scrolled through my contacts to find his telephone number. I dialed frantically but got his voicemail.

I was able to get out, "Hi Pat, this is Veronica at Ellis & Blackmoore. I think you might have the personal injury group's main fax number, but actually, please fax—" when Beverly walked in.

I stumbled. *What's the button to erase and re-record? Is it the asterisk? Or is it the pound sign? Do I just hang up? No, I can't hang up, or he'll get this cut-off message. I can't finish, or Beverly will ask who is faxing me signature pages, about what, what case, what contract, signature pages for what? All we do is file complaints and motions, no contracts. Crap. Crap. Crap.*

"I mean, uh, please call me back. Thanks."

"We got ten new cases today. I'm giving them all to Kate, but she can use your help. Go to her office when you're done making personal phone calls there." She glared at me from the corner of her eye.

Does she know something? "Okay," I said as I caught my breath. "Thanks."

She walked out. I grabbed the phone again, dialed, stood up with the phone to my ear, and used my foot to shut the door.

I left another message. "Please fax to the number at the bottom of *my* email signature block, not the general one or the one on Beverly's email. Thank you, thank you, thanks, oh um, here's the number so you don't have to go searching for it… thanks, okay, thank you."

Real smooth.

I heard a knock at the door.

What now? Please don't tell me Pat already faxed it to Beverly. God forbid.

It was Jada. I breathed again.

"You look like you could use this." She placed a latte and a penny on my desk. "I just found it in the elevator."

"No!" I said. "I mean thank you, and thank you for my coffee, but you're not supposed to pick them up."

"Oh yeah. I forgot… but what happens if no one picks them up? The city will be littered with pennies. Someone has to pick them up, no?" She tilted her head to stare at the blank walls of my office while I went back to clicking my mouse and typing as I searched "Filamina March wedding date," forgetting that I should have been in Kate's office to work on the new cases we'd just received.

"Love what you've done with the place. Ever thought of hanging even your diploma?"

Jada had only been in my office a handful of times. Beverly always gave her strange looks and never said hello. It didn't seem to make Jada uncomfortable, but I found it awkward and always suggested we meet downstairs.

"So, why couldn't you come downstairs?"

"I'm doing my homework."

"Oh, that's right. How was class?"

"Wonderful." I grinned, still scrolling. "Thanks for asking."

"Any cute guys?"

"No. No guys."

"That's too bad."

"Yeah." *Guys? I wasn't even thinking of that. How can I date anyone else? What will happen when John realizes the mistake he's made and comes running back to me? I can't be entangled with someone else.*

"What's your homework?"

"We have to present a news story next week." I looked up to explain. "A full *package*. An intro, the interview, B-roll, and a close. Don't you love the lingo?"

Jada was staring at me as though I'd worn my bra on the outside of my suit that day.

I felt my blood start to course and quickly went back to my computer screen. "Anyway, I'm doing my story on Filamina March."

"You're obsessed," Jada said under her breath.

"How's work?"

"I have to take a couple of mental health days off, starting tomorrow. I told Dan and Karen that if they want me in the office, they will have to clone me. And if they even think of calling me, I'll drop my work phone in the toilet bowl."

Jada had her own version of Beverly and Kate—Dan the Little Man and Karen Who Lost Her Broomstick. However, Jada's method of dealing with them was decidedly different than mine.

"How do you say that exactly? You literally said those words?"

"Yes. Those exact words. I think sometimes they think I'm kidding, and then they realize I'm not."

"You're not worried they're going to be pissed? I could never say that, even jokingly, to Beverly or Kate."

"What are they going to do? Fire me? Don't get me wrong. Dan and Karen are annoying, but when they're acting like normal human beings, we get along fine. We talk about our weekends, our lives, what's going on in the news, the weather even. But with you, with Beverly and Kate, they're socially inept. Believe me, I've witnessed it every time I visit you here."

"Shhh." The last thing I needed was Beverly listening at the door and storming in.

Jada rolled her eyes.

"So, what's Mark up to?"

"We haven't spoken in a few days."

"Wait, what? Why? A few days?"

"Yeah. We got into a huge fight. Thanks to my mother."

Jada's mother, the one and only JoAnn Graziano Santanelli, had some pretty strong opinions on how exactly Jada should be living her life. Actually, she had opinions on how everyone should be living their lives. And she wasn't afraid to voice them.

"What did your mom do?" I asked, but I already had my suspicions.

"The usual." Jada used a thick Queens accent she had perfected over the years to imitate her mother. "Ya goin' to be thirty and ya not married. Why not? Why aren't you two engaged? Doesn't that botha ya? When I was your age, I already had you. I had ya sister. Ya sister is younga than you, and she's already got a husband and that sweet little baby. What are ya waiting faw?"

"I don't get it though. Isn't she thrilled that you're a successful lawyer in New York?" I asked as I blew on my latte.

"No. 'Successful' to her is getting married and having babies as soon as possible."

Of course, I wanted John to propose and then I wanted to quit, but that was my plan, not my mother's. I would never want to be pressured into it. More significantly, I loved John and maybe still do, whereas Jada's feelings about Mark are uncertain.

"But you do want that someday," I said. "Does she think you don't want that at all?"

Jada shrugged. "She doesn't care. All that matters is that *she*'ll be happier when I'm married. And Mark uses it as ammunition, like 'maybe you should listen to your mother.' He would love to propose tomorrow. It'll be our two-year anniversary."

Mark and Jada had met at a law school alumni event. It was a typical wine-and-cheese reception in a large conference room at one of the big firms on Park Avenue. They'd both reached for a cheese cube at the same time and bumped toothpicks. It was a nice story. Everything about Mark was nice. He'd majored in chemistry at MIT, gone to Duke Law School, and was now a patent attorney. He wasn't a big drinker and didn't like big parties or loud places. He preferred to read and exercise, and well, that was pretty much it. There was nothing wrong with him, which might have been the problem. There was nothing too interesting about him either.

"Why don't you tell your mother to stop?"

Jada shot me a look from the top of her eyes, her chin tucked as if I should have already known the answer, which I did. Jada could stand up to anyone—her boss, her coworker—but not her mother.

She was examining her nails. "If that bitch at Princess Nails makes my cuticles bleed again, I will flip a manicure table."

I laughed.

"So you can't take a five-minute break?" she asked. "Why do you care so much? Do you get a grade? Or do you just want to be the teacher's pet?"

"I want a good segment for my reel," I said.

"What are you going to do with your *reel*?"

"I don't know. Maybe I'll send it to stations or online news sites. You know, there's so much media now."

"And make no money? How are you going to pay your rent and your loans, working for an *online news site*?" She said those last three words a little too mockingly, and all of my sympathy for her situation with Mark and her mother evaporated.

"Why are you being so negative?"

"I'm just being honest with you."

"Maybe I don't need you to be honest right now." My voice was louder than I'd intended. "Okay? Just be supportive."

"I am being supportive. I'm being supportive by being honest with you so you're not living in a dream world. I think you're wasting your time."

"Who asked you?"

"Do whatever you want." She got up so fast that the back of her chair hit the bookcase in my office.

"Thanks for the fucking support!" I screamed after her.

I sat at my desk for a few moments. *What the hell just happened?* Jada and I never fought. In fact, I couldn't think of another time when there'd ever been any tension between us.

Then I heard the handle of my office door turn. *She's back to apologize so quickly? Or did she forget something?*

The door flung open. It was Beverly. She was sweating and grimacing.

I was about to apologize for "having a guest over" and say that I was just about to go over to Kate's office when she said the words, almost in a whisper, "Trista Hines."

Fuck.

She walked slowly toward my desk, a piece of paper in her hand. "Can you tell me why I just received a fax from the client regarding the Settlement Agreement in the Stephens v. Hines case?" She said "Settlement Agreement" as if they were the most disgusting words she'd ever had to utter.

My heart raced. My throat dried up. "She doesn't have a lawyer and asked if she could make payments."

"I knew that name was on that piece of paper. No wonder there was no filing status for Hines." I could see the memory forming, the puzzle pieces falling into place. "You never filed the motion."

"Well, the client agreed—"

"I deal with our clients."

"It seemed like a reasonable deal and—"

"And nothing." She dropped the fax on my desk and pressed it down with her pointer finger. "Let me explain something to you, Veronica. I want the best for my clients, and *that* is why I do things the way I do them. I've been doing this for many years, and I know one thing to be true: every single one of these defendants will file bankruptcy eventually. Every. One. Of. Them. And then our clients will get nothing. I don't want that for my clients. I want them to get the most that they can *now*. Do you hear me? Now. How dare you take it upon yourself to do things any differently. And you, of all people!"

My face and neck began to burn.

"Where did you get this Settlement Agreement from? You drafted it yourself?"

I cleared my throat. "I found a template somewhere." My voice shook.

"Where? Somewhere on the Internet?"

"I can't remember exactly."

"Did Kate review it before it went out the door?"

I shook my head.

"Did I review it before it went out the door?"

I shook my head.

"So you drafted a document that no one else reviewed, no one else approved, a document you've never drafted before, and you let it go to the defendant's lawyer—"

"She doesn't have a lawyer."

"I'm speaking!" Beverly slammed her hand on my desk.

That was when my eyes filled with tears. My body was already stinging with nerves. It felt as though tingles of fear rose from within every inch of me and shot straight to my eyes.

Don't blink. Just don't blink. I blinked, and tears streamed down my face. "I thought I was doing a good thing."

"A good thing? And did you think I was never going to find out about this? If you would like to still have a job, there is only one way to fix this. Call this defendant and tell her the deal is off."

As she marched out the door, she pivoted back around to say, "And I already spoke to Pat Stephens. I talked him out of this. It's pointless, Veronica." She shook her head and added, "Boy, do you still have a lot to learn."

I stood and shut the door all the way. After a good cry, I pulled out the Hines file, found Trista's number, and dialed. I explained that since the agreement hadn't yet been signed by both parties, the client had "thought more about it" and decided it wasn't the way to go. I apologized profusely.

"I don't understand," she said.

Me neither. "At this point, I would suggest hiring a lawyer."

"I can't afford a lawyer." She sounded desperate.

"There are a lot of attorneys who handle cases pro bono, for free, for struggling small businesses. If you do a search, I'm sure you'll find someone." I wanted to add "Feel better" or "It's going to be okay," but it felt hollow, so I just apologized again and tried to hang up.

But before I could, she said, "Thank you again for trying to help me," which only made it worse.

I sat there, stung and stunned by all that had happened in the past hour. The penny Jada had found was sitting on the edge of my desk. I flicked it off.

Chapter 8

WHEN I TWIRLED JUST THE right amount of warm, gooey mozzarella, prosciutto, and crust around in my mouth, it was Heaven. And when the mozzarella oozed out of the corner of my mouth and fell onto my hand or plate, I peeled it off the plate or my hand and ate it. Mozzarella that good should never go to waste.

"Atta girl," Grandpa Sal said.

I looked up from my hot, crusty sandwich and saw hundreds of white stucco structures dotting up a cliffside. "Where are we?" Peering down, I took in the turquoise sea at the bottom of the cliff.

"Italy," Grandma Ant said with a tone that implied "Where else?" She put her sandwich down and dabbed her mouth with a napkin.

We were sitting at a dining area outside of a small café. Next door was what looked to be a tobacco shop with a drawing of a big pipe in the window. Beyond that were a few more cafés, a gelato shop, and a leather handbag store.

"Did you ever go to Italy?" I asked as my big Jackie O sunglasses slid to the tip of my nose. I lifted them with my forearm, not wanting to touch them with my deliciously greasy hands.

"We could never afford it," Grandma Ant said.

"You should travel more, Veronica," Grandpa Sal said.

"I can't take off from work." I didn't feel like rehashing the deep trouble I was in at my job—a job I desperately needed to pay off my exorbitant credit card bills because I would buy things to treat myself after a particularly bad day at the firm. *Talk about a vicious cycle.* "I'd love to go to Paris though. It seems so romantic and enchanting, like going back in time."

"Paris is beautiful," Grandma Ant said.

She must have gone since she's been dead.

We sat in silence for a few minutes, eating our sandwiches and drinking Coke from old-fashioned glass bottles.

"Ya enjoyed that class?" Grandpa Sal asked.

"Except for the part where I accidentally groped the teacher, yes."

"Was that funny or what?" Grandma Ant smiled. "Oh, how we laughed."

"That's just wonderful. I'm glad my life amuses you."

"So serious ya are," Grandpa Sal said. "You can't take it all so seriously, Veronica."

"I wish I hadn't told anyone about the class."

"Why? Because your friend thinks it's silly?" Grandpa asked.

I didn't answer but instead rescued a small piece of prosciutto that had fallen onto the plate and promptly delivered it to my mouth.

"What are you going to do, spend your whole life not doing things because"—Grandpa Sal spread his hands as if he were holding a big beach ball in front of him—"Oh no, people might laugh at ya?"

"I don't understand," I said. "Why can't my friend just be supportive?"

"When people have got something to say, Veronica, remember this: it's not about you," Grandma Ant said. "So it doesn't matter, and don't make it matter."

"I know." No, I didn't.

"Let me tell ya a story," Grandpa Sal said. "You see that place, that tobacco shop? Pietro used to run it. Pietro the pipe maker. He made wonderful pipes. Everyone loved them. But what Pietro loved more was singing. He had a pair of pipes. Get it? Pipes?" Grandpa laughed at his joke before continuing. "Anyway, he would sing all the time, in the morning, in the afternoon, at night. Always singing, while he made pipes, while he cleaned pipes. He wanted to be an opera singer. But everyone said, 'Why? You're better at making pipes.' But when the opera came to town, he went to see the—what do ya call it?—like a director or someone like that. And Pietro auditioned for him." Grandpa Sal was looking me in the eye.

"Let me guess. He became an opera singer and shoved it in everybody's face. Grandpa, I get the point."

"No! They said, 'You stink. Go home.'"

"Oh. That's a terrible story."

"Stop furrowing your brow," Grandma Ant said.

I unfurrowed.

"No, it's not," Grandpa Sal said. "Ah, well, maybe it is. I make these stories up as I go along. What do ya want from me, Veronica? Ya think I'm Charles Dickenson?"

"Dickens."

"Tomato. Tomahto."

"No, his name was actually Charles Dickens."

"Whatever you want to call him. The point is, you can't worry about what other people say even if they laugh at you or say, 'Why would you want to do that?' You have to do the things *you* want if you want to be happy, whatever the outcome, whatever people say. If you did what other people expected and not what you really wanted, you would—"

"Be a lawyer," I said.

"Let me tell ya something," Grandpa continued. "It has nothing to do with you—what they think, what they say. That's their problem. They have a problem with you doing something different because they're too chicken to do it themselves. And that's the truth."

"You don't know Jada. She's not a chicken."

"We don't know Jada?" Grandpa asked rhetorically.

"I know you know her. You see *everything,* but what I mean is she thinks the class is a waste of time. It's not—"

Grandma Ant suddenly spotted something in the distance and started waving her hands wildly. I sat up to see an older lady walking toward us.

"Ruth!" Grandma Ant called out. "Over here!"

Ruth seemed to bounce over to our table. "Antoinette, Sal baby, how are ya today?"

I noticed Ruth was carrying a small black satin clutch. She appeared to have taken great care in styling her silver hair. It was neatly curled, and she kept finger-combing the wisps near her ears. Her nails were painted bright red, and she was wearing a red dress and black satin heels that seemed a little high for a woman her age, but she was walking with no problem. Walking quickly actually.

"Ya got a hot date?" Grandpa Sal asked.

"No, smarty. I just came from my great-great-grandson's bar mitzvah." She said that with so much pride that she actually stood on her tippy toes. She had a heavy Brooklyn accent and pronounced smarty as 'smahty.' "It was in Jersey."

New Jersey to Italy. It's all possible here.

"Well, you look marvelous," Grandma Ant said before turning to me. "Perfect timing. Meet Veronica. Our beautiful Veronica."

I gave my grandmother a look that said, "Stop. You're such a grandmother."

Ruth smiled warmly and said, "Well, hello there." She stared at me a little too long.

Not wanting to be examined at the moment, I smiled back then stuffed the rest of my sandwich in my mouth.

"Where ya off to now?" Grandma Ant asked.

"Now, I've got a wedding. An old neighbor's great-granddaughter is getting married here in Italy. How nice is that? So I gotta get going, but very nice to meet ya, Veronica!" She waved and trotted off.

"That's our friend Ruth Stein," Grandma Ant said. "You meet the loveliest people here. You really do."

"Even the people you thought were the biggest pains in the ass when, ya know, you knew them when you were alive," Grandpa said. "For some reason, what can I say, they're different here."

"You knew Ruth when you were alive?" I asked.

"No," Grandpa said. "I'm just saying."

"How is she going to a bar mitzvah and a wedding and all these events?"

They both gazed at me, eyes wide, as if they were surprised I'd just asked that.

Grandpa Sal said, "She's dead!" as in "How else?"

"All right, let's stretch our legs now." Grandma Ant stood up, and Grandpa and I followed. "Let's walk over to the gelato place and see what they got."

We made our way along the cobblestone path, toward the town with narrow streets, and away from the seascape.

My grandmother pointed to a fuchsia sequin tank top on a mannequin in a window. "That's nice," she said. "To wear out with your friends or… on a date."

"Gram, please. I don't wear fuchsia." *Let alone a fuchsia sequin tank top.*

"Well, I think it's sharp-looking."

Grandma and I ordered two hazelnut gelatos and settled on a bench. Grandpa sat next to us with a cannoli that he'd almost finished eating already.

"We think you should go on the Match.com," Grandma Ant announced.

I almost choked on my gelato.

"Everybody's doing it," Grandpa Sal said. "And you gotta make sure your pictures are good. One up close and then the 'full body shot.' That's the biggest complaint, they say. That people don't have the right pictures."

"Wait. How would *you* know? And I don't know. Not yet. I—"

"She wants to mourn, Sal. She wants to mourn that fella John."

"She's got enough black clothes, this one." He motioned toward me, up and down with one hand from my feet to my head, then he looked me in the eye. "Mourning, Veronica, it's for the birds. Trust us."

"Now listen, if you do the Match.com—" Grandma Ant began.

"It's Match, Gram, not *the* Match."

"That's what I said. If you do this, just go on one date"—she held her pointer finger up—"we'll tell you where my engagement ring is."

"Hold on," I said. "I'm doing the class. Remember? In fact, I was about to say that you could tell me where the ring is now."

"Not so fast," Grandma Ant said. "Listen, we know if it were up to you, you'd waste too much time waiting for that John to come back. You gotta get on the Match, girl!"

I almost choked again, on nothing this time. "You got me to do the class, and now there's something else I have to do?"

"We said there were *two* assignments," Grandpa said. "Remember?"

"The class and the Match. And then that's it. We promise," Grandma said.

I spooned at my gelato.

"It's been nearly two months," Grandma said. "It's time."

"I know," I said. "I have to be honest though. Maybe I am... *was* waiting for John, but also the idea of dating scares me. It's a whole different world out there. Sometimes, I wish it were the 1940s. I was born too late."

My grandparents met in the spring of 1941. My grandmother was working at her parents' bakery on Stone Street in Newark. My grandfather worked at a barber shop down the street. Legend has it, he walked by during lunch one day, took one look at her, and wouldn't leave. He ate seven cannoli in four hours. They got married a few months later.

"The provolone's always sharper on the other side of the street," Grandpa Sal said.

"I've actually thought a lot about this," I insisted.

"We know you have," Grandma said.

"You didn't have to weed through a database of potential spouses." When they didn't respond, I added, "Life seemed so much easier then."

"Ha!" Grandpa Sal sat up. "We got married, and I was drafted a month later. We didn't see each other for four and a half years. Four and a half years. Not until the war ended."

Oh, yeah, I forgot about that. When Grandpa Sal finally came home, he surprised Grandma in the middle of the night. She'd always said she was wearing a mud mask, but she didn't care—she couldn't stop kissing him.

"Well, what I mean is," I attempted to explain, "it was simpler in some ways. At least with dating. That's for sure."

"In a way," Grandma Ant conceded. "But it was a different time. No one got divorced. If you married a good man, you were lucky... not like my sister Mary. Poor Mary."

Aunt Mary died before I was born. Whenever Grandma Ant talked about her sister, she would always say, "Poor Mary."

I never really knew what she meant. I'd asked a couple of times during our visits and when Grandma was alive too, but she never explained. I asked my mom too, but she just said, "Aunt Mary had a hard life."

I always assumed it was because she was older than her brothers and sisters and had to take care of them.

"All right, I know where we gotta go." Grandpa Sal rose from the bench and wiped cannoli powder off his sweater.

"Where?" I asked. "I'm not done with my gelato."

"Finish it," he said as he walked away.

Grandma Ant threw her empty gelato cup in the garbage can and followed him. I scooped one more bite and did the same then ran on the tricky cobblestone to catch up to them. Grandpa Sal turned a corner and opened a door to a building. As we walked down a long corridor, the walls got whiter, the floor got whiter, and the ceiling lights glared down.

"Where are we?"

"The hospital. 1951," Grandpa Sal said over his shoulder as he opened another door to another hallway. "We're gonna see poor Mary."

"Will she know we're here?" I wanted to meet her.

Grandma Ant shook her head. "We're just going to look in."

"Did Aunt Mary just have a baby? One of my mom's cousins?" I was getting more excited about this field trip.

My grandparents didn't answer. I assumed they didn't hear me.

We stepped onto a rickety elevator then walked down another corridor with bright lighting.

When we finally arrived at Mary's room, I wasn't sure what I was seeing at first. It appeared to be a small person balled up under the covers in a bed. I couldn't make out the face because her eye was bandaged and she was asleep with the other side of her face on the pillow. The other bed, where a roommate would be, was empty. Grandma Ant sat and studied her sister. I sat next to her.

It was quiet. There weren't many machines in the room or devices of any sort. No television. No phone. "Is she okay?" I asked.

"Her husband broke the bone." Grandma Ant gently ran her finger below her own eye, still staring at Mary. "Shattered the eye bone."

"How?" I asked.

"How? He hit her."

Oh my God. "Oh."

I reached for Grandma Ant's hand next to me. She squeezed it. None of us took our eyes off Mary.

"She called us in the middle of the night. I couldn't make out what she was saying," Grandma said. "But then I understood. Grandpa got the car running, and we raced to her. I was still in my housecoat. I didn't even run a comb through my hair."

Aunt Mary was perfectly still, other than the slow rise and fall of her tiny frame as she slept.

We stayed for a while longer until eventually, Grandpa Sal asked, "All right. Ready?"

"That's it? Is she going to be okay?" I asked. But they didn't answer. Grandma Ant stood, and Grandpa and I followed her out the door.

"Where's her husband? What was his name?"

"Vito." Grandpa Sal pronounced his name slowly, with a tone that said, *Good ol' Vito, how could we forget?*

"So she left him?" I asked. "I mean, after this?"

Grandma Ant stopped walking, pivoted around, and stared at me. "Sure, she picked up, took the kids, moved to another town, and got a wonderful job"—she threw her hands up—"ya know, with her eighth-grade education."

Oh.

Grandma Ant pivoted back around and marched ahead of us toward the elevator.

"That's not really what happened," Grandpa whispered to me.

"I know." I rolled my eyes. "Where is he now? I'm assuming he's on the other side?"

Grandpa shook his head and whirled a small circle in the air with his index finger. "On another tour of duty."

It took a second for that information to register. "He was reincarnated? Where is he? *Who* is he?"

Grandpa Sal shrugged. "Don't know."

"So... you believe in reincarnation?" We caught up to Grandma and all stepped onto the elevator.

"I don't have to believe in it," Grandpa Sal said as the doors closed. "It's not, how do ya say, one size fits all, Veronica. Some people don't learn it all the first time. Or the second time."

As we rode the elevator down, my mind swirled in a way that would give an entirely new meaning to "Hurricane Veronica." Or maybe Tornado Veronica like the window outside Dorothy's bedroom in *The Wizard of Oz*. Instead of the witch on a bike with Toto, I saw the concept of reincarnation go by and Grandpa Sal whirling a circle in the air with his finger, followed by Aunt Mary in a hospital bed, followed by a copy of each of my diplomas, my law license, then all of the significant news events of the past century. All of them were like flashes on a movie screen, then I heard "Up to you." But it wasn't John's voice, and it didn't make me angry or sad.

Damn right, it's up to me.

"Is the world my oyster?" I blurted out as the rickety elevator plopped to the ground.

"Oysters? Never cared for 'em." Grandpa held the elevator door as we exited. "Clams oregano? Clams casino? Now you're talking."

"Never mind." I exhaled as we walked out the door.

Chapter 9

I ORDERED PIZZA AND BAKED cookies in my studio apartment oven that was so small, it looked like it should be sold at a toy store. Still, it did the job and filled my place with the sweet smell of melting chocolate and dough. I heard a knock on the door and then "Matchmakers on call! Here to serve your matchmaking needs."

I swung open the door to find Jada and Lauren, both in jeans and ponytails, laughing in my hallway. I shooed them inside. "Honestly! I don't need my neighbors knowing how pathetic my love life is."

Jada pranced in and rested her purse and two bottles of wine on my coffee table. "This attitude of yours is unacceptable, Veronica. It's not going to cut it if you want to succeed on Match.com—or 'on the computer,' as my mother would say. She once asked me if I broke up with Mark, would I try meeting someone 'on the computer?' Are you baking something?" She sniffed the air as she took off her jacket and hung it in my closet.

A few days earlier, I had asked Lauren by text message if she would help me sign up for Match.com. She responded that she would be happy to and must have assumed I'd mistakenly left Jada off the text because she included her in the reply. Jada responded, without missing a beat and without any mention of our fight, which day worked for her and that she would bring wine. At some point leading up to today, I'd expected to get a phone call, email, or text from Jada with an apology or something to clear the air. But she didn't send anything. And neither did I.

"Yes, and I ordered pizza. That's something my grandparents would say. 'On the computer.'" I moved Jada's purse to the floor. "Okay. Let's get down to business. I want to get this over with. It feels like ripping a BAND-AID off or something."

"Jada might have a point," Lauren said. "You know, about having the right attitude for 'the computer dating.'"

Lauren and Jada made themselves comfortable on my couch. Jada picked up an old photo album I kept on the coffee table and started flipping through it.

Lauren continued. "If you're dreading this, it might not be the right time. The way I look at it is even though I haven't met my husband yet, I've been out with some nice guys, some fun guys, and some not-so-nice-or-fun guys, but I'm meeting people. I'm having fun."

"Oh my God, look at Alison Dreier," Jada said, glued to the photo album. "She always looked miserable in pictures. What the hell was she so mad about?"

Is she avoiding eye contact with me? She's acting like her normal confident self. Maybe she doesn't feel awkward at all. But shouldn't we talk about it? Or shouldn't one of us apologize?

"I ran into her at Bloomingdales last year," Lauren said. "She met her husband *on the computer.*"

"Really?" I headed to the kitchen to check on the cookies.

"Really!"

I took the cookies out of the oven and, having no counter space, rested them on the stove. I scraped up three hot ones and brought them over to the couch on napkins.

We ate cookies and pizza and drank several glasses of wine, then Jada announced, "All right, sign-up time. Lauren, I've never done this, so you lead the way."

All of a sudden, I didn't want to rip it off like a BAND-AID anymore. I'd lost my nerve somewhere between cookies and pizza, and the wine wasn't working as the liquid courage I'd hoped it would be. I tried to convince Jada and Lauren to watch a documentary on Greta Garbo. "It's only an hour! She was a fascinating woman. She became a recluse."

Jada grabbed the remote control. "And that's exactly what you're going to become if you don't start dating."

I've only been single for two months, I wanted to say.

"No more stalling. Let's do this." Jada turned the television off. "Recluse," she muttered, shaking her head.

Back to her old self. I guess I'm the only one who feels awkward about our fight. Maybe it was no big deal to her. So why should it be to me? Maybe we don't have to talk about it.

"Okay, you don't have to get off the couch." Lauren got up and walked over to the bistro set in the corner of my living room. She straightened up in front of my laptop. "You just sit back like you're in the psychiatrist's chair. I'll ask you questions, and all you need to do is answer."

"Okay," I said, glancing at the ceiling.

Jada headed to my closet, browsing as if she were considering what to buy.

Lauren began. "How old are you?"

"Almost thirty."

"And by that, she means twenty-nine," Jada said. "God, Veronica, don't age yourself." She kicked up her right leg to get a better view of my leopard peep toes that were now on her feet.

After a few other basics—my sign (Libra), my nationality (Italian American), my religious beliefs (simply spiritual), my political beliefs (moderate)—and uploading some pictures (a few tan close-ups and a couple of full-body shots), Lauren asked, "What are you looking for in a mate?"

"*Four. Things,*" Jada said mockingly.

"This is not your profile," Lauren scolded her.

A while ago before I met John, I had come up with my *four requirements*. That was after fifteen years of dating and a few serious boyfriends. I firmly believed in my rules, reasoning that they were based on experience, rooted in my own personal—and painful—research.

It started with Rob. He was my first "real" boyfriend. We met freshman year of college and dated for two years. After two years, I realized we never really laughed together. I sat at the edge of my bed one day and thought: *I like to laugh, and he isn't funny. We should break up.*

After college, I dated Victor for one year. He was absolutely hilarious—always telling me some story that made me laugh so hard I cried—but he was also perfectly content living at home and not using his Boston College degree for anything other than going to the alumni tent to tailgate before football games. He worked for his father's heating and cooling business, and when I suggested that they take it global or at least expand, he said he wasn't the type to sell out. *Sell out? It's heating and cooling!* I broke up with him. He was not ambitious, and I needed ambitious, I concluded.

I watched Jada examine a pair of suede open-toe boots with fringe and put them back. Lauren reached for another cookie.

After Rob and Victor, I came up with the four requirements. I realized I needed someone with a sense of humor and ambition. Those were the first two. I also realized that trustworthiness was very important to me. I wondered at first why that one came up, but it dawned on me that was based on experience too. Two words: The Perm. My father left my mother for another woman. That made three, and the last requirement was simple—I had to be attracted to him, of course. I am in a human body, after all.

Oh, and he had to be one hundred percent Italian. I didn't even list that as a requirement. It was just a given. I'd never dated a guy who wasn't a "pure blood," as Jada mockingly referred to it. But neither had she if you looked at her track record, though she never mentioned it, and it never seemed that important to her.

Looking back, John had all of my requirements: Italian, attractive, ambitious, he wasn't a cheater, and he made me laugh. But it still hadn't worked out, and I didn't know why. But I refused to give up on my formula. Jada suggested I get a copyright.

"Smart and ambitious. I kind of lump them together." I held up one finger. "Funny. Trustworthy. Oh, and he doesn't have to be good-looking, but I have to be attracted to him. But don't write that."

"Yeah, you can't write 'good-looking' as one of your requirements, but you'll just know from their pictures," Lauren said.

"What about Italian? Can I say that?"

Lauren scrunched her nose and shook her head. We moved on.

"What do you like to do in your spare time?" Lauren sounded so official, as though she were taking my medical history.

I realized I was furrowing my brow. I unfurrowed. "Well, I used to like to work out. I liked to run, but now, you know, I have no time. I like to read. I love biographies, especially. I like the History Channel, oh, and true crime stories too. Dateline always has something good. I'm obsessed with HumanInterestStories.net."

"Bor-ing." Jada did a twirl while staring down at her feet in my charcoal-gray patent leather pointy Mary Janes.

Lauren clucked her tongue.

"I'm kiddding," Jada said, drawing the word out. She kicked up the other leg and did another twirl.

"Can I just say I'm an old soul, obsessed with news but not politics or sports, and I hate my job? And that I just want to fall in love, get married, have kids, and quit?"

Jada glared at me with her hands on her hips. "Not if you actually want to go on any dates."

"Okay, let's think," Lauren said, scanning my apartment. "What's on your bookshelf?"

Jada marched over to my corner bookshelf. "Let's see here. *Audrey Hepburn: A Life In Pictures*. Ever notice no guy likes her? Only girls like her. *Something Borrowed* by Emily Giffin. She's a lawyer. Did you know that? *Good In Bed* by Jennifer Weiner. Got that, Lauren? Put that in the profile."

"Do not put that in my profile." I sat up. "It's not that kind of book anyway, Jada."

"What else? What's this? *Understanding Mean People*. Seriously, Veronica?"

"You'd have that book too if you worked for her bosses," Lauren said, defending me.

"Thank you, Lauren." Still, I didn't think Jada would need that book if she worked for Beverly or Kate. That was the difference between us.

"Okay, listen," Lauren said. "You like to travel. You like going out to dinner. You like museums and going to the beach."

"Yeah." I nodded. "I like museums when I have the chance to go."

Lauren typed quickly. She was always so eager to help. She reminded me of my mom.

"All right, let's upload your photos, and you'll be all set."

Hearing that caused my stomach to flip, but then it was all a bit anticlimactic when she finally declared that I was "all signed up."

"Let me see this." Jada sauntered over to the computer in my black-and-gold wedges.

I nudged my way in to give my profile a once-over. *Well, there I am. A single twenty-nine-year-old female lawyer in NYC, looking for a male within ten miles of me who is funny, college-educated, and has no piercings. Okay then.*

Lauren grinned. "Happy dating! Actually, my grandmother always said 'There's a lid for every pot.' So, happy lid searching."

"Thanks," I said as I reviewed my new profile. "By the way, what's my password?"

"Jada told me to make it PenniesFromHeaven. All one word." Lauren winked.

Jada had obviously told her about the pennies. I was okay with that. I'd always pegged Lauren for a believer. "I like it. Thanks."

After they left, I sat on my couch with a cup of tea and my laptop closed in front of me. I was curious to check out who might be on Match.com, but I wondered if it was better to be less active and let the boys come to me. I sipped my tea and glanced at a framed photo propped on my bookcase that I'd bought at a vintage shop in SoHo. The black-and-white image showed seven ladies lined up on a porch, hands on hips, dressed in fancy fringe dresses, and ready for a fun night. In white script on the bottom right, it read, "Newark, NJ 1927."

No flappers ever had to go online to meet men. They just went out dancing.

I reached for my middle finger, feeling the urge to twirl Grandma's ring. Then, I put my tea down, opened my laptop and searched. I searched until I couldn't keep my eyes open any longer.

Chapter 10

I woke up in the morning and immediately opened my laptop. *Has anyone winked at me since last night?*

Hmm, he's cute. Syd? He checked out my profile. Why didn't he send me a message? A shaved-head type. I like the boldness of the shaved head. And he wears it well. Nice face.

So I did it. Barely still awake, I sent my first Match.com email to a guy named Syd Blackman:

Hi there, I like your profile.

What does a creative director do? I'm a lawyer. You don't want to hear about what I do unless you need to fall asleep.

Where in the city do you live? I'm on the east side, in Midtown.

Not sure what else to say. Feel free to ask me anything!

That was easy. If I was going to get my feet wet and make some mistakes, I figured it might as well be with someone who was clearly not going to be my husband. He was cute, but I was pretty sure his family hadn't changed their name to Blackman when they'd come over from Italy.

I got in the shower. When I got out, I already had a little '1' near my envelope. My heart skipped a little. *I've got mail!*

Nice to "meet" you, Veronica.

Yes, I'm a creative director. I come up with those commercials that make you want to buy all the stuff you don't need. I like it a lot. But sometimes, we hear from the lawyers if we don't, for example, put helmets on animated lollipops riding motorcycles. That was an actual email I got from Legal last week. "The lollipops in your spot should be wearing helmets." But overall, it's a fun job.

Midtown is nice. I lived on the Upper West Side for a few years but just moved downtown.

I laughed while reading his message until "Upper West Side" made me think of John. I tightened my towel around me, and with my hair still dripping from the shower, I sat down on the couch to draft my reply:

That is funny! I suppose you do want your lollipops to be law-abiding. Thank God for the legal department. I'm taking a news reporting class to try a different job on for size. See what it feels like. Just for fun.

Where are you from originally? I'm from New Jersey—Bellefield—it's in North Jersey, not too far from the city.

Only child. Not spoiled. :) A Libra—the scales. :) What else would you like to know?

P.S. This is my very first correspondence on Match. I'm a little green.

After I hit Send, I wondered if I'd been too hasty revealing my novice status on Match.com. I finished blowing out my hair then checked my messages. *I guess I didn't scare him off.*

Reporting sounds like it could be interesting. I watch a lot of CNN. That and NFL network.

I'm from Jersey too. A town called Materdeen.

What else would I like to know? Hmmmm. Do you like bowling? I understand the risk in asking that question. So if I don't hear back, I won't be offended. ;)

I pushed aside some hangers in my closet, trying to figure out what to wear.

Bowling?

Yes, I'm addicted to this website, HumanInterestStories. net. My handle is RosannaZotto2.0. I can explain in person.

I haven't bowled in a long time. I have to say that's a funny question. :)

I hurried to the bathroom to put on my makeup. I was hovering too close to being late for work. I slapped on some concealer, bronzer, and mascara then hurried back to my computer:

Human interest stories. I will have to check it out.

A funny question, yes. But I have a good reason.

A good reason? I zipped my skirt and slipped into my heels.

Well, let's get these feet wet.

Sure, I'd go bowling if that's what you're asking. But may I buy you a drink first?

Before I was out the door, he replied:

No, you may not. I'm buying. Let me know what night.

I practically skipped out the door. *Well, what do you know? I may have just set up my first Match date. I'm a natural!*

Considering I'd almost been fired over Trista Hines, I had been trying to be extra early to work. But I missed the mark on that particular morning, arriving at eight thirty. As I opened the door to my office, I could hear Beverly's squishing shoes coming down the hall. She passed right by my office with only a grunt. I was momentarily relieved that she hadn't stopped in or said anything, but then I immediately worried about what that meant. I texted Jada. —I might be getting fired any day now. So, I might as well take a long lunch. Want to meet at 1?—

"You have a date already?" Jada appeared stunned as we waited in line for our salads. "Wait a second! Who is this guy? You haven't been on Match for even twenty-four hours yet."

"I know." I smirked.

"Besides, the fact is that he sounds nothing like your type. He's not Italian. He's bald? He's creative, did you say?"

"That's why he'll be a perfect first date for me. I figure I should go out with someone who's not Italian and therefore obviously not my husband. You know, to kind of break me into the whole online-dating thing."

"That doesn't sound very fair to him."

I hadn't thought of that. "Well, I don't know. It's just one date."

"Sounds like a plan, I guess," Jada said as we crossed the street. All of the awkwardness from our prior fight seemed to be completely gone, and I was grateful for that.

"Thanks for helping me sign up." I bit into a cucumber. "I'm really glad I did it. I think this is what I need. Even if I don't meet the love of my life, focusing my energy on new people and—"

"I cheated on Mark."

My forkful of salad never made it to my mouth, and a few pieces fell to the ground.

"What?"

"Don't make me repeat it," she said.

"When?"

"The other night." She looked down, moving her fork through her salad.

"Why didn't you say anything yesterday?"

"Because Lauren was there! I'm not telling anyone. *Anyone*. Please, Veronica. I'm only telling you. I just have to get it off my chest."

"Hold on, how did this... with who?"

"I don't even know where to begin with this story." Jada put her uneaten salad back in the paper bag and pushed her sunglasses back to rub her eyes. "Mark has been in Miami for work, so I went out with Michelle—you know, my friend from college. And her older brother Todd, who I used to *love*, just showed up at the bar... I wasn't expecting that—for him to be there. She didn't say he was going to be there. So of course, I drank too much, and of course, he conveniently lives two blocks from the bar, and we all went back there for an after-party, and, I don't know, everyone left but me."

I opened my mouth to say something or ask a question, but nothing came out.

"But listen, this whole thing never happened as far as I'm concerned. I just want to forget it happened. I'm not telling Mark. I would never. I can't. But I just had to get it off my chest. I decided the minute I left Todd's place that I wasn't going to tell a soul, but it's been eating at me. But now... I'm forgetting it ever happened." She appeared to feel better then, exhaling and taking a big gulp of her iced tea.

"Well, just because you're forgetting it ever happened, doesn't mean Ted, or Todd, I mean, isn't going to say anything to Michelle or anybody else."

"I swore him to secrecy," she said. "I threatened his life."

"Oh, I'm sure he's shaking in his boots!" *Is she serious?*

"I don't think he'll say anything."

"And how could you do that to Mark? I mean, yeah, you've been lukewarm about him for two years and probably should've broken up with him a long time ago, but he doesn't deserve to be cheated on!"

"Are you fucking kidding me?" Jada slammed her iced tea bottle down and pushed her chair back from the table. "I'm confiding in you. I don't need your judgment!"

Whoa. I picked up my salad and my tote bag. "Even if he never finds out, you made a fool of Mark. I am judging you. You should be ashamed of yourself."

"You're just jealous. I'm balancing two guys, and you're stuck online dating and wishing you were in London."

Ouch. I walked away, slamming my mostly uneaten salad in the trash on the way out of the park. I didn't let the weight of her words truly pierce me until I relived them in the bathroom at work, where I let the tears fall freely. *Two fights in one week with my best friend who I never fought with before. What is happening?*

Less than an hour after walking away from Jada, with my eyes and nose still red from crying, I was on a train headed to court in Kingsberg, New York.

Beverly phrased it this way: "Stop reading your silly websites. You're going to court."

It was funny how Beverly would hardly ever let Kate or me near any clients, but she trusted us enough to send us to court on their behalf. I thought she liked not having to leave the office for anything other than a smoke break.

"Kingsberg. The Stephens v. Hines case. Your favorite matter. Consider this your last chance to save your ass after the stunt you pulled. File the motion and get an order to satisfy. You know what that means. Get the—what is it? A doughnut truck? Get the doughnut truck and sell that baby for cash. Time to stop making the doughnuts." She laughed at her joke.

I didn't correct her that the truck sold mainly cupcakes, not doughnuts.

"Do not come back without that signed order. Stand over the judge while he signs it if you have to!"

After racing through Grand Central Station and barely making the train, I wiped the sweat from my brow and checked my phone. I had a Match.com message from Syd, asking if I would actually be up for a drink that night. I replied: —Your timing is impeccable. What a day this is turning out to be. I'm already thirsty.—

My next instinct was to text Jada with this new development. And then I remembered. I put my phone in my bag as I stared out the window at the passing scenery of houses, swing sets, and pools.

Then, I sat outside Judge Fila's chambers for an hour. I made it there by two o'clock, but his secretary told me to have a seat.

What will I say if the judge asks me if we've tried to settle at all? I can't say, "Yeah, well, my boss believes no defendant will ever stick to a payment plan. She calls them all losers. Ha. Ha... Ah, she's a riot."

When the door opened, two well-dressed men in dark suits emerged. The door shut. Judge Fila's secretary and law clerk were not at their desks. I didn't think I should just get up and knock on the judge's door, so I sat there, biting my lip and flipping through the file, which didn't have anything useful in it, and I probably knew more about this defendant than any other case. After ten minutes, the door opened.

Judge Fila was in his seventies, tall and slim with thin silver hair. "Hello there. May I help you?"

"Yes, I just filed a motion for default judgment downstairs, and we're also seeking an order to satisfy the judgment. The case is Stephens versus Hines." My throat was dry. My palms were soaked. I heard John's voice. *Grow a pair. You went to law school, and you're almost thirty.* I reached for Grandma's ring. *Fuck.*

"Come on in." He held the door open.

I sat down on the brown leather chair in front of his desk.

"Would you like a candy?" Judge Fila pointed to the bowl of Werther's candies on the edge of his desk.

"I'm fine, thank you." I barely glanced up from the file on my lap, making sure I had all of the filings in their proper order for him to review.

"Don't want to ruin your supper? Have a candy." He lifted the bowl this time. "When you're my age, you'll look back and say, 'I wish I ate more candy, less broccoli.'"

Fine, I'll have a damn candy. I peeked up toward the candy bowl and reached forward when I saw the penny—a shiny penny in front of me, next to the candy dish. I looked at Judge Fila and smiled then grabbed a candy and sat back.

"So, how may I help you?" He folded his hands and peered over his small glasses perched on the tip of his nose.

I explained the facts regarding my client Pat Stephens's foot and how Pat had an attorney who filed a complaint in the wrong county, then corrected it. But by then, Pat had lost confidence in that attorney, so he came to us. By that point, the defendant, Trista Hines, had never answered the complaint. So we filed a motion for default judgment, and after so much time, we would like an order to satisfy the judgment that would allow us to collect any assets that would satisfy my client's damages. Or one asset—a cupcake truck.

I left out the settlement agreement discussions.

"So, you haven't heard from the defendant?" the judge asked. "There've obviously been no settlement discussions?"

I accidentally swallowed the entire candy whole. *Ouch.* I crossed and re-crossed my legs and tried to ignore the pain as the entire thing worked its way down my chest.

"Well, we tried," I said. *I tried.*

Suddenly, there was a loud knock on the door, which jolted me and moved the candy further down. The door opened slowly, and a woman about my age, dressed rather casually for court in white sneakers and a gray tank top with light jeans, ambled in.

"Hi. I'm Trista Hines," she said.

If I hadn't accidentally swallowed the candy, it would've fallen out of my mouth.

"Come on in." Judge Fila welcomed her.

She smiled shyly as she sat in the chair next to me.

I expected Trista Hines to be short and petite with dark-brown hair. I don't know why. That was what she sounded like on the phone, as nonsensical as that was. In person, she actually had light-brown hair, the kind where I could tell she'd been blond as a little girl. If her hairdresser hadn't run off with her man, she would probably have pretty blond highlights. She was tall and thin with a tattoo of a butterfly on her right shoulder blade.

What the fuck? How did she know I'd be here?

"I'm sorry to bother you, sir." She cleared her throat nervously. "Ms. Buccino explained last week that they'd be filing the, uh, paperwork? I've been losing sleep over this, and then, just about an hour ago, I decided to call Pat Stephens myself, and we talked for a bit. He seems like a nice guy. But he said he didn't know what could be done because he knew you"—she looked over at me from the corner of her eye—"were actually down here as we spoke. So I raced down here and asked a few people downstairs what to do, and they told me you were the one, the judge, I mean, on this case."

Seeing Trista, someone who appeared to be more nervous than me, who clearly had bigger problems than me, tugged at my heart again. She was desperate. It also sounded as if she and Pat wanted to make a deal, but he was under the impression he had no power to do that. I had to fix this. Once again. *Fuck you, Beverly.*

I asked Judge Fila to excuse me so I could make a phone call to my client.

Ten minutes later, the settlement agreement was back on. Pat was, naturally, a little confused by yet another turnaround of events, but I reminded him he had every right to settle if that was what he wanted, that he was the client after all.

"I keep saying, 'What the hell am I going to do with a cupcake truck?' I'd rather get some cash every month to pay for my physical therapy," he said. "That's all I want."

I explained to Pat that, while Beverly was a lot of things—to which he replied, "Yeah, she's funny"—she was not unethical. I explained we simply had a difference of professional opinion.

He understood and said he was going with my advice. *So fuck you again, Beverly.*

Pat and I had such a good conversation that I even felt comfortable enough to say, "Let's not mention this to Beverly."

He laughed and agreed.

When I returned to Judge Fila's chambers, I think he was as delighted with the news as Trista. He held up the unsigned order and tore it in half. We shook hands, and Trista and I walked out.

Outside of the courthouse, with the sun shining, Trista hugged me and promised, "You'll never see me again. I mean, in a good way."

I headed back to the train station, feeling equal parts satisfied and terrified. The train back to the city wouldn't be leaving for another hour, so I stopped at a Starbucks and sat by the window. I couldn't believe I'd put myself in the same situation again. I couldn't believe I would be lying to Beverly again, hoping she never found out what I'd done. I tried not to think about it and called my mother to tell her about the penny on the judge's desk. When I hung up with her, I stared out the window and heard John's voice. *I think all that stuff is bullshit, but believe what you want.*

About six months into our relationship, we went to St. Bart's for a weekend. We still hadn't said "I love you" at that point. That should have been the first warning sign. Instead, I told myself that everyone moves at their own pace. In fact, it took John over a year and me saying it first.

We'd stayed at a beachside resort that I was glad I wasn't paying for. We had our own private chateau with a butler, maid, chef, and plenty of alcohol. John didn't drink that weekend. He was there to relax, not get hammered, he said. I, on the other hand, took the liberty of imbibing before, during, and after almost every meal. It felt like a waste not to, what with the bar in the living room, and the butler offering it up on a tray. The thing I remembered most was the veranda just off the living room with a queen-sized lounge chair. It was more of a bed than a lounge chair. We spent most of our time there. John, reading the financial news and typing on his phone. Me, drinking and looking at the waves.

That was where, tipsy and brave and wanting to share something personal, I first told him about the pennies, and that was when he first responded with, "You know that's bullshit, right? I mean, believe what you want if it makes you feel better, but don't be conned by those crystal-ball-reading lunatics who spout that kinda stuff." I tried not to be offended. *Not everyone has to be a believer*, I had told myself.

At Starbucks, I peered out the window at all of the people going somewhere rather than spending the hour, or afternoon, or day in an office. I thought about Jada and Judge Fila and work and the penny and my mom and believers and John.

I can't believe I'm going on a date tonight. I wonder what John is doing. I wonder if we're living parallel lives right now. Maybe he's thinking of me while he drinks English tea and is going on a first date tonight. Actually, since London is six hours ahead, he might be on that date right now. I hope she's awful.

When I got back into the city, I thought of stopping at Bloomingdales to buy a new top for that night but decided to do the responsible thing and go right to the office. It was the least I could do since I was currently the worst employee in New York City.

"Is it done?" Beverly asked, entering the elevator as I got off.

"Yes." I swallowed. It suddenly felt like that Werther's candy was working its way back up.

"Good. Get yourself dinner. We got a bunch of new cases, and we have to finish another motion to be filed first thing tomorrow morning. You're preparing it. It's going to be a long night. Pack a toothbrush."

I was relieved she didn't seem to want to know any more about what happened in court. She probably thought it was straightforward and taken care of.

Unfortunately, I still sensed I was on 'probation,' and therefore, in no position to sneak out for a drink with Syd. So I walked into my office, plopped down in my chair, and cancelled my date with Syd. He was understanding, writing back, —I've been there. We'll reschedule.—

I threw my phone in my tote, and before getting to work, I checked my email.

There was a message from my father—the first I'd heard from him in weeks since I ran out of Aunt Marie's house—asking me to review a contract with a new vendor for his restaurant.

Is he kidding me? No mention of Aunt Marie's. No apology whatsoever. Maybe he's related to Jada. Maybe we really are sisters. I stared at the message for a moment.

Fuck you. Like I need this right now. I deleted it and got back to work. *A lot can happen in a day.*

Chapter 11

"How do I know the penny was you?" I asked my grandfather. We were sitting at a table at Il Giardino in Little Italy.

"That's our sign," my grandfather said.

"I know, but maybe Judge Fila just left a penny on his desk?"

"Exactly."

"What do you mean 'exactly?' How do I explain what the pennies mean to skeptics like Jada or John? To me, it means you're there for me. I know it. I believe. But how do I explain it to the non-believers?"

"First of all, Veronica," Grandpa Sal said, "don't worry about explaining anything to anybody. Just know this: it wasn't a coincidence. No such thing." He sat back and rested his hands on his belly, staring out the window as though he were trying to figure out where to start a very long story. "Remember you shared a cab with a lady? It was raining, she had"—he did a waving motion by his head—"the blond hair?"

I thought about the night I went to John's to get—and forget—the wrong ring.

"Let's just say there are a lotta ways in which we're all... uh... connected. Some people would call it a coincidence. Call it what you want." Grandpa Sal held up a finger as if to say 'hang on' and took a moment to cut into his veal piccata and take a bite.

I tapped my fingers on my water glass. "I have no idea what you're talking about. The blond lady? What about her?"

"Now, help me out here, Antoinette, if I don't say this right." He sat back again. "The penny on Judge Fila's desk was there because it is our sign that says, 'Hey, my little *brasciole*, you're not alone. Breathe, would ya?' It's about perspective, Veronica. You gotta learn to relax and you'll, ya know, start to see things differently. The penny helped you relax. It didn't change that Judge Fila fella. It changed you."

"No. Judge Fila was a nice person, and it made me relax."

"If you were still anxious, you might not have seen that he was a nice person. You would have refused the candy, gotten it over with, and ran out the door. But we wanted you to relax. We wanted to help you. And we knew what was coming. Ya know, the Trista gal."

"So the pennies are your way of saying, 'Hi, we're here with you, and you'll be fine.' I already knew that."

"Now, how did it get there, ya wanna know?" he continued. "Well, Judge Fila did just leave a penny on his desk. It went like this. So, let's see, six months ago, was it?" He scratched his neck as he collected his thoughts. "A young man was in the judge's office. He drove to the courthouse and had to get his parking garage ticket, you know, what do they call it? Validated, right? He was sifting through his pants pocket before he left the judge's reception area to find his parking garage ticket. He pulled it out along with a load of change that scattered everywhere. He reached down to pick up his change. He got most of it, except a penny. Thanks to me, he left a penny there."

"How did you get him to miss that one penny?"

"Energy." Grandpa Sal winked at me and continued. "But that's not the whole story. Judge Fila's new secretary, she gets up from her desk an hour later and picks the penny up. She put it on her desk. Later, she and the judge are talking, and he says he's going to need all the luck he can get because his daughter's getting married on Saturday, and the weather better hold up because it will be outdoors under a tent in, where's that place in Long Island? What's it called? The Hamptons. Judge Fila told his secretary how it was his daughter's second marriage and hopefully, this one will be happier, and he doesn't mind paying for this one too even though she offered to pay for it, and she was a good kid even though she's not a kid anymore. His secretary gave him the penny and said, 'Here's your good-luck charm.' The secretary is not one to offer good-luck charms. She doesn't even know why she offered it. But we do." He winked again. "Am I getting this right, Ant?"

Grandma nodded.

"He walked back into his office and put the penny next to the candy. For you. Well, he didn't know—doesn't know—it was for you. He thought it was for him, but you get the point." Grandpa Sal went back to cutting his veal. "So there you have it, my little *brasciole*. Not that interesting, but you asked."

"All of the ordinary events in life, Veronica, they're not so ordinary after all." My grandmother twirled her pasta. "The weather held up for the judge's daughter. And this will be a long and happy marriage. She married for love this time."

"She married for love." Grandpa repeated Grandma's words then added, "She also happens to be that lovely blond-haired lady you shared a cab with on that rainy night. Remember? She said you're doing the right thing."

"The blond lady was Judge Fila's daughter?" I asked. "How weird is that?"

"Close that mouth, Veronica. What are ya catching, flies?" Grandma Ant said. "And not weird at all. You know how often connections like that happen, and you never know about it?"

"So what's the point of it all? That lady in the cab was the judge's daughter and the reason there was a penny on his desk for me to see. I'm not sure I get it, but—"

"You wanted to know if the penny was just a penny. How it all happened. Well, that's how it all happened," Grandpa Sal said. "We can see what's going on in your life. We see everything. And, ya know, we know when you're going to need us."

As I stared down at my chicken parm, my grandmother reached out to hold my chin in her hand and examine me as if I were some fragile figurine she'd just finished dusting in her breakfront. I gently moved my chin back away from her hand.

"How sharp you look when you dress in your suits, Veronica," Grandma Ant said. "I say to myself, 'That's my granddaughter walking down the street. Look at her, how beautiful. The cat's meow, she is.'"

I couldn't help but think of how uncomfortable I felt in suits—both literally and figuratively. "It's all very deceiving." I finally dug into my food. "In case you haven't noticed, I suck at my job."

"No. We don't see that," she said. "You might not like it. It's not your passion, but you're not as bad as you think."

"Because of work, I had to cancel my Match date. So who knows when I'll even be able to set up another date and actually go out with anyone. You might as well just tell me where the ring is. I feel naked without—"

"Nice try," Grandpa Sal said without looking up from his veal.

We sat in silence for a little while, eating and drinking and taking in the atmosphere. Il Giardino was a restaurant with an open air skylight. You could see the apartment building above and people's clotheslines.

"It's weird. My boss, Beverly, she can be so harsh, but she's funny too. I wish I could laugh at her jokes; I wish we had that rapport. But it's hard to overcome. I can't forget the other times when she's just so mean."

"You should try to forget," Grandma Ant said. "That's forgiveness. People talk about forgiving and forgetting. That's what forgiving is—forgetting."

Okay, this is getting too philosophical. I just wanted to vent about how strange my coworkers are.

"You hold onto things, Veronica," she continued. "Good and bad. With work, with your friends, with your father."

And I definitely didn't want to turn this into a conversation about my father or anyone else.

"Finish eating," Grandpa Sal said. "Let's go somewhere."

We all took a last bite of our meals. I saw from the corner of my eye that my grandfather had retrieved a cannoli from somewhere and ate it quickly before dusting the powder off his sweater and directing Grandma Ant and me out of the restaurant. "Let's go. Come on." He waved us out the door and down the street.

We turned a corner and entered a familiar building.

"I don't want to see Aunt Mary again." I stopped walking. "It was upsetting, and I—"

"Different time," Grandpa Sal called back. "This is a happy occasion."

I resumed following them, and we again took the rickety elevator up a few levels to the long hallway. Nurses in crisp, white caps were busy behind their stations and didn't notice us. We walked into a room and saw Aunt Mary again. But this time, she was younger and beautiful and holding a bundle wrapped in a pink blanket.

"Aw," I said. "Who's that? Oh, Mommy's cousin?"

"My godchild Annette at one day old... long before the black hair dye and the chain smoking. Ya know, before you knew her," Grandma Ant said, smiling.

I tiptoed forward to get a closer look at both of them. Suddenly, I heard a knock behind me.

It was Grandma Ant—not Grandma Ant now, but as she was then.

"Gram! You're—"

"The cat's meow," she said. "Yes, I was."

I was going to say "so young."

Grandma Ant lingered at the door.

"I didn't know if you'd come," Aunt Mary said.

"Well, I'm here." The young Grandma Ant removed her white leather gloves and rested her glittering black clutch on the table next to the bed. "How could I not welcome my niece? Let me look at her."

Aunt Mary handed Cousin Annette to Grandma Ant, who kissed her forehead. "Thank you for coming," Aunt Mary said.

"You don't have to thank me."

"I feel awful about the last couple years," Aunt Mary said. "I've wanted to call and—"

"Forget it. I'm sorry too. Let's forget it and kiss this baby over and over." Grandma Ant nuzzled Annette.

Aunt Mary laughed, and Grandma Ant scooted onto the bed next to her, still holding the baby.

"What are you talking about?" I asked my grandmother.

"She's my sister." Grandma Ant adjusted herself, half-sitting on the windowsill. "I love her. We are very close, and we were very close in, ya know, the physical world. But there was a time when, let's just say, we weren't so close."

"That's one way to put it," Grandpa Sal said.

"Around the time Grandpa and I were supposed to get married, Mary became engaged to Vito. After us! They became engaged after us. But ya know what she did? She went straight to our church—St. Gerard's in Newark—and she booked her day for as soon as possible."

"That bitch!" I laughed at my own joke.

Grandpa Sal snorted and laughed one of his silent laughs with his hand on his belly.

"It was a terrible thing to do," Grandma continued. "We knew Grandpa was going to be drafted. He was drafted a month later, and we didn't see each other for four and a half years. But Vito, he was 4F." She folded her hands as if that rested her case.

"What's 4F?"

"He was ineligible!" she shouted as though I should have known that. "He couldn't serve. So she didn't have to rush to get married. If anyone should have gotten married sooner and had more time with her husband—as husband and wife—it was different back then, ya know? We didn't live together until we were married. If anyone should have had more time as a wife, it was me. I had to kiss him goodbye a month later!"

"So, did you go to their wedding?" I asked. "I would have skipped it. I mean, honestly, that's a crappy thing to do now that I think about it."

"Of course I went. I was the maid of honor. But let me tell you, I was very hurt, very upset. After my wedding, and after Grandpa got drafted, she had her husband home with her. Now, I didn't know at the time how Vito would turn out to be, but as far as I knew, she rushed her wedding ahead of mine and then had a husband home with her."

"Did you tell her?"

She shook her head. "I stopped speaking to her." She held her hand to her mouth for a second. "For two years."

My mouth dropped.

"I refused to speak to her," she continued, not taking her eyes off the scene of her, Mary, and Annette. "If there was a holiday or a birthday or Sunday dinner, I would go to my parents' early and then leave early, or I would say, 'Oh, I'm spending it with my in-laws.' When Grandpa was in the service, I made sure to see my in-laws every day because that was the right thing to do, and because I didn't want to go to my parents' house or see or speak to Mary. It broke my mother's heart, but I was stubborn."

"So, what happened?" I asked. "How did you reconcile?"

Grandma pursed her lips then grabbed a tissue from up her sleeve.

She used to do that when she was alive too, keep tissues stuffed up her left sleeve. I always thought that was odd. She shook her head in response to my question and pointed to my grandfather to take over.

"Vito beat Mary up so bad, she was in the hospital for a week," he said. "She almost lost the baby"—he jutted his chin in their direction—"Annette."

"When I found out what had been going on, I was so..." Grandma Ant's voice cracked, "ashamed of myself... for being so petty. I couldn't—" She cried harder. "I couldn't believe how I'd acted. Every time I thought about it—ya know, during the time we didn't speak—I was so sure I was right. I was the one who had been wronged. But then when I found out what she had been going through—"

Grandpa put his arm around Grandma.

I turned back to study Aunt Mary, Annette, and Grandma. Aunt Mary lifted Annette's little hand, and they marveled at each of her fingers. Grandma Ant kissed the palm of each of her hands and stroked her wispy baby hair. Aunt Mary looked at Grandma, complimented her earrings, and asked if she'd heard from Sal. They looked comfortable with each other. Just like sisters. It was hard to believe anything had ever come between them.

Chapter 12

IT WAS A PARTICULARLY BUSY morning, and I hadn't even started working. First, I retrieved the deleted email from my father and replied:

> Hi, Dad. Yeah, I'll take a look at this contract. This is not the kind of law I practice so definitely not my expertise, but I'll let you know if anything pops out at me.

Then, I texted Jada. —Hey, I want to apologize. It's complicated.— *I suppose.* —But I still want to be there for you as a friend, literally and figuratively. Let me know if you want to grab lunch.—

She replied right away. —I can't meet for lunch today.—

My heart dropped at her curt reply.

But then she sent another text. —I'm sorry too, by the way. Let's forget it. We're cool. K?—

I wasn't sure what she was apologizing for. Cheating on Mark? Or maybe, finally, acknowledging that she was not being supportive about my class. I replied. —K. Let me know when you're around.—

Over the course of our entire friendship, Jada and I had bickered as though we were sisters, but it was part of our teasing relationship. Not serious. Not about anything that mattered. But in the past couple of weeks, we'd both stormed out on one another. Maybe it was me. After all, I'd also stormed out on my father. Or maybe it was the stress of the new challenges each of us was facing in our own lives. Whatever it was, I hoped it never happened again.

She replied. —I can probably have lunch tomorrow or later in the week. Just been crazy around here! How was your date?—

After I explained what had happened and how I had to cancel on Syd, she replied. —I'm sorry. Keep me posted on all your dates. I want to hear!—

I spent the rest of the day working, reading HumanInterestStories. net, and researching Filamina March. Before I knew it, it was time to sneak out and go to class.

As if on cue, my door burst open.

"Veronica!"

I squinted. "Hi. I have a migraine," I told Beverly. "I see spots, and I can't see half of my computer screen."

She sighed and stared at me from the corner of her eye. "We got twelve new cases," she continued. "Start reviewing them." She paused as I dramatically rubbed my left eye while she spoke. "And don't pull another, what was it, doughnuts? Cupcakes? Don't pull another cupcake crusade. I've been doing this a lot longer than you, Stevie Wonder. The defendants never pay over a long term. First few months, yeah, everyone's happy, but they never make the whole payment to our clients. Better to not prolong it, and just grab whatever assets they have and auction them off. Better for our client—"

I cracked my neck loudly.

"Oh fine, go home. Be here at seven thirty tomorrow morning. We have to get started on these," Beverly said before dropping the new files on my desk and marching out.

I grabbed my tote bag and raced to the elevator. While it stopped at every floor on the way down, I checked my phone and saw a message from Syd, asking about rescheduling our date. Although I couldn't help but smile as I saw his name pop up on my screen, I figured I would do the practical thing and nip it in the bud. He wasn't Italian after all, so there was no point, and as Jada had pointed out, it wasn't really fair to him.

I decided to go with a polite and little white lie in reply. —Hi, Syd. Forgive me for not reaching out first since I was the one who had to cancel. So, oddly enough, my ex-boyfriend recently came back into the picture, and we're going to give it another chance. I'm so sorry. Bad timing, I guess. I wish you all the best in dating and everything.—

I felt bad lying to him because I got the impression he was a nice guy, but between work and class, I had to use my limited time to date wisely. I had to go out only with those dates who had the potential of being something more.

I figured my intuition was correct because, not a moment later, I received a Match.com email from a Greg Salerno. I replied to Greg. He was thirty-four, worked in finance, had gone to Lehigh, and had played hockey in high school.

Veronica Salerno. I like it. Okay, stop. That's pathetic… but it does have a nice ring.

A lot of people in law school were like Elena. She had that unwavering confidence that didn't come from being the prom queen, but from being the president of the Key Club—a total, unabashed dork who didn't appear bothered by the fact. She either didn't pick up on her own eagerness or missed the social cues that being such a gunner was not cool. Or maybe she just didn't care. Either way, it served her as an adult. I wished I could chip away at my own self-awareness, wished I were a little less conscious of how I may have seemed to others, or most of all, wished I just didn't care.

Elena volunteered to go first, naturally. The assignment was to present a story idea, including the who, what, where, when, why, and how. We were to present it as a video story: B-roll, interviews, voice-over, intro, and outro. Also, it had to be local—in the New York tristate area.

Elena's story idea was about an exhibit that was coming to the museum in South Street Seaport—a study of the human body with exhibits of deceased Asian men and their preserved remains. She proposed to interview the museum director and learn why and how they got that exhibit, how long it would be there, and what we could learn from it. *Interesting.*

Asa's story was about students from the Fashion Institute who were designing dresses out of egg cartons. She proposed that she would interview them, their professor, and try on one of the dresses. *Cool.*

Jo's story was about a group of ex-pat British Arsenal fans, how they met every week at the same bar, how some Americans had joined, and how soccer was becoming more popular in the States. She proposed to interview the founder of the group and the bar owner. *Fun.*

I was next. My story suddenly seemed awfully dark. But for once, I didn't care. I proposed to interview Filamina March's wedding party—maid of honor, bridesmaid, and best man. My idea was to retrace the love story of Filamina and her husband from the beginning. Were there any signs? Any overheard snide remarks? Any foreshadowing of trouble in the future? I'd planned to use their wedding photos and photos from her bridal shower and bachelorette party as B-roll.

Silence.

I swallowed. *Too soap opera-ish?*

Then Dave said, "That's pretty ambitious."

That's a good thing, right?

"Well, here's what I didn't tell you last week," he said. "You're all going to actually produce your stories. These are all going to happen. And we're going to put them on the NewYork3News.com site."

I felt my throat get dry. "I thought this was just for class, just an exercise of our dream story."

"I lied," Dave said. "Well, I didn't really lie. I wanted each of you to pick something that you were sincerely interested in. Now, I'm thinking out loud here. We do cover crime at NewYork3News, but it's not our best section on the site. This could be really good. I mean, you're not going to get the wedding party—you could try—but maybe you could get a neighbor. Let's go for a neighbor." His arms were folded as he tapped his fingers while he thought some more. "Yeah, Veronica. Let's talk after class. My boyfriend is from the same area as where this family lives, so I know it's not that far. Still considered New York area news."

I nodded.

"The other thing I didn't tell you last week is that not only are we going to actually produce all of your stories, but whichever story gets the most hits, that person will get a freelance gig with us. Not full time. Don't quit your day job just yet. But a few stories a month, and you'll get paid for each story. Great for your reel. Great for networking. Great for landing that full-time job sooner or later. All right, uh, Veronica, you can sit down."

As I took my seat, Asa whispered, "Crazy story. That's going to be good."

Jo, overhearing, glanced in my direction and nodded. Having been around Beverly and Kate so much, I'd forgotten what it felt like when other people had faith in me. Then I noticed Elena was saying nothing. She had her head down, reading something in her notes. That, I was familiar with.

"So, your story might be a little more work than the others, but I think it could be really good," Dave said to me as we spoke after class. "So for next week, find a neighbor. Let's set up an interview, pick a date, and we'll coordinate with the camera crew."

Camera crew? Oh, crap. When the hell am I going to have time to track down neighbors of Filamina March? Let alone find one who is willing to talk on camera. What the hell did I get myself into?

"Sound good?" Dave asked.

And how the hell am I going to do this in between work and dating and… work?

"Sounds great," I said.

"You can do it," Jada said as she bit into her turkey wrap. "You'll figure it out. Let me know if you need help with, whatever, questions or whatever."

"Thanks," I said. "How's Mark?"

"Good," Jada said, a little perkier than was typical of her. "We're going to that new restaurant on Fourteenth Street tonight. Rusignuolo's. I think I'm saying it right. I heard it's amazing."

"Oh, fun!" I replied, also a little perkier than I'd intended.

"Are you excited for your date tonight? What's his name? Greg?"

"Yes. Greg Salerno. I didn't expect him to schedule a date so quickly. I'm freaking out. And it's been awhile since I've been on a date. I mean, I don't think I've ever been on an official first date other than John. You know how it was in college and law school. We always kind of knew the person we were going out with. I don't know. It's weird. I'm nervous."

"You better call me right after. I want all of the details."

"I will. I hope I can sneak out of work without incident. I'm running out of excuses lately."

"Diarrhea," Jada said.

"Huh?" I stopped eating my sandwich.

"Best excuse ever. No one can make you stick around if that's the case."

"I guess." I placed my sandwich down for a moment.

"Although, knowing Beverly, she'll probably tell you to go to the store and get a butt plug and get back to work."

"Ew!" I laughed so hard, a few people in line at the counter turned around.

This made Jada laugh so hard she had to consciously swallow her food so she didn't choke. We laughed until we cried. I supposed we were officially back to normal.

At six forty-five, when I sensed the coast was clear, I went to the bathroom and freshened my makeup. Then, I never went back to my office and headed straight for the elevator.

Please don't let Beverly be coming back from a smoke break when I get downstairs. I made a beeline for a taxi when I got outside. I shut the door and said, "Seventy-First and Third," the location of Jamie's Bar on the Upper East Side, which was Greg's selection. Then, I heard my name.

"Veronica!" Beverly shouted, cigarette in hand.

Oh crap.

I rolled down the window. *Should I yell "diarrhea" across the sidewalk on a busy street?*

Before I could say anything, she said, "Don't be late tomorrow morning. Client meeting at eight."

"Okay," I replied. *Is that it?* I guessed I was off the hook for the night. As the cab waited for the light to change, I tried not to look in Beverly's direction, but something caught my eye. It was another figure, another person, standing next to her, cigarette in hand, puffing away madly: Kate.

I didn't know much about Kate, or anything at all really, but I would bet she took up smoking just to get in Beverly's good graces. *Now that is a true kiss-ass.*

The cab sped away, and I was on my way to my first Match.com date. My heart was pounding, and my palms were sweaty. I kept wiping my hairline in case I had beading sweat. *What if I can't recognize him from his picture? What if he can't recognize me? When the hell is John going to realize he made a mistake and come crawling back to me? When will I stop asking myself stupid questions?*

I arrived early. I headed straight to the bar and ordered a martini. I reached to twirl my grandmother's ring but felt my naked fingers and cracked my knuckles instead. After ten minutes, I was convinced I was being stood up until someone tapped my shoulder.

"Veronica?"

Well, hello. He could have been John's younger, darker brother. He was tan, with wide shoulders and thick, brown hair. He'd just come from work and was in a suit that fit his well-built frame perfectly.

"Hi!" I felt my shoulders drop as he pulled up the barstool next to me and ordered a vodka on the rocks.

We talked about the usual – how long we each lived in the city, where we went to school, work. He did something in finance, which should have reminded me of John but didn't. We moved on to friends. He was still friends with his college and MBA school buddies, though most were now married and moving to the suburbs.

When we got to family, I felt the twinge I sometimes felt when the topic was brought up. *Are his parents still together? One big, happy family? Or, like me, does he come from a "broken home," as John would put it?*

"My parents are divorced," Greg said.

"Mine too," I said.

John was always so proud of how his parents were married for over thirty years. They'd had a huge party for their thirtieth anniversary. It was before John and I were dating, but I saw the photo album on a visit to his parents' house. It was propped up on their mantle.

"That's from our party. Look at it. Thirty years!" his mother had said.

I couldn't help but notice that there were only two photos of John's parents together, cutting a cake. The rest of the photos showed his father talking to guests at their tables and his mother either sitting down eating or talking to—probably yelling at or bossing around—the maître d'.

"My mother ran off with her boss." Greg chewed on a straw.

Oh. We have a lot in common, I suppose. Should I tell him about my father?

"Yup, she was his *secretary*. Can you believe that? I don't know why she would want to leave my father. He's a great man. She's a bitch. I haven't seen her in twenty years. She ruined holidays. She ruined family vacations." He shook his head and reached for his drink. "She ruined everything."

Wait. Did he just call his mother a bitch? I felt my chest tighten. "Did you—sorry—did you just… call your mother a bitch?"

He stopped chewing on the straw. "Yeah, are you going to defend her, lawyer girl?"

"No." I feigned a laugh. I didn't want it to get even more uncomfortable, but I knew one thing for sure: I did not want to sit through an entire dinner with this guy. I wasn't even sure that was where it was going—we'd only agreed to meet for drinks, after all—but after another twenty minutes, before it could go any further, I reached for my wallet and placed a bill on the bar.

"Leaving?" He was back to chewing his straw, and it appeared, examining me from the bottom up as I maneuvered off the barstool.

"Yeah." I gently placed my hand on my stomach. "I'm sorry—I—have—I don't feel so good. It's—yeah—I have to go."

"Feel better." He smirked. And I thought I heard him say something to the effect of "All right, well, hey, call me," as I ran out of the bar and right into a taxi.

I called Jada as soon as I was in the cab. "Okay, he was really cute, but he called his mother a bitch."

"What?"

"I think he has anger issues. He was really good-looking, but I don't know, creepy. I had to get out of there. I used the diarrhea excuse."

"No, you didn't!"

"Okay, not in so many words."

"Well, issues or not, diarrhea or not, you went on your first Match date. I'm proud of you. Your feet are officially wet!"

I sat back as the cab made every light on Third Avenue, and watched all of the stores pass me by. Intermix. High-End Home Furnishings.

"Yes, officially wet." I exhaled. "Splish splash."

Chapter 13

IN THE CASE STATUS MEETING with Beverly and Kate, the Stephens v. Hines case came up again, and Beverly said, "I know that motion was filed along with a motion to seize assets to satisfy the judgment. So, let's monitor that for collection." I nodded eagerly, then returned to my office, shut the door, and pulled up the Case Status spreadsheet.

We—Beverly, Kate, and me—all had access to the file. We were supposed to be updating it regularly. I scrolled through and noted over four hundred lines on the "Active" tab. That meant we currently had over four hundred ongoing cases.

That's a lot of money in Beverly's and the firm's pocket. And that's a lot of cases to keep track of. I know she has an issue with what I did and would go ballistic if she knew what really happened at court—even though I did nothing wrong since it's up to the client ultimately, and all I did was give him a second opinion that he went along with—but I also know Beverly. She's not the most organized person, and she will forget about keeping track of this eventually.

So, I cut the row with the Stephens v. Hines case and pasted it in the "Closed" tab. Beverly only ever reviewed the Active cases, the cases we needed to wrap up in order to collect our percentage.

I reached for my grandmother's ring to twirl. *Crap.*

Then, I checked my email and set up Match.com date number two, hopeful that he couldn't be worse than the first guy.

Moments later, Rich LaFiorno replied that "drinks would be cool."

Cool. I moved on to my other assignment.

I Googled "Filamina March address," and hundreds of articles came up, mostly related to her husband and the upcoming trial. Not surprising. When I tried "Filamina March address Anton, NJ," I found that the doctor and his wife owned a number of properties even within the town of Anton. So which Anton address was it?

Hmmm. I've narrowed it down to one of three addresses, but they all look like the house I've seen on the news and HumanInterestStories.net. Large brick houses. Set back. Red door. They own three houses in the same town all with red doors? These people are truly bizarre.

And I know my own door is going to burst open any minute. I have to do this now, and I have to be sure I have the right one. I'll have to use one of these people-finder sites. But which one? And they all cost something. And once I find the Marches' address, will I be able to find their neighbors? Will anyone be willing to talk to me?

A few more clicks and I found myself spending $159.99 to be absolutely certain I had the right address. *This class is now costing me more than I expected.* It turned out to be worth it since it confirmed one of the addresses I'd narrowed it down to—the one where the attempted murders had happened. Even better, the site provided names and telephone numbers of all of the Marches' neighbors. And that was how I found Selma Renner.

"Hi, Selma? Uh... Mrs. Renner?"

"The one and only! You're talking to her."

"Hi! My name is Veronica Buccino, and I'm calling about your neighbors, the Marches." My throat felt a little dry. "Do you have some time to chat?" I stared at the closed door of my office and willed it to stay shut. *Please don't let Beverly walk in.*

"Well, today's your lucky day, Veronica. Usually, I'm at bridge at this time, but we pushed it off to eight o'clock because my friend Barbara's getting a mole removed. And any other day, who knows if you'd catch me. I have my bingo, my mahjong, my canasta. I'm very busy. On Sundays, I go food shopping. I take my friend Millie. She doesn't drive. And you know what? I don't cook. So I drive us to the A&P, and then she'll make me a tray of lasagna. Or last week, she made this terrific dish. It had, uh, some kind of meat and—"

"That's so nice. Wow, yeah, you are busy. Let me ask you—"

"You better believe it. I'm always going. The ladies at the center say, 'Look at her. We can't keep up with Selma Jean.'"

"That's great. Well—"

"Oh yeah, grass doesn't grow under my feet. But right now, I'm free. So you're in luck."

"Great. Well, about the Marches—Dr. March and his wife—I'd love to talk to you—"

"You got questions. I got answers."

My other line started to ring. It was Beverly.

Shit.

I knew I had only moments to set up a date with Selma Renner. I knew I had to do it then and there because Beverly would be at my door any moment.

"I'm not sure if you've been interviewed yet about the ongoing court case, but I'd like to set up a day to come to you and do an in-person interview with a cameraman from NewYork3News. It'll be very casual, and we won't take too much of your time."

"Oh, so this is for the TV news? What station are you with?"

"It's called NewYork3News.com. It's an online news site, covering events and stories in New York, New Jersey, and Connecticut. It's not on TV. It's on the Internet, on the computer. But it's video. You can watch it like a TV." I was speaking like they do at the end of a car commercial on the radio, fast and factual. "So what day next week are you free?"

"My great-grandniece is a reporter on TV. In Florida. Her name is Juliette Markel. You know her?"

"How nice. No. Nope. Doesn't ring a bell. How about one week from today?"

My phone rang again. It was Beverly.

"Well, she's in Florida. But I thought maybe you all knew each other."

"No, don't know her. So this day next week would work?"

"Let's make it two weeks from today. That's better. Ya know, this isn't my first time on TV. There was a hurricane last year. Hurricane, um, oh what was it? Hannah? I can't remember. It was a big one, and the people who live at the center would not evacuate, and they interviewed some of us. Now, I don't live there, but I said how I don't blame some of my friends for not wanting to leave. You know, not wanting to have to pack up their things, their medications."

"Okay, good, so you've done this before. So, I'll confirm with the cameraman and call you back. I look forward to meeting you, Mrs. Renner."

"That woman is a slut."

"Excuse me?"

My phone rang again. Although it was Beverly again, I was relieved to know I still had a few more seconds before she barged through my door.

"Well, you know, Dr. March was a philanderer too. That's what got them in all this mess. But she's no Mother Theresa, his wife, let me tell ya. Oh, I'll fill you in when we get together, Veronica. All right, doll. Take care."

As I hung up, Beverly opened the door and let it swing so hard, it hit the wall. "I was calling you."

"I was in the bathroom."

She eyed me suspiciously. "I heard you on the phone."

"I was just getting off a quick call with an old friend of my grandmother's." *Where the hell did I pull that one out of? At least it was better than the truth: I was lining up an interview for a class I'm sneaking out of here to take, and I'll be calling in "sick" in two weeks to conduct it.*

"By all means, use firm time and the firm telephone to catch up with old family friends. That's what it's there for." She squished away in her orthopedic shoes.

She must have forgotten what she was planning to ask me, and I didn't follow up.

Nine hours later, I snuck out on a "coffee run" in order to meet Match. com date number two. I walked into Cellar Bar and made it through half of a head swivel before I heard my name from a slightly nasal voice.

"Veronica?" I saw a dark-haired guy with a stocky build approach me and embrace me as though we hadn't seen each other since childhood. I hugged him back and held in a giggle.

We found a seat at the bar, and although he had thick dark hair and deep dimples, I didn't want to kiss him. And I didn't want to kiss him after three glasses of wine either. I was relieved that he didn't suggest we get dinner.

I was supposed to go back to the office but instead went home, kicked off my heels, poured myself another glass of wine, and pulled out my laptop. If these dates didn't lead to my husband, the least they could do was entertain my friends. I wrote an email to Jada and Lauren with the subject line: Date Report #0002.

Excuse used to get out of work before 9PM: Going on a Starbucks run at 7PM; never went back

Name: Rich LaFiorno.
Age: 32.
Occupation: Electrical engineer.
Rating (from 1 to 10; 10 is my husband): 4

We met at Cellar Bar in the Bryant Park Hotel. Nice dimples, but I didn't want to rip his clothes off. We talked about work (he's an engineer; he explained it in detail; I zoned out) and families (he's got a mom and a dad and a brother and a dog named Scruffy) and friends and where we went to school and who we might know in common and vacations and restaurants and summer share houses (Hamptons, Fire Island, Spring Lake) and books and TV shows and how do you like Match so far and, oh dear God, there are absolutely zero sexy sparks. By my third glass of wine and the thirty-third topic of polite conversation, there was nothing left to talk about, and we just pecked on the cheek and said goodbye. I had that same feeling of wanting to get out of there like I did with date number one, but for a different reason, of course.

Oh well. Next...

Jada promptly replied to this date report with:

119

Yawn!

Lauren replied:

> I was waiting for a report on date #0001, but then I got
> the scoop from Jada. Ick! And this #0002 sounds nice
> but yeah, yawn! Whatever happened to Syd? Was that his
> name?

I didn't know how to answer Lauren's question, or how to explain
the real reason—because I wanted to marry an Italian, and he wasn't
Italian, and he would have been a good first date to get my feet wet,
but now what was the point?—over email, or text, or in person, without
sounding calculating and a little ignorant. So, I chickened out and just
replied:

> One 'Ick' and one 'Yawn.' I guess it can only get better
> from here!

The next night, I couldn't set up any less-than-spectacular dates because
I had to go to class.

"She sounds fucking amazing," Dave said after class. "What a find."

I couldn't help but grin one of those big grins that in a few moments
I would have to say to myself, *Close your mouth. You look crazy.* I glanced
at my feet and then back up.

"Veronica, I think you have something huge on your hands. The
potential for a major story. Isn't Rosanna Zotto supposed to interview
Filamina? She's probably not going to get much out of her, and it's
probably going to be a short interview, like most are for TV news. But
you have the potential for a huge story. For breaking news. She called
her a 'slut'? Depending on what this Selma knows, she could add a
very interesting perspective. No one else has found her—I have no idea
why—let alone interviewed her. I want to ask you something—"

*Oh crap... no. no. no. Damn! Screw him. I found Selma. This is my
story, my interview. He is not taking this away from me!*

"I'm up for it. I can do it!"

"Excuse me?" Dave appeared confused.

"Are you going to try to give this story to one of your reporters? Do you think I can't handle it because I didn't go to journalism school or because I'm a lawyer, and I've never been on camera? You're wrong. I can do this."

"I was going to ask you if you feel comfortable writing a complementary piece to go along with the video story."

"Oh." I saw the corners of his mouth curl up slightly. "Sure. You'll obviously look at it before it goes on the website, right?"

"Of course. I'll be editing it and so will the editor. But you'll be writing it. I know you're a lawyer, and you're very busy, but I just wanted to see if you'd be willing to do that. I think it could really complement the video story. We like to give people something to read. We found people don't always click on the video. It'll be more work, and no one else in the class will have to do a written portion along with their story, so I wanted to make sure you're on board."

"Sounds good." *I suppose I should learn how to write like a journalist and not a lawyer at some point soon.*

"Great." Dave stood. "Oh, and you'll get a byline. That's always nice. We still have to make sure the video is superb, of course."

Superb? Of course! Superb.

The next day, in between Googling "How to Not Write Like a Lawyer," dodging Beverly, and being insulted by Kate, I set up a lunch date. I sipped on a Diet Coke at the sushi bar where we'd planned to meet. AJ was late, but when I heard "Veronica?" in a deep voice and turned around to see a tall, tan guy with bulging biceps beneath his white-collared shirt, I decided that I didn't mind waiting.

What I did mind was his personality. After two strikes of rudeness, I decided that instead of sitting through lunch with a pit in my stomach waiting for the third strike, I had to get out of there. I told him I had to go back to work and couldn't eat after all.

I spent the rest of the day trying to get some work done in between Googling "Elements of a Feature Story," before I was back home on my couch by nine o'clock. With my laptop and a glass of wine in front of me, I typed up Date Report #0003:

Excuse used to get out of work before 9PM: None. I made it a lunch date.

Name: AJ Vitiello.
Age: 36.
Occupation: Something in finance, who the hell knows.
Rating (from 1 to 10; 10 is my husband): 2

I will make this quick. We met at a sushi place on the Lower East Side. I was leery of lunch on the first date, but I agreed because I liked his name. Veronica Vitiello. The alliteration was appealing. Shut up, Jada. Anyway, I didn't get to eat. I got out of there. I will give him this: he's really cute, dark hair, broad shoulders, all the good stuff. And everything was going seemingly well until the hostess came over and asked if we would like to be seated for lunch. At that moment, his phone rang and—ugh—he took it! With the hostess still standing there! And he talked to whoever it was for a while! The hostess and I were just hanging on until she excused herself, and I just sat there. How rude! And how awkward!

After that, we talked for a little while longer, and I told him about my news reporting class. He replied, "Why would you want to do that? You're a lawyer. You're going to waste all that education and time and energy you spent passing the bar? Don't you think that's stupid?"

Check, please! I told him I had to go back to work.

Oh, P.S., I am D-O-N-E with Match. Done. I met Mr. Angry, Mr. Boring, and Mr. Rude with a side of Negative.

I'm going back to meeting men the old-fashioned way—B-A-R-S!

Oh, P.P.S, I did see a penny on the sidewalk on the way out. Anyway, I'm drinking alone in my apartment now. Good night.

Lauren quickly replied:

Your grandparents were telling you the next one won't be such a jerk like this AJ!! And, wtf?! I think it's wonderful that you're taking that class. I want to hear more about it, actually.

Jada replied.

Did you request jerk and/or clunker in your profile?

I replied.

Yes, right after the "lives within a ten-mile radius" requirement.

I turned my computer and phone off and went to sleep.

Chapter 14

"WHAT'S IT LIKE TO DIE?" I'd been strolling through Central Park with my grandparents. I put on my sunglasses as we settled on a bench.

"Oh, it's wonderful." My grandmother closed her eyes and let the sun hit her face. "It's a party. Everyone you ever loved who went before you is there to greet you. And everyone looks just like you remember them."

"How could they look like you remember them?" I asked. "They're stuck at that age for eternity?"

"It doesn't work like that," my grandfather said. "When we visit with you here, we look like you remember us—ya know, very good-looking," Grandpa said.

Grandma opened her eyes to roll them and went back to letting the sun hit her face. "And it's meant to help you, how do I say, to put things in a human form, so you can relate and understand. But we're not actually somewhere. This isn't a—what's the word—physical place. We're still who we are, but we just look like this during our visits. I don't know if I'm explaining it right. Think of it like this—if the whole world were blind, then you'd only see people for their souls. That's how it is when you die. *Capisce?*"

The more I thought about it, the more I liked the idea that it didn't matter what anyone looked like because we were all, at our core, energy. We all had our own energy, our own soul, our own center, and in the end, that was all that mattered.

"So, where do you go when you die?" I asked. "I don't get that part."

"You go to the other side. And that can be anywhere you want.

You've seen how that works," Grandma Ant said. "And that moment when you pass, that welcome party can be anywhere, so to speak. You can choose a big, open space, standing on clouds, whatever it is your heart desires. I chose a memory, a place—my parents' bakery on Stone Street, where I met your handsome grandfather."

"I chose my parents' house in Newark," my grandfather said.

"Do you know you're dead?" I asked.

They both laughed and answered "yes" at the same time.

"It's not scary?" Even though I believed in life after life and that my loved ones who had passed before me were still with me, the idea of death scared me... maybe because I was still alive.

"Not scary at all," my grandfather continued. "When I walked into that house, it was just like I remembered, and then I saw my mother. She walked out of the kitchen, wiping her hands on a dish towel, like she'd just finished cooking. Just how I remembered her. You know, she died when I was in London, serving."

I thought of my grandfather as a young man in his early twenties. He must have been so scared to be in another country and to be at war and to hear such awful personal news. He must have felt so alone. My grandmother must have been so worried, not knowing when the war would end, and when or if they would ever see each other again.

And there I was, sitting between them. *Me? I hate work, and I can't find a guy.* I felt equal parts lucky and silly at that moment.

"Life went on, and I got to see my mother again," Grandpa Sal said. "And I see her now. And when I walked into the house, and she was there, it was something else. She looked like a healthier version of how she looked back then."

I knew what he meant. Grandpa died when I was fifteen. Right before he died, he had lost some color in his face. Something just didn't look right for a few weeks before. He'd suddenly appeared older to me. But right now, he had rosy cheeks, his full head of gray hair, and his big belly. My grandmother liked to say his hands were chubby, and his fingers were fat little sausages. He wore a gray sweater vest with a neatly ironed white collared shirt underneath, and his favorite black pants. I wondered if, even on the other side, my grandmother still picked out his clothes for him.

"She hugged me," Grandpa Sal continued. "And she said in Italian, 'Welcome home, Salvatore, my baby.' We hugged for a long time." He sat up straight and put his arms out. "When I let go, I saw all of these people—my father, my brothers, my sister, aunts, uncles, cousins, all the ones who went before. They were all there, and they were all so happy and looked so good, and they were all saying, 'Welcome home, Sal!' and they were hugging me."

I rested my head on my grandfather's shoulder for a second. He put his arm around me and kissed the top of my head.

When I sat up, I asked, "But all along, while you were alive and they'd already gone to the other side—like your mother, for instance— didn't you see your mother? Didn't you visit with her on the other side like I'm doing with you?"

"Yes. But it's different. When you're both finally on the other side, it's—I don't know how to say—but you both understand. You're not still going through life. You don't have all that confusion or fogginess you have when you're alive, learning the lessons. It's different when you've both passed, when you're both in the same place."

I turned to my grandmother. "What about you?"

"My passing? Oh, it was so beautiful," she said. "Beautiful" sounded like "Beauty–ful." "I walked into my parents' bakery, and Salvatore was there, and he looked so handsome like he does now, and we just hugged. I didn't want to let go, but when I did, I saw everyone. I saw my sister, I saw my brother, and I screamed when I saw my parents. Oh, how I screamed. And I met people too. My grandparents, who I never knew, but ya know, when you do meet, it's like you've always known them. Because, well, ya always have. It's wonderful." She closed her eyes again and faced the sun. "Absolutely wonderful."

Grandma Ant died seven years before when I was twenty-two, but here, she looked just like I remembered her. Her short, curly white hair was still thick and shiny, and all of the wrinkles I'd tried to memorize before she was gone were still there, but somehow her skin looked suppler and more radiant. Her blue eyes had their color back, and of course, she dressed to impress in a dark-blue sweater with a rhinestone pin in the shape of a leaf on her collar. I loved that pin. I wore it with a black sheath dress I had with a big collar.

"Aren't you sad that you left people behind?" I'd never asked them this before.

"Nah. It's not like that," Grandma Ant said. "You feel *sorry* for the people you've left behind. Life on Earth, ya know, in the physical world, as we say, that's the hard part."

So, I gathered that once someone passed, the irony was that some people on Earth felt sorry for people who had died when, in reality, it was the other way around. I thought about that for a while, and then my grandfather said, "Listen, *brasciole*, the thing is, don't worry so much about who's passed. They're all right. See—" He made a hand motion as if to offer himself up as proof. "You're still living your life. It's not easy. We know."

"It hurts, though, when someone you love is gone," I said. "Like when I graduated law school, I remember thinking that I wished you were there, and yes, I know you were there, but I wished you were alive, and we could talk about it and get a picture, at least!"

"Who needs a picture?" Grandpa Sal asked.

"And what if, God help me"—I glanced up at the sky—"I get married. You won't be at my wedding."

They laughed. I looked at them both from side to side.

"Oh, we'll be there," my grandmother said. "And we were there at your graduation party. We wouldn't have missed it for the world! We were dancing and talking amongst ourselves. We were there with our parents and our grandparents and our brothers and sisters. We had a great time. And the food! God bless Bella Notte!"

"How were you eating the food?" I asked.

"Veronica, you might be in that world, let's call it, and we might be in this world, but we're there too," my grandfather said. "Our worlds can cross... what's that term... two dimensional? No, three dimensional, that's it. You think of your world as three-dimensional, and that's wrong."

Before I could even begin to wrap my head around that idea, Grandpa Sal added, "You know, whatever we thought of Dominic all those years, Bella Notte always had great food. I gotta give him that."

"What do you think of him now?"

"Your father?" Grandpa Sal asked. "He's like almost every other soul in a human body. He has good qualities and not-so-good qualities. Hardly anyone is all of one thing, *brasciole*. People are complicated."

That's a nice way of saying it. Yes, he is.

Eventually, we got up from the bench and headed to the boathouse. "You went on a lot of dates from the computer," my grandmother said. "From the Match. Didn't it feel good?"

"Feel good? No, not really. The guy who called his mother a bitch? That was awkward." I shook my head as we walked to a nearby table and sat down. "They were all awkward. I'm going back to meeting guys the old-fashioned way—in bars—so you might as well tell me where the ring is."

"Ha! Not yet," Grandpa Sal said.

"Well, let's talk about what it was you didn't like about these fellas," my grandmother continued, determined as usual. "How did you feel after each of the dates?"

"Depressed."

"Exactly."

"Exactly what?" I stared at her. "How does that help me? You wanted me to feel depressed? That's why you told me to go on Match? Thanks a lot. And I mean, literally, like a stab in my chest, pangs of depression. Is that what you wanted?"

"Of course not, Veronica," Grandma Ant said. "That feeling—let's call it, like you say, a pang of depression—pay attention to that. That's your gut talking, your instincts. That's your body telling you this person is not for you."

"Gram, I love you, and I know you're trying to help me, but I don't need my body to tell me that one guy was a jerk or the other guy didn't excite me, and you know the rest, blah blah blah."

"Yeah, well, always remember to listen to that feeling, as uncomfortable as it may be. That feeling is another way of receiving the signs, of knowing whether or not you're on the right path. So, pay attention. Blah blah blah."

"Don't I have enough homework? Don't I have enough things to do? Enough assignments?" I sipped my lemonade that had suddenly appeared. "I'll add that to the list: pay attention to those other signs in the form of a stabbing, cringe-like feeling. Got it. Noted."

"So, that list of requirements of yours?" Grandma Ant continued. "All right, they're good. It's good to know what you want. But let me say this, Veronica—funny is the most important. Life is long. Looks fade. Funny is forever."

I had to giggle to myself. *Okay. That I can agree with.*

"Your computer dates. Why were they all Italian?" she asked.

"I—well—I don't know. I'm one hundred percent Italian American. I very much identify with that." I shrugged.

"Who cares if your husband is Italian?" Grandpa Sal asked.

"Wait! What?" I held up my hand in protest. "Growing up, I felt like you were always encouraging me to end up with someone Italian. I mean, I don't know if you really ever said that, but I felt that."

"Your mom's lovely Don isn't Italian. We love him. You love him. Our Connie loves him. That's what matters."

"Well, it's important to me." I wasn't sure how to explain it, other than how much I identified with that as a trait of mine. Proud to be one hundred percent Italian American.

"Or is it important to your father?" Grandpa Sal asked.

Ugh, no.

"Things like that—Italian, Irish, Jewish, black, white—they really don't matter," Grandpa Sal said.

"Oh, really? Grandpa"—I looked him straight in the eye—"I've heard things you've said about other cultures, other people."

He laughed. "Ya see, when you're alive, sometimes you can only see so much. But when you get here, and ya know, you look back on your life—well, you see what a bozo you were at times. Or worse."

I had to smile at this.

He continued. "None of it matters in the end. You can't judge a person for a damn thing except their soul"—he pointed to his chest—"who they are and not the body they're in."

"I love that. There are no labels, only souls. Judge a person based on their soul, not the body they're in—even if the body is a handsome Italian."

"You got it, my little *brasciole*," Grandpa Sal said.

"Why don't you give the computer dating one more try?" Grandma Ant held up her finger. "One more date."

"Please don't call it computer dating."

"I call it the Match; you don't like that. *Madone* with you. Whatever it is, do it. One more, ya hear?"

"All right, all right." I fiddled with Grandma's ring. "I'll give 'the Match computer dating' one more try."

"Now you're talkin'," Grandpa said.

Chapter 15

I woke up at six fifteen the next morning and grabbed my laptop.

> Hi Syd. This is the Italian lawyer girl from NJ who got back with her ex. I have a confession to make. The truth is: I do have an ex, but he has not re-emerged. I'm so sorry that I lied. I had been getting messages from a few other guys, and I decided to set up dates with them. I didn't know how to explain that. It was silly and stupid. Oh, and as it turned out, those other dates were all disasters. Serves me right, I suppose. Anyway, I shouldn't have lied. If you'll still have me, I'd really like to get to know you. May I buy you a drink one night this week? Signed, The Lying Lawyer (insert lawyer joke here)

After I showered, I grabbed my phone, wiped the steam from the screen, and saw a message from Syd.

> Hi Veronica. Morning person? Me too. Hey, thank you for coming clean. And thanks for trying to let me down easy last time. The truth—"I have a bunch of dates lined up with more promising guys"—might've hurt. Lucky for you, I'm very forgiving, particularly of cute, Italian, female lawyers from Jersey who lie sometimes. So, let's meet up. Is Thursday good? And one thing—you're not buying. Lying? Yes, but you're not buying. Drinks on me.

I couldn't remember another morning when I'd gotten ready for work with a smile on my face the entire time. There's a first time for everything.

"So work is crazy?" I asked. It was past two p.m. on a cloudy but warm day in Bryant Park. Jada and I were lucky to snag a table.

"Yeah." She pulled her salad out of the brown paper bag.

"Deadlines? Are Dan and Karen away?"

"Yeah. I mean no, they're not away, but we've just had a lot of work. So, you're going to quit Match?"

"Well, I was, but I'm going on one last date. Remember the bald, Jewish, creative guy I had originally slated to be my first Match date? I want to see what he's like in person. His emails are hilarious, and I just feel like I should try one more Match date before I quit. Just one more."

"So, go out with him."

"We are. Thursday. I have to be honest though, part of me is thinking, yeah, he is really funny and cute in his pictures, but another part of me keeps asking what's the point? Is he my husband? I don't know. But I'll go. I'll go!"

"Because his last name doesn't end in a vowel?"

It suddenly sounded so ridiculous. I laughed as I chewed my salad.

"Well, the rest of the dates were all good on paper, and they were disasters," Jada said. "So what have you got to lose?"

Exactly. "In other news, I'm covering a story on Filamina March for my class, and I spoke to this elderly neighbor of hers, and oh my God—hysterical—you would so—"

"I'm about to have an affair." Jada sat back and took a deep breath. "With Todd." She put her head in her hands.

What? "Okay," I said slowly, resting my fork. "You're *about* to have an affair?" *Well, stop yourself. It's that easy.*

She nodded.

I tried a different tactic and wasn't sure who I was trying to calm down more: her or me. "Who uses the word 'affair'? What is this? A soap opera? Is he about to discover a long-lost love child with a rare tropical disease?"

She didn't smile. "He's been calling and texting, and he wants to see me, and… I want to see him. Very much."

I looked her in the eye. "Well, then, you have to break up with Mark."

"I know."

"It's one thing to make that mistake you made that one night. But you can't do it again. Even if he never finds out, you'd still be making a fool of him." *Says the girl who lied to Syd. But that's different. It was a white lie. And I came clean. And I lie to Beverly all the time, but that's different too. She's a beast.*

"Stop preaching, please. I know what I have to do. I just need your support." Jada put her elbows on the table. "I know it's time to end it with Mark. I just don't know how to do it."

I wanted to scream, "Well, it's about time! You've been lukewarm about him for two years. But did you really have to cheat to get to this point?" The words were on the tip of my tongue. They were dying to come out, but I checked myself and just said, "I'll help you. I'm here for you. Call me before and after. Like pre-game and post."

"Thanks, Coach," she said with a sigh.

"This is good. You have to trust your gut. You're doing the right thing."

We both got busy with work and didn't meet up for lunch again the rest of the week, but I spent the next few days writing and re-writing breakup transcripts for her that she would then nix altogether just before we got to the final draft. Then we would start all over again. I did this in between coming up with questions for Selma Renner and all while dealing with Beverly and Kate and trying to get some real work done. Still, I also found time to Google "Syd Blackman" at least ten times. Apparently, he'd been the brains behind some of the commercials that I actually didn't fast-forward through, some of the few funny ones. *Who knew?*

Syd selected the place to meet. It was called Est, a French steakhouse with a long, dark wood bar at the front. I arrived early and parked myself at the bar with a strawberry martini.

He had asked where I worked and then picked the restaurant because it was close by. *Thoughtful.*

When he walked in, I recognized him immediately, but he was even cuter in person. Shaved head, black button-down, jeans. After exchanging a peck on the cheek that wasn't as awkward as the hug I'd received from date number two, he leaned back to examine my drink and asked if I was sufficiently hydrated. He ordered a vodka and soda.

Adorable face, broad shoulders, perfect teeth, and scruff on his chin. But not too much scruff, not a full goatee. He had just enough hair there, ironically. It worked. *It all works on him. He's sexy.*

"You can wear jeans to work?" *That's my first question? What is wrong with me? Am I nervous? I didn't expect him to be this cute in person. Holy shit, I'm nervous.*

"Yeah." He looked down at his casual attire. "I'm guessing this wouldn't pass at the law firm?"

I shook my head. "You're lucky."

"Yes, I am." We locked eyes.

I looked away, suddenly self-conscious in my suit. But one round of drinks later, I was laughing harder than I'd ever laughed on a first date in my life. I had felt comfortable enough to tell him about my news reporting class and my first "encounter" with Dave.

"Did he say 'If you needed a tripod, you could've just asked'?"

I wiped the tears forming at the corner of my eyes. *I hope my makeup is not running. I hope I still look cute, at least kissable.*

"So, a news reporting class?" he asked.

"Yeah." *Don't make fun of it or ask me why a lawyer would want to be a journalist. Don't ruin it.*

"That sounds interesting," he said.

"It is." I took another sip of my second martini.

"Do you have homework?"

I told him all about Filamina and her neighbor Selma and how the interview was coming up in a little more than a week.

"You could practice on me before your interview. I can play the role of old Jewish lady and nosy neighbor. I've known a few in my lifetime."

"Oh, that could be helpful," I said. "So, what's your job like?"

"Well, I come up with ideas for television commercials, pitch them to clients, and then go to the shoot, wherever they're filmed—usually in L.A., but sometimes in pretty cool places like Prague, New Zealand, or Uruguay."

"That sounds amazing. Do you like it? Like, does it fulfill you?"

"Every day. I mean, of course, there are frustrations. Frustrating clients sometimes, things go wrong, but I think about how I was a kind of shy kid, and now I'm traveling all over, seeing my ideas turned into mini thirty- and sixty-second movies. It's good... It's really good."

"That's great." I was mesmerized. "What's it feel like to not hate going to work every day?"

He laughed. I noticed his perfect teeth again and his lips. *Nice lips.* "What's it feel like to hate going to work every day?"

"You don't want to know."

"You need Rosanna Zotto's job. That's your calling."

"Ha! If only."

"Let's toast," he said. "I'm not a big toaster, so I don't know why I'm doing this, but here's to finding your calling." We lifted our glasses. "And to old Jewish ladies and bowling. Shall we?"

For once, I didn't want the date to end. I didn't want to run home and write a date report in my pajamas. "We shall."

It turned out bowling was Syd's litmus test. Any girl who flat-out refused couldn't be much fun, he figured.

As it also turned out, I was a terrible bowler. At one point, Syd said, "Stop bowling like a lawyer. Bowl like a journalist. Bowl like Rosanna would bowl."

Then, I got a strike, and even though I thought it was just a coincidence, something about it felt magical. Maybe it was this cute guy who had remembered things I'd told him and who was trying to inspire me. *And what a difference that makes. I'll take this feeling over a pang of depression any day.*

After several beers, sliders, and strikes by Syd, it was close to two in the morning, and all I wanted to do was to kiss this guy. But it didn't happen. Not a real kiss, anyway. He hailed me a cab, opened the door for me, and kissed me quickly on the lips.

I sat back, watching the streetlights pass, tasting beer and burgers on my lips, and wondering when I would see him again. *My first great Match date. Finally.*

Chapter 16

When I woke up the next morning after only five hours of sleep, my eyelids felt heavy, but I didn't feel tired. I was excited to write up my date report about Syd.

> Name: Syd Blackman.
> Age: 36.
> Occupation: Creative director (which sounds too good to be a real job, I know).
> Rating (from 1 to 10; 10 is my husband): 8.7
>
> Not what I expected. At all. Best first date I've ever had. Laughed my ass off. What a difference to actually type up a date report that doesn't leave me forlorn.
>
> He is adorable too, and can you believe this? We went bowling until 2AM on a school night. Bowling! I know!
>
> I had some beverages in me and really wanted to smooch his cutie face, but it didn't happen. I don't know why.
>
> Jada, I got your text. We can analyze at lunch. I'll meet you downstairs at noon.

As I showered and got ready for work, I actually turned off Rosanna Zotto and turned on the oldies station. I was in the mood for music.

I scrolled through my "#OldSoul" playlist and blared Darlene Love's "He's Sure the Boy I Love." Then, I sang off-tune and applied extra under-eye concealer.

I checked my phone and saw Jada had replied to my report. —Bowling?!—

I laughed, but before I could respond, Lauren did.

—Oooooooh!!!! Go out with him again! Who knows? If you get married, maybe he'll change his name to BlackmanoJ and you can still have an Italian last name!—

I smiled and got concealer in my eye. I typed back:

—You're so funny, Lauren. I don't know if it will lead to marriage, but I'd really like to go out with him again. We left it with a peck on the lips and "I'll call you," so I hope he calls me.—

"What are you waiting for?" I asked Jada.

"I just haven't found the right words."

I wanted to say, "What about all the words I've been writing and re-writing for you?" But I didn't.

Jada put her sunglasses on before she lifted the plastic lid from her container of steaming hot soup. It was a hot day, but I guess she was in the mood for soup. I ripped the plastic off my fork and opened my salad. "You can't just tell him the truth, right?" I asked.

"Never! I mean, he'll eventually find out that Todd and I are together. I just don't want him to know the timeline. Let him think I met Todd after."

"So"—*How do I put this?*—"you foresee you and Todd being serious right away?"

"Yeah. We've been talking and texting constantly. He mentioned that he's going to Barbados next month, and I think he wants me to go with him. A partner at his company has a place and offered it to him for a week."

"And you only hooked up once?"

"Yeah. But it's different. Different than Mark. I don't know how to explain it. I can't wait to see him again. I'm excited about this."

I understood. "Well, before this goes any further, before you go to Barbados, you have to do the right thing with Mark."

"I know, Veronica." Jada dipped her bread again and bit down hard.

"Maybe just send a text that says, 'Can you come over tonight? I want to talk about something.'" I swallowed as I thought of John telling me we had to talk at dinner that night. "That will prepare him a little, and then you can say all the things we've been practicing—that you've been doing a lot of thinking, and while things might seem status quo, your feelings have changed."

"Okay. Okay, I will."

"Start with the text. Send it now." *If this is delayed any longer, Jada may find herself actually having an affair. And that is not happening on my watch.*

"All right, yeah, and then I can say 'let's take a break' and then after a couple of weeks, I can say that I think we should go our separate ways."

Poor Mark. I didn't think he was the one for Jada, mainly because she hadn't been sure he was the one for the entire time they'd dated, but he was still a good guy. I couldn't help but feel sorry for him because I was pretty sure he was about to get his heart broken.

She typed, showed it to me, then took a deep breath and hit Send.

"You're doing the right thing."

"I know." She stared toward the street.

"What's Todd like, by the way?" I asked.

She beamed. "Amazing. Handsome. Successful. Fun to be with."

"I can't wait to meet him."

"So, what else is going on? That sounded like a fun date with the Jewish guy. Too bad he's not Italian."

I laughed to myself. I was about to analyze the date in person, excited to relive it, but then Jada asked, "And how's that class going? Will I be able to see this video story?"

"Yeah, it'll be on the website. And you can read the story too... with my *byline*." I grinned.

"That's good." Jada didn't lift her head as she scooped the last bits of her soup.

"How cool is that?" I stared at her. "A byline!"

"Very cool. I'm proud of you." She finally lifted her head.

You better say that.

"Listen, when you meet Todd—I just thought of this—don't say anything about Barbados. It's not confirmed yet or anything. I mean, I'm pretty sure we're going, I just don't want him to think I was telling anyone."

"I won't." *Break up with your boyfriend first.*

When I got back to the office after lunch, Margaret stopped by for another lottery collection. "Any day now. I can feel it," she said.

I handed over my money then checked my email.

> Miss Veronica, I wanted to thank you again for working out the agreement on my case. I thought you'd like this good news—the first payment is not due until the 1st, but Miss Trista already sent me a check! Better than driving around Queens, trying to operate a cupcake truck with my bad foot. And my physical therapist will be glad about finally getting paid! And I'll send my payment to accounting directly and not Beverly, like you said. No worries. Thanks again, Pat.

This is an odd sensation. What is this feeling? I think it might be... pride? In my work? My lawyerly work? This is a very strange sensation, indeed. Certainly never felt this before. Too bad it's something I have to hide from my boss.

Later, at a meeting in Beverly's office, I was asked a question I didn't know the answer to—*now this feeling, this sensation of feeling like an idiot, I am much more familiar with.* Then, Kate asked if "we could please concentrate"—*yes, this feeling of wanting to smack her with a three-hole punch and knock myself out too, I know this feeling well.* We were getting up from the chairs in front of Beverly's desk when I accidentally spilled tea on Kate's binder full of sample complaints. It really was an accident, and I did apologize, but I didn't feel that sorry.

I hadn't been paying attention at all during the meeting. I was too busy relishing the idea of having helped Trista and having pleased Pat at the same time. I was also reliving my date with Syd and wondering when he would call. I wondered if he was texting me at that moment while I was trapped in Beverly's office.

When I got back to my office, I noticed I had a text. I almost tripped and spilled more tea as I lunged for my phone.

But it was from Dave: *Reserved the camera crew. All set.*

I wanted to squeal. *Camera crew.* I felt so Rosanna.

I immediately dialed Selma Renner's number to confirm. "Hello, Mrs. Renner?"

"The one and only."

"Hi, this is Veronica Buccino from... from NewYork3News." I felt another odd sensation, hearing myself say that, but I liked the sound of it. I was so used to being Veronica from Ellis & Blackmoore. "How are you?"

"Hello, Veronica. I'm doing marvelous. When's my television debut?"

"We're confirmed for Monday. Full camera crew."

"Oh, dear. I forgot to call you. No, I didn't forget to call you. Why am I saying that? What happened was I realized I didn't have your number. I've gotta leave for Florida on Monday. My sister is not doing too well. She's not active like me. So I have to go to Florida. Can we move it up? Let's do, uh, let's see, not tomorrow, but the day after."

Are you frigging kidding me?

"Um, I don't know if we'll be able to get a camera crew that quickly." My heart raced. "Let me check."

"Why don't you check? And I better go to the beauty parlor and get my hair set. Wait until I look into that camera. I've been waiting to tell the full story about those two—those Marches. It's about time if you ask me. All right, lemme call Dottie at the salon. She does all the girls' hair. It's very difficult to get an appointment, but wait 'til I tell her it's for TV."

"Internet," I quickly corrected. "Wait! I have to see if I can get a camera—" Too late.

"Bye, dear." I heard a click.

I called Dave, who was not flustered by this news. "Let me check the schedule again," he said coolly.

If it worked for NewYork3News, then that would give me not even two days to prepare for my first on-camera interview. I'd been preparing all along, but I wasn't prepared for it to happen so soon.

As I rested my elbows on my desk and rubbed my eyes, not caring if I smeared my mascara, the phone rang.

Fuck. Too much stimulation. I think I'm going to curl up in the fetal position.

And then I realized it was my cell phone, not my office phone. *Syd!* But it was Dave. "Your lady is in luck. Two days from now. All set."

"Thank you."

"Don't sound so excited," Dave said.

"Sorry." I laughed. "I'm in the middle of something. Thank you, really. I'm excited."

I hung up and confirmed with Selma. "And Dottie can fit me in, so we're all set," she said.

Then, I stared at my phone. It was the middle of the afternoon. Surely, I should have received a "Had a great time" text by now. Something. But nothing.

So I did something. Like Jada earlier that day, I bucked up and sent the text.

—Thanks again for drinks and bowling last night! Hey, are you around tomorrow night? I'm going to be interviewing that older Jewish lady in two days and want to practice so I don't make a fool of myself. Let me know!—

I hovered over the Send button for a moment until something told me to "Just do it," and I did. Then I tried to busy myself with work while I waited for a response, but it was too boring to capture my attention. Instead, I reviewed my questions for Selma, checked HumanInterestStories. net, and checked my text messages every seven seconds.

After what felt like nine years, but was actually only forty-five minutes, I got a reply.

—Hey, I was just going to text you. Glad you got home OK. I'll bring my best 'Sylvia on Her Way to Mahjong in Boca.' Where should we meet?—

Yes. I typed, —Thanks! Looking forward to meeting Sylvia. I'll think of a place.—

Three minutes later, he replied. —Sylvia is looking forward to meeting you. She heard you're cute.—

Chapter 17

"IT'S WEIRD BECAUSE I WANT to do this so badly. I want to do this interview on camera and write a really good article. But I don't know. I'm..."

"Shitting a brick?" Grandpa Sal bit into his cannoli.

We were at an ice cream shop in Midtown, sitting at a metal picnic table out front. Grandma Ant and I were both having double-scooped chocolate ice cream in sugar cones.

"Watch your language, Salvatore," Grandma said as she carefully took a spoon to the top scoop like a lady.

I took a bite of my top scoop and spilled some chocolate sprinkles on my lap.

"It's just an expression, Ant," Grandpa said. "It means that you're scared. My nephew, Carlo, used to say it all the time. Vinnie's son. He used to say—"

"Okay, okay, don't say 'shit.' That's my point." Grandma Ant was still spooning at her ice cream cone.

"You just said it." Grandpa Sal pointed at her.

"Yes, I'm scared." I instinctively reached for Grandma's ring, but my bare finger was becoming more familiar. "I'm torn. I want to do it. But if Dave said the camera wasn't available, I have to be honest, part of me would've been a little relieved. On the one hand, I live in a constant state of anxiety at the job I hate, but I'm also anxious about a job I could love. I can't win!"

"How the hell did ya ever make it through law school?" Grandpa Sal asked. "You're afraid of your own shadow."

"Grandma's ring," I said. "So just tell me where it is."

"No," he said. "Carry on."

"So, let's say," Grandma Ant said. "What if you back out? How would you feel?"

"Back out?" I asked. "Are you kidding me? You! You are the one who encouraged me to do this in the first place."

"I'm not saying back out. What I'm trying to find out is how would you *feel* if you backed out?"

"I would feel like sh—crap."

"Like shit, how?" She pointed at Grandpa as he said, "Hey, now."

I glanced at the street to think for a moment. "I would feel like a coward. I would feel like I let Dave down."

"And then months from now? Years from now? Let's say you're still doing the law," she said.

"Ugh." I swallowed. "Depressing. I'd regret it. I'd think 'Why didn't I do that? It was one video story and one written story, and it could have been so much fun, and it could have led to something great.'"

"Now, think about this, what if you do it, and the worst happens? It's the pits, let's say."

"Don't say that! I would feel like a failure. That's what I'm afraid of. I can be a failure as a lawyer because, who cares, it's boring. But I don't want to fail at something that I love."

"I'll bet ya anything you'd rather feel like a failure, a little down in the dumps, if that were to happen, than to never know. To wonder. To feel regret."

"I guess."

"Guess what?" Grandpa Sal asked. "Guess the numbers for the lottery. This, my little *brasciole*, you *know*."

"Of course, I'm going to do it. I would never back out. I'm just nervous. Please just pray that I don't bomb."

"You're going to be great," Grandma Ant announced. Then she spotted something across the street and started waving. "Ruth! Over here, Ruth!"

The little Jewish lady we'd seen in Italy scurried toward us from across the street.

"She moves at some clip, huh?" Grandma said under her breath.

"Hello, Gorgeous! Hello, Handsome! Hello, Beautiful!"

I looked around. *Am I Beautiful?*

"Where ya off to now?" Grandpa Sal asked. "Don't ya ever stop to take a breath?"

"Hey, when you're as popular as me, you get a lot of invitations."

They all found this hilarious. I smiled politely and devoured my ice cream cone.

"Let's see," Ruth said, "I just came from seeing my friend Angie Castro. She just died. I had to go welcome her. She was so excited to see me. Now, I'm on my way to a bris in Brooklyn. My niece's daughter had a beautiful baby boy."

"Gah bless," Grandma said.

"Good. Go. Get outta here. Ya make us look lazy," Grandpa said.

Ruth laughed and swatted in his direction before taking off.

"Enjoy!" Grandma called after her.

"Being dead seems like so much fun. I have to ask—what's the point of living, of going through it all and experiencing all of the crap when it's so wonderful and easy here?"

"We are all souls who want to—what's the word—evolve," Grandma Ant said. "It's our nature, and it's a good thing. You want to set out and go through it, the challenges, the hard stuff. That's how ya learn."

"Veronica," Grandpa piped in, "you don't have it as hard as some people. You do have some challenges. We see it. A lot of it's in here." He pointed at his head. "The doubts, the fears, the worry, the anger."

"I'm not angry."

"You're not angry with your father?"

"No," I said defensively. "He's just, ugh, the way he is, and I have to deal with him."

"Anyway, one of the best things you can do to evolve, as Ant says, is to learn and give thanks at the same time."

I'm not angry with my father. I wouldn't say "angry" is the right word.

"Over here, Veronica," Grandpa said, waving.

"Ya gotta count your blessings. What are you grateful for?" Grandma Ant took a sip of espresso that had appeared.

I took a deep breath and exhaled.

"Just because I'm a worrier or I'm overly introspective or... whatever."

144

I paused to gather exactly what I was trying to say. Grandpa huffed and made hand motions as if to say, "Let's get on with it." "Listen, just because I hate my job doesn't mean I'm an ingrate. Okay?"

"We know," Grandpa said. "It's a process. Believe me."

"From the top." Grandma Ant clapped her hands. "What are you grateful for?"

"My job, I guess. I mean, I know. I know I'm grateful to have that job. Um… my education, all of the opportunities I've been given. I know I'm lucky. Even the opportunity from class, from Dave. Honestly, it's amazing."

They were listening closely, and from their nodding, I assumed I was doing this right. "And I'm grateful for Jada even though, you know, it's been a little challenging lately with her. She's a good friend. Lauren too. And well, you both. Thank you for listening to me. And my mom. She's so sweet and just the best mom ever and um, hmmm…"

"Terrific," Grandma said.

"Practice'll make better," Grandpa said.

"Perfect," I corrected him.

"You don't have to be perfect."

"My mother keeps a gratitude journal," I said, just remembering. "She's done it forever. Ever since I was little."

"We know," Grandma Ant said.

"You told her to do that?"

"No," Grandma said. "Think about it. We didn't know this while we were still alive. No one in our generation kept those types of journals, whatever ya want to call them. And she started doing it when you were young—while we were still alive—so no, not from our suggestion."

"From someone else's," Grandpa Sal said.

"Who? Her grandparents? Did they meet with her and help her? Like I meet with you? Here? Like, you know, not in 'real life.'"

They both nodded. "During the divorce especially," Grandma Ant said. "But she's a forgiving person by nature. It was a hard time, and keeping perspective helped her. I know that."

So, my mom was helped by her grandparents too. I liked knowing she hadn't been so alone and must have felt supported even if she didn't remember the specifics when she was awake.

"Is everyone guided by someone? What about people who don't handle divorce or their problems so well? Are their guides failing?"

"No!" Grandma laughed. "Well, yes, everyone is guided by someone, but no, their guides aren't doing a bad job. No such thing. No such judgment. It's—well, ya know—everyone's path is different. Different lessons, different purpose, different path."

"Honestly," I said, "all of this really is easier said than done. Don't worry so much. Be forgiving. Be grateful. Easy for you to say! You're dead."

"As a doornail," Grandpa said.

Chapter 18

"Name three things you're grateful for," I said. "Anything. Whatever comes to mind."

Syd sat back to think about it. He was in a black button-down and jeans again. *His uniform, I guess.* We were at a Greek restaurant on the Lower East Side, seated next to each other at a table with a white tablecloth and a window view of the street.

"Uh, let's see. I'm grateful for my work, that I do what I love."

"So you're really excited to get to the office in the morning?"

"I don't know about excited. I don't dread it. I'm excited when I get to create something that I'm really proud of. And then there's the flip side. If there's something I really want to work on, or a client who I really want to create something for, and I have these great ideas, and then the client goes with some other idea or some other agency... that sucks." He picked up the bottle of red wine, and before refilling his glass, he lifted his eyebrows toward me and generously replenished my glass.

"If Beverly, the partner at my firm, said we lost a case or a bunch of cases to another firm, I would think 'who gives a sh-crap?'"

While I was saying crap, he was saying, "Rat's ass?"

I laughed. "Who says that?"

"A lot of people from New Jersey, no?" He was laughing too.

"I don't think so."

People like my father, maybe. I didn't say that, and I tried not to think it. I got to the office early that day to draft a long and what I hoped was a helpful email to my father about another vendor contract he'd received.

"I'm no career coach, but I think not giving a crap is a sign that this might not be the job for you," Syd said.

"Uh, yeah. Okay, what else?" I sipped my wine.

"Let's see. My family. I have great parents and a great sister who is one of my best friends, and my nephews, Dylan and Sam, are healthy, rambunctious, and nuts. Does that count as one big one?"

"Yeah. That's the family umbrella." I dipped a pita wedge deep into the hummus bowl, and as I lifted it to my mouth, a clump landed on my black dress. Luckily, it missed Grandma Ant's black-and-white beaded necklace that I was wearing. I quickly grabbed my napkin and scooped it up, lifting most of the hummus and then dropping it again. *Crap.* "Don't mind me. Hurricane Veronica here." I shook my head and continued to wipe at the stain with my chin tucked in.

"Who cares?" Syd asked. Then as I looked up, he took a pita wedge, dipped it in the hummus, and wiped it on his black shirt.

My mouth dropped. "What'd you do that for?"

"That's what dry cleaners are for."

I put my napkin down. "Yeah… I guess that's what we pay them for."

"Exactly," he said. "Relax. It's just hummus."

As I sipped my wine, I peered over the top of my glass to peek at the stain on his shirt. "What were we talking about?" I asked. "Oh, right. One more."

"Right. Well, I'm grateful that I survived cancer."

I wish my reaction had been more graceful. I couldn't help that I straightened up and widened my eyes. "Oh."

"Yeah, they found a tumor growing around my spine when I was twelve. Chemo, the whole thing, lost my hair." He pointed to his head. "I guess that was foreshadowing."

I didn't know what to say. "I'm sorry."

"Don't be sorry. It was a gift. I mean, of course, I wouldn't want to relive it, but it changed me. It changed my whole family. No one in my family—mom, dad, sister—gets off the phone without saying 'I love you' ever since the day I was diagnosed. And for me, I was such a nervous kid before that. After cancer, I just wasn't anymore. I wasn't afraid to go for the things I wanted. Live the life I wanted. Not become an accountant like my father, but follow my passion. My personality changed. I wasn't the shy, nervous kid I was before. That's what my tattoo is for."

"You have a tattoo?"

"Not very Jewish of me, I know."

"Doesn't that mean you can't be buried in a Jewish cemetery?"

"Not my problem." He pulled back his shirt to reveal a tattoo on his inner arm. "Gadal. It means 'grow' in Hebrew."

I studied it.

"Not like grow hair." He tapped his head. "But grow as a person. So, what are you grateful for?"

I put my elbows on the table and said, "I think my dead grandparents send me signs." I quickly grabbed an olive and talked while working around the pit. "Yeah, my grandmother and my grandfather, they send me pennies. It's usually when I'm worried about something or at big moments in my life. It's nuts, I know."

"Pennies, did you say?" He leaned in.

"Yes, pennies." Another olive. Another pit. "I'm weird. I know."

"I think my grandmother is a fly."

I stopped chewing and covered my mouth. "Huh?"

"My mom's mother. I think she comes to me as a fly. I can't remember how it started. I think I was at my cousin's daughter's bat mitzvah, and there was this fly in the temple who wouldn't leave me alone, and then I had this weird thought like, 'What if it's Grandma?'"

"And you know it's a sign, right?" I asked. "Like it's not physically her, like if you killed the fly, you wouldn't be killing your grandmother. It's her but not literally."

"Exactly. It's her way of saying she's here. When my oldest nephew was born, it was the middle of February, and there was a fly in the delivery room."

My eyes widened again.

"My sister is on video saying, 'It's the middle of February. What is there a fly doing in here?'"

"I love it." *He gets it. Syd Blackman is a believer.* I realized I was grinning. "Some people think it's nonsense. But I can't help it. I know what I know."

"Me too," Syd said.

That was when I kissed him on the lips. Now, his eyes were wide. *I hope the hummus isn't too garlicky.*

He smiled and put his hand on my waist and kissed me back. Closed mouth, long, simple kiss.

He smells amazing. I don't think he's wearing cologne, but he smells musky, or is it cedar? I don't know, but it's delicious. I wanted to linger there, just breathing him in.

"I hope this isn't what you're planning for your interview," he said. "I didn't realize it was that kind of class."

"It's the new style of interviewing. Didn't you know?"

"So, what do you like to do besides read human interest stories?"

I have no idea. "What do you like to do in your spare time?" I asked.

"I asked you first."

Damn. "Well, didn't you read my Match profile? I like to read and work out when I can, which is practically never, and travel when I can, which is practically never. And shop. Go to movies. What about you?"

"Well, I might have mentioned I like the Jets. I might have downplayed that a little. I never miss a snap. I've watched every game for the past twenty-six years."

That's some commitment. And you'd get along with my cousin Christopher.

"And I like hiking. There are really good places in Nyack. And I love hockey. I play with my cousin in a league in Midtown. We both played in high school."

"Hockey? Do you get beat up?"

"Not too bad. I also ride bikes with my cousin. We've done a couple of century rides for charity. You know, hundred-mile bike rides?"

As I watched him talk about the Jets, hiking, hockey, bike riding a hundred miles, and even his job, I noticed how genuinely happy he appeared. Animated. Engaged. Maybe it was the cancer. Maybe I'd met too many cynical New Yorkers. Maybe I was one of them. But this person enjoyed things. He enjoyed life. It was refreshing.

What do I enjoy? Reading human interest stories? Hey, it's something.

What did John enjoy? Now that I'd thought about it, pretty much nothing. He'd rushed through his workouts—weight lifting only—so that he could get back to work. He hadn't enjoyed movies because people checked their phones and were rude and ruined it. He hadn't liked any sports. He'd played football in high school, but the kind of money the players made these days left a bad taste in his mouth for the whole sport and what it had become. I sighed.

"What was the sigh for?" Syd asked as he sipped his wine.

I shrugged. Then, with both hands, I held his face and kissed him again.

Greek wine is dangerous. I was pretty sure we were making a scene, but I didn't care.

"So, what are you going to ask the old Jewish lady?"

For a moment, I had to think about what he was talking about. "Oh. Um. Selma?"

"I'll be Selma. What do you want to ask me? I can't do an old lady voice, but I'll answer the way she would. I'll answer the way my grandmother would."

"The fly?"

"The fly."

"Um, okay. So, how long have you lived next door to the March family?"

"Too long."

"Why too long?"

"They're loud. They're hooligans. They don't pick up after their dog. Oh, and their kids are dirty, and they smell. They run around with no shoes on their feet."

I laughed and inhaled another pita wedge. "That sounds awful."

"You know, you're very attractive. You look like that Rosanna Zotto." Breaking character, Syd noted, "By the way, I went on that site you like and signed up as TheJewishAlRoker. Look for me."

We laughed more. And drank more. And kissed more.

We didn't prepare much more for the interview, but I was having too much fun to think about it.

Chapter 19

"I WISH I'D PREPARED MORE."

I was talking to my mother from a cab headed to the NewYork3News offices. She had called to wish me luck.

"You'll be great," she said. "Just ask what you want to know. That's what other people want to know, right?"

"Yeah." I reached for my grandmother's ring. I hadn't reached for it in a while. I think I'd finally forgotten I lost it. But now I remembered, and my stomach flipped twice—once at the thought of losing it, and once at the thought of how my first on-camera interview would go. Then, it flipped again when I said a little prayer that Beverly wouldn't call me while I was at my "doctor's appointment."

"Call me when it's over," my mom said. "What time do you think it'll be?"

"I don't know, but if it's early enough, I should probably go back to work."

"Don't do that. Go celebrate. This is a wonderful thing. I'm so proud of you."

Don't be proud of me yet. This could be a big frigging bust and waste of everyone's time.

As the cab pulled up, I saw a white SUV parked in front of the building with NewYork3News.com painted on the side. And then, at that very moment, I received a text. —Bowl like Rosanna.—

This made me giddy. I pushed my shoulders back and walked into the lobby.

When I stepped off on the seventh floor, I was a little taken aback.

I was so used to law firm surroundings that the lack of a receptionist, the closed-off glass entrance, and the large statue of Betty Boop holding three Emmys on a tray was a bit of a culture shock. *Do I knock? Is there a doorbell? Should I text Dave?*

As if on cue, Dave walked around the bend and spotted me. As he opened the glass door, he announced, "There she is, our crimes and courts reporter."

"Ha! We'll see about that."

"You'll be great. Come on in. We're almost ready, just have to finish changing the batteries in the camera and testing the microphones. Want some coffee? Water?"

"I'm good, thanks." I sat down in Dave's small office while he marched through the hall and called out directions to people. "Vince, what about camera two?" "Joe, where's the cable from yesterday?" "Doug, you're coming, right?"

Dave's walls were covered from floor to ceiling with newspaper clippings, printouts of articles, and tons of photos of him with various people—Dave with the police commissioner, Dave with the mayor, Dave with... *Is that Rosanna Zotto?* I got up to get a closer look, but before I could decipher whether it was Rosanna or not, Dave came back and startled me.

"Ready?"

A few minutes later, we—Dave, Vince, Joe, Doug and I—piled into the van. Vince the Prince, as they called him, was the main cameraman. He was no more than five-eight and a hundred twenty pounds but seemed to have no trouble carrying the enormous camera. He said he'd worked for his father's construction business as a teenager and was used to carrying heavy things. Later, on the dashboard of the van, I noticed a picture of Vince carrying his wife up their wedding aisle.

Mean Joe Dean was the editor, and from the short amount of time I spent with him that morning, I found him to be not very mean at all. He lived in Hoboken with his fiancée, Carlene. She would eventually be Carlene Dean.

There was also Doug, the intern. He was a college student at NJIT who worked as a production assistant and invited me to a birthday party for one of his roommates that night at his off-campus house. I thought that was sweet, but I said I had to go back to work after we finished the story.

Everyone called Dave Kennedy "Mr. President." I still thought of him as my teacher so it felt a bit voyeuristic to see him in this other environment.

As we pulled away from the office, I quickly checked my phone. There was a text message from Jada. —It's done. Mark picked up the last of his stuff this morning before work. I feel so relieved. Will fill you in later.—

She obviously forgot about my big day today.

I tried to quickly think of how to respond to Jada—*Congratulations?*—but after a few minutes, I decided I had to concentrate on the task at hand and what I needed to accomplish. I put my phone away and reviewed my notes. I was busy going over my questions and hadn't realized that we'd made it off the island of Manhattan in record time, but once we were in New Jersey and on the Garden State Parkway, it happened. At around Exit 153, it sounded as if we'd driven over a metal brick.

"What the fuck was that?" Joe asked, and after thirty seconds and another half a mile, it was obvious.

No. Not a flat tire. No! Please! I can't reschedule. She's going to Florida. And I can't take any more time off of work. And I can't postpone this because I'll lose my nerve. Please, not a flat tire.

"Flat tire," Doug declared, getting back into the truck.

"All right, I'll call AAA," Dave said. "Veronica, can you call this lady and let her know we're going to be late? Or reschedule?"

"Okay." *I'll tell her we're going to be late.* I stepped out of the van and put my palm up to my ear to muffle the whiz of cars speeding by.

"You see, Veronica, I thought my day would be free," Selma explained. "But my friend Angie Castro died. It was a long time coming. First, a stroke. Then, she broke her hip. Then, you know how it goes, she was in and out of the hospital. So anyway, today is the wake, and I have to go today because my day tomorrow will be very busy, what with me going to Florida. So you'll have to be out of here by noon. She was a very good friend, my Angie. A very good friend."

Noon? "Okay, sure."

That was how Dave, Vince, and I ended up in a filthy red suburban taxi cab on our way to Selma's while Joe and Doug waited for AAA. Apparently, Uber wasn't quite as prevalent in these suburban parts of New Jersey. It was eleven o'clock in the morning, and the cab driver was eating a hot dog and drinking a small carton of milk. He was an elderly man with white hair and a large belly, and he asked us all what we did for a living. When he found out I was a lawyer, he asked me about filing bankruptcy.

I was reviewing my questions for Selma and wiping the sweat from my forehead and palms, but I tried to help. "Maybe you can call your creditors and work out a settlement agreement. Lower payment terms over the course of a longer period of time, maybe?"

He made some noise that sounded like "Rahhhh." Then, he said, "I tried that, but you know how these bastards are. It's a conspiracy—"

"Right here! If you could stop right here." I looked at the big brick house with the red door set back from a long, neatly mowed front lawn. I recognized it from Google's street view. I'd tried to get a good look at the Marches' house, when I tried to confirm the right address, and when someone on HumanInterestStories.net said the Marches had never replaced the window with the bullet holes, which could supposedly still be seen.

I couldn't see it.

I stared at the Marches' house, up close and personal. It was much bigger than Selma's house next door and had two lion statues at the edge of the circular stone driveway. It appeared rather peaceful, actually. *Looks can be deceiving.*

Dave paid the driver, who asked for my number. I told him I didn't bring any cards with me, and Dave shut the door before he could ask for a piece of paper to write my number down.

I brushed my black pants with the back of my hands and adjusted Grandma Ant's red-beaded choker around my neck.

"Why don't you knock on the door while we unpack some stuff here and get the camera going?" Dave said.

As I walked toward the door, I checked my phone. 11:05. *That should be enough time. I think. I hope. What do I know?* As I was about to ring the doorbell, the door swung open.

"You must be Veronica." The familiar voice came from the Joan

Rivers lookalike—sans plastic surgery—with Dolly Parton's boobs. Selma had on large, black-rimmed glasses that took up half her face, and she was wearing what my grandmother would have called a "housedress." It was pink and green and white and loose and rather low-cut. "Don't you look lovely?" she said. "I love that necklace you're wearing. I used to have one just like it."

"Nice to meet you, Mrs. Renner. Thank you. It was my grandmother's." I reached out to shake her hand.

She grabbed it with both hands and scrunched her nose to move the lower part of her big bifocals up so she could get a better look at my necklace. "Your grandmother's? You don't say?" she said under her breath. "They don't make 'em like that anymore." She backed away and held her hands out as if to get a better look at me, like a proud grandma. "Well, come on in. Are those fellas down there with you?"

"Yes, those are the camera people. They're just setting up."

"What can I get ya? Water? Coffee? Ever have a Manhattan Special? They're so refreshing."

"Water would be great, thank you."

Selma's couch wasn't covered in plastic, but the rest of the place was a cliché. Mauve carpeting. A glass candy dish on the coffee table. Several framed photographs sat on top of a piano that stood in the corner against a mirrored wall. And the whole place smelled like a combination of Bengay and Chanel No. 5.

She came out with three glasses of lukewarm water in plastic cups. "Forgive the plastic. I'm very busy. Who has time to run the dishwasher? And, ya know, it's just me. My Harry passed. My kids don't come over. I go to them. That's how it is these days."

"No problem. So maybe while the camera is getting set up, we'll do a pre-interview, go over some questions—"

"No time. I gotta get to the funeral home early. I'm bringing the cookies. Store-bought. I don't bake. She has a ton of family, and there'll be a lot of kids there. So we figure they'll be in the room downstairs, having cookies and juice while the adults pay respects."

Dave and Vince knocked. "Come on in, fellas!" Selma called toward the front door.

Dave and Vince carried the equipment into Selma's living room.

I walked toward Dave. "I was thinking we could do this on the piano bench because it overlooks the window, and you can see the Marches' house."

"Sounds good," Dave said as Vince handed me the microphone.

I wiped my brow.

"Can I be on the right side? This is my good side." Selma pointed at her left cheek.

"Sure." I sat down, crossed my ankles, and adjusted my jacket. Dave equipped Selma with a microphone, attaching it to the collar of her housedress.

"If it falls off, you might have to pick it up," she said. "I can't bend so good. Let's face it, I haven't seen my feet in seventy years."

I noticed a copper clock on Selma's wall. The time was now 11:20. *All right, we better get started.*

"Dave, I'm thinking I'll go right into the questions," I said. "We can do the intro out front afterward and then get some B roll."

"You got it." Dave tapped Selma's microphone then backed away. "In three, two…"

I pushed my hair back and straightened my necklace. "Tell us, Mrs. Renner, how long have you lived next door to Dr. March and Filamina March?"

"Let me think. Let's see. They moved in around the time my grandson was getting married. So, four, five years, let's say. I remember being picked up in a limousine for the wedding, and the Marches' kids were young. They were playing out front. And they were all looking at me, like the queen had just stepped out of her castle. I had on a pink dress. It was beaded. It came to about—"

"Sounds beautiful. So, in these past few years, you've witnessed, at least from a neighbor's perspective, the Marches' life, really. You were home on the night of the first attempt on Filamina's life when someone fired a shot through their living room window."

"Yes, I was. Filamina came out in her bathrobe. The police were called. It was something else."

We talked about the second and third attempts, Dr. March's mistress, her arrest, her plea deal, her shady past, her insistence that Dr. March was the mastermind, and finally, Mrs. March's reversal of her divorce petition and now staunch support of her husband. The copper clock read 11:45, and we hadn't yet covered anything that was not already available on HumanInterestStories.net and every other news source.

Crap.

"So, why do you think Filamina is supporting her husband? Why is she standing by her man?"

Selma looked away from me and right into the camera. "Because she's a tramp."

"And why do you say that?"

"Get up!"

"Excuse me?" I got up and looked over at Dave, who just shrugged. *Helpful.* Something told me to go with it, so I did.

Selma then lifted the seat of the piano bench and pulled out a black square case. "Sit back down."

After we sat, Selma opened the case and pulled out a pair of binoculars. "I have binoculars, and I'm not afraid to use 'em. I'm eighty-five years old. Ya gonna arrest me? Ya gonna sue me? Go right ahead." She spoke directly at the camera. "I see everything!"

"What have you seen?"

"My grandson got them for me." The copper clock read close to 11:50. "I think we went to a baseball game, and he gave them to me, and I used them for a minute, maybe. I hate baseball. Puts me to sleep. But I use them a lot now, ya know"—she glanced back to the camera—"around the house."

"So, you've seen things with your binoculars?"

"Let me tell you, of all the people who don't bother closing their shades, these people put on some show." She pointed toward the Marches' house with her thumb.

"What *specifically* have you seen with your binoculars?" I repeated, louder this time.

"Dr. March might have his lady friend, yes. But Filamina March is no saint. She has had a number of boyfriends, let me tell ya. Different men over while her kids were upstairs sleeping. Do you know how many times I came home from bridge or from bingo or from poker—I used to do a poker night, but all the people in my poker club died—anyway, I would see her with a man, who was *not* Dr. March, in the living room doing who knows what—I never did those things with my husband. We were married fifty years before he passed. We had a beautiful marriage. He was a wonderful man, my Harry."

"So, if she had other boyfriends, why do you think she doesn't just leave Dr. March and be with one of them, or just be single and free to... ya know?"

Selma stared me straight in the eye. "Will Dr. March be able to perform surgery in prison?"

After a second, I realized she expected me to answer. "No, I suppose not."

"Exactly! No surgery, no money. She's got it made, that Filamina. She doesn't work. Her husband pays for everything. And she does whatever she wants."

I suppose she does, but it doesn't sound like a happy marriage or life.

"Makes a bit more sense now, huh?" Selma asked. "Some people will do anything for money. Shame," she said, practically under her breath before announcing, "But there's more."

"Oh?"

She got up and walked toward Vince. He backed away a little, but she crept closer and gently tapped the camera. She pivoted around quickly and gave me a look as if I should have known what she meant.

"Okay." I stood and gently led Selma back to the piano bench. "And what's the something else you're referring to?"

"Cameras," Selma whispered when we sat back down. "He's got that place *wired.*"

"Dr. March has cameras in his house?" I asked.

"All over the place."

"How do you know this?"

"My other neighbors, on the other side in the gray house, they have this beautiful bichon frise named Pippy. Oh, she's such a good dog, my Pippy. Anyway, one morning, Dr. March sees me going for my morning stroll and stops me, and he says, 'Mrs. Renner,' like he's so respectful when I can see right through him. Anyway, he says, 'Mrs. Renner, our neighbor's dog, that little white one, I think she made on my front lawn.' I said, 'Not Pippy.' Long story short, he said, 'Yes, Pippy, and I have the tape to show you if you want.' I said, 'You show it to me right now.' I went right into his house, into his office or whatever you want to call it on the first floor, and he showed me on his computer. And not just the front, but the backyard, the side of the house, and every room in the house! He has cameras in every room in the house! So anyway, I said I would talk to Pippy's parents. But can you believe it? Every room in the house!"

"Do you think Mrs. March knew this?"

"And they were never very nice to Pippy. I saw how they looked at her. If she ran up to sniff them or the kids, they'd look at her like she was dirty. I don't trust people who don't like animals."

"Do you think Mrs. March knew about the cameras?" I repeated. Another glance at the clock. *11:53. She can be a little late. I'm sure they're not waiting around for the store-bought cookies.*

"Well, that's my point. She didn't know at that time because when he heard her coming down the hall, he got rid of that on the computer. I don't know what he did, but it was gone. He pressed some button, and it was not on the computer anymore. I might be old, but I know things. I know she had no idea. But of course, now she might know, and that might be the reason."

"So you think he caught her with one of her boyfriends?"

"Yes, Veronica, he caught her with one of her boyfriends and probably threatened to show all the other mothers on the PTA. She's president of the PTA, she's mother of the year, mother of this and that. She's a tramp, and you better believe he's blackmailing her with the naughty cameras. I know it!" She was slicing the air with her hands now. "PTA! Mother of the year! This. That! Enough."

"Well, that's quite an allegation, Mrs.—"

"And another thing, they might look a certain way, every hair in place, their lawn so neatly manicured, and they have nothing to do with Pippy or anybody's dogs, for that matter. No pets of their own. Nothing out of place. Everything always has to be perfect. Just so. He's very controlling, that Dr. March. You know, those perfectionist types. I don't trust them either. Not for a second!"

"Do the police know about these security cameras?"

"Not as far as I can throw 'em!" She was staring right at the camera then shifted back to me. "What'd ya say, dear?"

"The police must know about these security cameras. He's going on trial. They've searched the March house. How is it that this has never been reported?"

"Every time the police wanted to talk to me, I was in Florida. I called them a few times, and no one ever called me back. Then, there was this newspaper. Oh what was the name? It escapes me. The fella called, wanting to interview me, and I said I'll be in my Sunday best, and he said 'Oh no. There won't be any pictures.' I said forget it. I went to Florida and never called him back. Oh, look." She was pointing at the copper clock. "I have to get going now."

"I'm sure the police subpoenaed the security company."

"Maybe. Maybe that's how they tracked down those hit men. All five hundred of 'em. Not too sharp, eh? But ya know, I don't know. I think this was all Dr. March's doing. He's smart. He's a disgrace of a man, a real pig, but he's smart. He probably wired it himself and then, ya know, got rid of everything. All right, dear, I gotta go."

"Why hasn't one of her boyfriends come forward and told the world she's not what you think? That she has ulterior motives?"

"Maybe they all have ulterior motives too." Selma shrugged. "It's a dirty world, sweetheart, and there are dirty people rolling around in it."

"So, Filamina probably thinks he's guilty too but wants to keep everything status quo. Continue to have her cake and eat it too?"

"Cake, cookies, cupcakes, brownies. That broad enjoys it all. Speaking of cookies, I'm late. But how'd I do?" Selma smiled at the camera.

"Great. Thank you again, Mrs. Renner. You've definitely got an interesting perspective as a neighbor, and your theory would explain Mrs. March's reasons for supporting her husband and even, possibly, another motive for Dr. March. You've given us a lot to digest." I was trying not to rush through the words. "We thank you for your time." I almost forgot to look at the camera until Dave waved. "For NewYork3News, I'm Veronica Buccino."

My shoulders dropped.

Selma touched my arm. "You're very good at this, dear. A real natural."

"Aw, thank you." I glimpsed up to the ceiling and held my arms out. "This is so much more fun than being a lawyer!"

Dave and Vince looked at each other and laughed as they started to wrap up the extension cords.

In a matter of minutes, we were packed up, and as Selma walked us out the front door, she handed each of us a bottle of Manhattan Special for the road.

Before we called a different cab company, we shot the intro outside between both Selma's and the Marches' houses. I had memorized it and did it in one take. After that, as we waited for the cab, I was finally able to breathe normally for the first time that day.

While we headed back to the city, Dave propped the camera on his lap to show me the raw footage. I quietly sipped my Manhattan Special and watched the interview. That was when it hit me.

Chapter 20

"TALK ABOUT DIRTY LAUNDRY." I gulped my mango martini.

I had decided not to go back to work after the interview. I went back to my apartment and attempted to start the written portion of the story. After a couple of hours of staring at a blank page, I called Syd to meet for a drink at a Midtown bar.

"You're not the one exposing it," Syd said. "Selma is. It sounds like she really wanted to put it all out there."

"I felt great right after, like I'd really done it. I went out there and uncovered this new angle to this story I've been fascinated with for so long." I shook my head. "But then, watching the footage, it seemed so tawdry, so lowbrow. And I can't stop thinking, just wow, I can't win. The law is boring and intolerable, and journalism is exhilarating but leaves me with a guilty conscience."

"You don't always have to do that kind of journalism. You can do other stories that are more inspiring."

"I guess. *If* I do any more stories. I'm making one hundred and fifty dollars for this. Can't exactly quit my day job." I swallowed the last bit of my martini when I noticed my phone ringing.

Syd gestured for me to take it.

"Hiiiiiii!" It was Jada.

She did remember after all. "Hi! You sound happy."

"Yes. I'm very happy. And very drunk. I skipped work today. We just went to the Yankees game. Are you at the office?"

"I didn't go to work either," I said. "I had my interview for class today."

"Oh! That's right. How was it?"

"Good." I sighed.

"Where are you now?"

"I'm at Lilly Bar with Syd."

"Cool. We'll meet you."

We?

Forty minutes and another martini later, Jada arrived, sweaty and ruddy-faced but giddy. Todd was tall and blond and also looked like one might look after drinking outdoors at a baseball game all day. Syd and I made room for them, and Jada and I made introductions.

"So, you're a Yankee fan?" I asked.

"Not really," Todd said. "A client gave me the tickets."

"How long have you lived in the city?"

Todd was staring at a TV screen over the bar. I thought he didn't hear me. Jada tapped him. He brought his attention back and rested his elbows on the table before answering, "Ten years."

Maybe these are superficial questions, but this would be the part where you ask Syd if he likes baseball, or ask about my journalism adventure today, though I'm sure Jada didn't mention it because she hasn't even asked me herself yet.

"So, I met the funniest lady today." I proceeded to tell them about Selma.

"Hold on," Todd said. "You're a lawyer, right? So, what is this for?"

"Yeah, I'm a lawyer. This is for NewYork3News.com. It's an online news site."

"Is that your *other* job?"

"No. It's silly, but I took this news reporting class, and this assignment I did turned into this interview I did today."

"It's not silly," Syd said.

"She's a lawyer," Jada said. "We met in law school." Jada then turned to me with a sheepish look. "I told him that, but I guess he doesn't remember. We've been drinking in the sun too long."

"What kind of law do you do?" Syd asked Jada.

"Corporate. I don't love it, but I love the paycheck. I'm not going to sign up for a news class any time soon."

I smiled. *Fuck you, Jada.*

"Why not?" Syd asked. "Doesn't it sound fun?"

Jada just grinned. Her smile was patronizing in its width, I felt. *What the fuck?*

"All right, I've had a crazy long day," I announced. "I'm going to pass out."

Syd put cash on the table, and we all exchanged goodbyes and handshakes. Syd walked me to the corner to get a cab.

"I don't really want to go home," I said. "I'm actually not that tired."

"Me neither. Let's get out of this neighborhood so we don't get busted by your friends."

We went to Steel Rose Bar where more martinis were drunk, and in a redux of Saturday night, more kisses were exchanged. We were making a scene, I was sure, but I didn't care. What I did care about was not going too fast. I wanted to do more than kiss him, but it still felt as though it were too soon.

"How long have they been dating? Jada and that guy?" Syd asked.

I lifted my head from his shoulder, where I'd been taking in his delicious musky cedar scent. "Just a short while." *Her boyfriend just picked up his things this morning.* "But there's a whole backstory there that's not worth rehashing right now," I said, swiping the air.

"So, when was your last relationship?"

"Not too long ago. We dated for two years, and then he moved to London." I'd been so consumed with other things that I hadn't thought much about John lately.

"Is that why you broke up? Because he moved?"

"Yeah, kind of."

"Kind of?"

"I was convinced he was going to propose, and he didn't. Instead, he said, 'You can come to London if you want. It's up to you.' So yeah, I politely declined that offer."

"What an invite."

I sipped my drink. "What about you?"

"My last relationship was two years ago. We also dated two years. Her name was Jessica. She was Italian too."

"You like the Italian girls."

"They're the best."

"Why'd you break up?"

He shrugged. "She cheated on me."

"Oh, how awful. I'm sorry. That's horrible."

"Ahh, it's all right."

"Who did she cheat on you with?"

"Her boss."

"Ugh. Did you suspect?"

"No, but when she told me, 'I'm sleeping with my boss,' that pretty much tipped me off."

I couldn't help but laugh. He laughed too.

"Why would she do that?"

"I don't know. She was one of those girls that always had a boyfriend, was never single. I think she saw herself approaching thirty and just went nuts. Had to have all the fun she missed out on."

"Are they still together?"

"Well, we're not Facebook friends anymore so I don't know, but I can send her a message and find out if you want."

"That's quite all right. So, you're still in touch?" I hoped he would say no.

"No. I was kidding. If they are still together, I guess that's good. I don't wish her anything bad. Honestly, she's a nice girl. She just had a roving vagina. Kind of a deal breaker."

"What about the fool factor? Don't you feel like she made a fool out of you?"

"At the time, yeah. I was angry, but it was a long time ago now. I got over it and moved on."

I had known Syd for such a short time, but I already felt like I was getting to truly know who Syd Blackman was. I'd known John for two years and only broached the past relationship topic once or twice. He would just say, "The past is the past." I thought at the time that was a good point of view. I didn't want to know the gratuitous details, but I realized later, it wasn't the gratuitous details that I was seeking… it was what he'd learned, who he was. Discussing past relationships helped each person understand the other person. That was when I told Syd about the four requirements. He almost spat his drink out.

"Are you always so methodical? Do you organize your socks by color?"

I laughed and lightly slapped his shoulder. "No!" *John does.*

"Do I meet the four requirements? Oh wait, I'm not Italian. I must have slipped through the cracks."

"It's not a perfect system," I teased.

"So I have a chance of advancing to exclusive status then?"

I nodded, but I didn't say "Yes." We sat awkwardly, sipping our drinks for a brief moment.

"So," Syd started.

My heart dropped. *I'm not ready to have this conversation. This day was eventful enough.*

"When do I get to see the interview?" he asked. "How soon will it be up?"

I felt my shoulders go down. "I don't know. They have to edit it, but probably soon, maybe even tomorrow. And in the meantime, I have to do the written part to complement the video story. I hope I can write like a journalist and not sound too lawyerly."

"Did I mention yet that my cousin Rachel works at CNN? She got her master's in journalism at Northwestern. I can ask her to look at your story for you."

"Really? I don't know. I don't want to bother her with my little online story. I'm sure she's busy at CNN."

"It won't be a bother to her. She's really nice. It doesn't have to be anything formal. She could look at it, and we could all go talk about it over drinks."

"I don't know. I'm an amateur at this. It's too embarrassing—"

"Veronica, give yourself some credit. You're trying something new. It's not going to be perfect the first time, but you're smart enough to know to ask for help and network and ask the right people."

"Yeah, I guess you're right. Okay. Yes, please ask Cousin Rachel. Thank you."

We smooched. And drank more. And smooched again.

When the bill came, I insisted on paying. He protested.

"No, you helped me prepare," I said. "You played the role of old Jewish lady. It made all the difference."

As he opened his wallet, I noticed all of the bills were crinkled and folded and stuffed in odd ways. For some reason, it made me smile.

"What are you smiling about? My old-lady impression? I was good, but maybe you haven't been around that many old people."

"That's not it." I laughed. "That's definitely not it."

"Well, listen, I know you're a big, fancy lawyer, but you're not paying on dates with me."

Then, he paid with a hundred-dollar bill that appeared to have been washed and dried in the laundry and stuffed in his sock for a week.

We walked out, holding hands, and as we stood on the corner, I spotted a penny at my feet.

"Do you pick them up?"

"No. In case they're someone else's sign."

"Good, because I like you, but I don't want to start going around town picking up pennies. Well, for you, I would, but—"

"It's okay," I assured him.

I like this bald Jewish man. Very much. Is he my husband? I don't know. Why does my mind always jump to the future? Stop thinking, Veronica. In the cab on the way home, I looked out the window as we sped across town.

What if the Marches sue me? Crap! I wish my brain had an Off button.

Chapter 21

"SHE'S A RIOT, THAT SELMA, isn't she?" Grandma Ant asked.

I was in my living room in the fetal position on my couch while my grandparents sat at the bistro set in the corner. "Where's the ring?" I asked without looking at them.

"We'll tell you when—" Grandma Ant said.

Grandpa Sal cut her off. "When the time is right."

"No!" I sat up. "I fulfilled my end of the bargain. Where is it?"

"We'll tell you soon. Ya gotta get to a point when it'll be clear to you that—"

"Antoinette!" my grandfather pleaded.

I shook my head and curled back up again. *I'm fighting enough battles. I'll deal with that later.*

"That Selma reminds me of our friend Ruth. You met Ruth. And we know Selma's husband, Harry. What a nice fella. Isn't he nice, Sal?"

"Oh yeah," Grandpa Sal said as he put the last bite of a mini cannoli in his mouth. When he was done chewing, he said, "All right, *brasciole*, talk."

"I feel like Jerry Springer."

"Which is it? Do you want to be a lawyer? Or do you want to be a news gal?" Grandpa Sal asked.

"I don't want to be Jerry Springer!" I rolled over to yell this. "I'd like to be the kind of journalist who is less Jerry, more O... as in Oprah Winfrey."

"What about that Rosanna Zotto?" Grandma Ant asked. "She's

going to interview the wife, and she *was* going to interview the mistress. Isn't that, ya know, like Jerry?"

"Well, no, she would have done it in a respectable way. Plus, she's with a big news organization. She's not a freelancer like me. I could get sued!"

They said nothing.

I covered my face. "I have to talk to Dave. He'll be so disappointed, but I have to tell him I'm not comfortable with this."

"All right, talk to him. See what happens," Grandma Ant said. "About the interview, you were nervous before it, weren't ya? And then you did it, and then you were almost jumping up and down! We saw. Now, didn't that feel good?"

"Yes, but at the expense of someone's privacy. I know she's a cheater, and he's a cheater, and yes, I'm hard on cheaters." I flipped over my pillow. "My father. Jada. I know that about myself. Maybe I'm a little judgmental, a little unforgiving. I'm working on it. You *see*, right? But I don't know if even the Marches deserve this. I wouldn't want my mistakes shown to the world." I threw my head back on the pillow. "I finally do something fun, but then I feel like crap about it. I can't win."

"None of that," Grandpa Sal said.

Grandma Ant said even louder, "Hey, hey, now. All right, they won't all be like this—the sex and the cameras and the whatnot. You're learning, Veronica. Rosanna Zotto wasn't built in a day."

At that, I smiled.

My grandmother added, "Or Oprah. Ever see any of her old shows? Good lord. Ya know, Gah bless her, but oh, those old shows."

I thought about that for a moment. "I'll talk to Dave, and if he insists on going forward, I guess I'll have to live with it. Just pray nobody sues me. And yeah, I guess everyone does start somewhere."

"You guess right." Grandpa stood up. "Now, let's go eat. I want macaroni."

"You just had a cannoli," I pointed out.

"Sue me." He walked toward the door without looking back.

Chapter 22

PLEASE PICK UP BEFORE BEVERLY comes barging in.

Dave was not a phone person. *Voicemail. Frig!*

"Hi, Dave. This is Veronica… Buccino. I, I just want to talk to you about the story. About Filamina. About Selma. If you could call me back when you get this, please? Thanks."

I will now send him an email and mark it urgent. Has anyone ever really used the red exclamation point? I am about to make history.

> Hi Dave, I just left you a voicemail. Not sure how to put this, but I am having a bit of a moral dilemma about this story.

Before I could explain by email, I heard "Veronica!" and my office door burst open. I tried to quickly close out of the email, but instead, I hit Send.

Fan-friggin'-tastic.

"Hi, Beverly," I said.

"Quit emailing your friends about the latest royal family gossip. Who cares? They're all nuts on the other side of the pond." She snapped her fingers. Actual snaps.

Who the hell snaps their fingers at people? Beverly.

"We've got work to do. Grab your pad and a pen. Meet in my office."

An hour later, with five new cases in hand, I returned to my office to see this:

Ha! You may be a fancy law firm associate, Veronica, but you are a newbie journalist. Typical first story nerves! Don't sweat it. Put your feelings aside. Welcome to the biz.

BTW, the video story is being edited as I write this. Please finish the written piece as soon as possible. Need to see a first draft. We want the video and accompanying written piece to run as soon as possible.

Shit.
I replied.

Okay, I'll work on the written portion, but are you around to speak later?

I'm not sure Dave understands what's at stake here. Maybe if I speak to him, he'll agree that it's all too sleazy, but since I did such a good job, he'll give me a more Oprah-like assignment in the future. Here's hoping.

A dedicated law firm associate would then go through each of the five cases she was just handed, learn the facts, and start preparing the necessary filings.

This was what I did: moved the stack of case files out of the way and onto the windowsill after accidentally spilling Earl Grey tea all over them. Then, I Googled, "What is a lead sentence?"

As far as Dave was concerned at this moment, we were moving forward, and he wanted to see a draft as soon as possible. So I figured I'd better start working... by not working on my actual job.

Well, for starters, it's spelled "lede" in the news business. It's also the first and most important sentence of my news story.

Maybe this would work: *Dr. March, the man on trial for conspiring to murder his wife, has many skeletons in his closet, and according to a neighbor, so does his wife.*

Maybe?

Or maybe this: *Filamina March may be the devoted wife of Dr. March, the man on trial for conspiring to have her murdered, but she's also allegedly a raging slut.*

Definitely not.

How about—My phone rang. It was Kate's line. I didn't pick up. I needed five minutes to craft a lede, then I could do my real work.

While many have wondered why Filamina March is standing by her man, a longtime neighbor—

My phone rang again. It was Kate. Again. I didn't pick up again.

While many have wondered why Filamina March is standing by her man, a longtime neighbor believes she knows why. And it's not out of pure devotion.

That could work.

"Veronica!" Beverly pushed my office door open and hollered, "Kate is looking for you. She's not going to be here tomorrow. You need to handle something for her. Go to her office."

I grabbed my yellow legal pad and knocked gently on Kate's door before walking in. "Hi," I said. "Beverly said you need me to handle something for tomorrow while you're out."

"Mm-hm," was all she muttered as she pecked away at her keyboard.

Well, okay then. How long do I sit here? I wonder if she'll thank me for handling whatever it is. Ha! I could dream on. Oh, and of course, I forgot my phone so I can't do any pretend scrolling to alleviate the awkwardness while she pecks away. I'll just have to sit here like a lump, waiting for her.

Finally, she pointed to the stack of files at the corner of her desk. "Those are my cases."

I nodded.

"From the meeting?" she asked, as if she wondered whether I could hear her.

I nodded again.

"That we just had with Beverly?" Her eyebrows rose.

Yes, I'm understanding you. Do you want me to nod harder? The meeting. I was there. Get to the fucking point, bitch! I didn't say that. I just nodded more vigorously.

She sighed and shook her head like an actress wondering why she had to work with such amateurs. "I'll be out tomorrow. There are motions that need to be filed for each of them." She turned away, picked up the phone, and started dialing.

I picked up the files and walked out, slamming her office door behind me. Hard. It felt good. It would have felt better if she had anything on her walls that could've come crashing down and shattered into a million pieces.

I went back to my office, threw Kate's files on the windowsill next to mine, and continued working on my Selma story.

Seventy-two hours later, I had a first draft. And I learned that Dave does in fact use the phone, such as when he wanted me to stop tinkering with the story and "send the damn thing already." A hot story like Selma's would normally have been up on the site within a couple of hours, he explained, but since crimes and courts wasn't their most popular section, they were letting me "train" on this story and take a little longer.

"You have twenty-four more hours," Dave had told me.

I appreciated the extension and the one after that and didn't mean to keep pushing it, but I couldn't stop tinkering with every paragraph before writing the next one.

I printed it while Beverly was on a smoke break. Then, I took a break of my own, sipping tea and staring out of my office window at the cars zooming down the street, the protesters shouting on the corner, and the people walking by. I thought about all I'd learned in the past three days, including Beverly's uncanny ability to interrupt me every time I was just on the brink of crafting the perfect sentence about Filamina, or Dr. March, or Selma, or Selma's binoculars. But I was still able to crank out a first draft. A first draft was better than nothing.

"Don't you want to win the most number of hits contest and get another freelance assignment from us?" Dave asked yesterday.

I'd forgotten about that. All I cared about was writing the best story possible. My name would be on it, on the Internet forever, for all the world to see. I didn't want it to *just* be good. It had to be "Dominick Dunne for Vanity Fair" good with a thorough background of the case, the bizarre facts, and why Selma's big reveal even mattered.

Dave was getting impatient. "Dominick Dunne didn't write breaking news for a daily. Send it *now*."

Still, he didn't strike fear in me like Beverly did. "I know, but Dominick Dunne was straightforward while also being lyrical and erudite. I want to be lyrical and erudite! I promise, I'm almost done." And I continued to tinker.

I also learned that as an independent contractor in the eyes of

NewYork3News.com, if the Marches sued me for this story, I would be sued personally and have to pay for my own defense. *Friggin' fantastic.* Dave, however, thought the likelihood of that happening was "less than zero." *I'm not good at math, but I think that means not likely.* And he stuck to his decision to run the story.

I learned that Syd's cousin Rachel was extremely understanding. Although we scheduled an after-work meetup then a lunch, I had to cancel both times because of work. *Leave it to work to get in the way. At least Syd and Rachel seem to understand.*

I learned that Todd didn't talk about ex-girlfriends. He wanted to leave the past in the past. Todd didn't talk about the future either. He didn't want to worry about it in the "here and now." Todd also didn't talk about the status of relationships. He wanted to let things happen naturally and not "put labels on it." Todd drank a lot. Todd worked a lot. Todd got home really late. But Jada was the one who looked tired.

In the category of "Things I didn't learn in the past three days because I already knew," was that I liked Syd. A lot. But in that case, I was the one who didn't want to put a label on anything.

"So, are you still on Match?" he asked with a smirk over drinks later that night when, unfortunately, Rachel was the one who couldn't meet up. *Ships in the night.*

"No." I leaned toward the bar and reached for a napkin I didn't need.

"Me neither," he said.

"But I…" I tried to find the right words. "I don't want to label anything just yet. I mean, it hasn't been that long, and I'm enjoying this phase, this time, and you know, I also got out of that long relationship and I—"

I was finding a lot of words, but from the concerned look on his face, I wasn't sure any of them were the right ones.

Then, reaching behind his neck, he said, "I don't like labels either."

I nervously straightened the napkin underneath my cocktail.

"I cut them out of all of my shirts," he said. "They itch."

I laughed hard. He did too. Then I downed the rest of my cocktail.

A moment later, I was still smiling and studying his cute lips when I realized his smile was gone. That concerned look was back. So I turned away and ordered another drink.

Chapter 23

I DIDN'T KNOW WHAT TO say to make Jada stop crying.

"It might be a blessing in disguise," I offered, but she didn't respond and just blew her nose loudly, which prompted stares from the other diners.

Earlier that morning, Jada texted me. —Todd ended it. Can you meet for lunch?—

Ended it? It just began.

When I met her at the diner, her eyes were red and puffy, and she was in yoga pants.

"I couldn't deal with work today," she'd said.

I understood. "He's a jerk. He'll regret it," I tried again as I sat across from her, but she didn't respond to that either.

I realized in that moment I'd never seen Jada cry. "Hey, if Dan or Karen walk by and you get busted for not being in the office today, you could say your allergies are killing you, and that's why you're not in the office today. One look at you, and they'd believe it."

At that, she smiled briefly.

"You should get a massage or go shopping," I continued. "I realize this is bad advice, but go buy something. Seriously. Something fun and pretty. It'll make you feel better... even if just for a minute."

"Maybe."

I exhaled. "I have to be honest," I said. "I'm surprised you're this broken up after such a short time with Todd."

She shrugged and reached for another tissue.

"Did your mom or sister know anything about Todd?"

She shook her head. "They only know I broke up with Mark, and you can imagine my mother's reaction."

Jada was in no mood to do her famous imitation of her mother, but I knew it involved her customary guilt trip about marriage and babies and the clock ticking. When I checked the time, I realized we'd been sitting there for over two hours.

"Thank you," Jada said, hugging me hard, as we parted at the corner.

I practically ran back to the office, praying the whole time I wouldn't cross Beverly's path.

No such luck. She spotted me getting off the elevator and told me to come to her office. "You don't think I know that when I go to the bathroom, you sneak out? When I go to have a smoke, you dash out of here? And every excuse in the book! Come on! You could write a book, Veronica. Ever think of doing that? Veronica Buccino's Not Very Interesting Excuses Book—I have a migraine, I have to go to the dentist, I have to go to the doctor, I've got to save the whales. You barely work! This is not a playhouse. If you had half of Kate's work ethic, you might not always be scrambling through that pad of yours, looking for things you never researched."

I had planned to tell her I was going to pick up a prescription before the pharmacy closed so I could meet Syd and his cousin Rachel that night. Finally.

But Beverly was on high alert when it came to me. *Still, maybe if I finish all of the work she's about to give me, I can get out of here at a decent hour. Syd said his cousin printed out my article and will go over it with me paragraph by paragraph. And I cannot cancel a third time. And Dave is blowing up my phone with "Damn, you're a perfectionist. I should just write the article at this point."*

"Now, here are six case files." She pointed to the stack at the edge of her desk. "We need motions filed on each. Get started on that."

I stood up without making eye contact and grabbed the files off of her desk.

"Maybe now you'll get something done today. I want to see all of the motions when I get in tomorrow morning," she said as I walked out of her office.

I went through each file faster than I ever had before. I didn't break to check my phone or email or even to look at HumanInterestStories. net, but I'd still only gone through three of the six cases by seven that night. We were supposed to meet at eight thirty.

I suppose I have to cancel now.

As I reached for my phone, my office door opened. Beverly was on her way to take a smoke break but made sure to stop in and ask, "Hey, Cupcake Crusader. How far along are we?"

"I got three of them done."

"Type faster." She fished for a cigarette. "You're skating on thin ice, in case I didn't make that clear." She shook her head as she walked away, calling over her shoulder, "All six on my desk by tomorrow morning."

Yes, I heard you the first time, Grumpy. I stood up and slammed my office door shut.

"Hi!" Syd sounded happy when he picked up on the first ring.

"Hey." I hoped my tone prepared him at least a little bit for what was coming next. "So, Beverly reprimanded me today for leaving early. I know eight is not early for normal people, but it's practically a half day to her. And it doesn't help that I had to take two hours for lunch to be there for Jada. Long story. Anyway, I can't believe that I have to do this, but I can't meet up. I'm so sorry. Please apologize to Rachel." I swallowed. "Again."

"Oh… okay. Can you maybe do ten p.m.? We can push it. Rachel's ready for you, and I think she'll really help you. From the little I talked to her about it, she has some really good feedback—"

"Syd, I can't. If Beverly sees I've left even for a minute… I can't even think about it. I'm not Rosanna Zotto yet." I laughed nervously. "I need this job." I took a deep breath. *Okay, wait. Let me figure this out. If I could somehow get one or two done before ten and then manage to sneak out of here at ten, I could come back after midnight and finish the rest. That might work.*

"That's your problem, Veronica. You think you need that job."

Huh? I felt my neck get hot. "Easy for you to say." I tried to sound like I was joking. "Would you like to pay my school loans and credit card bills and everything else? Actually, I *do* need this job."

"And that's why you'll never get out of there." He wasn't joking. "I don't want to sound like your friend—who you spent two hours at lunch with today? Anyway, maybe that class was a waste of time. If you're not going to go for it, all in, what's the point? Go ahead, stay at the job you hate. Not just tonight. Forever."

I felt my blood rush through my veins. *Is he kidding me? Like I need this right now?* "I don't have a choice!" I screamed into the phone.

"Yeah, actually you do," he said.

"What the fuck do you know? And thanks a fucking lot for understanding." I hung up.

I sat at my desk for a few minutes, waiting for my hands to stop shaking, for my heart to stop racing.

Then, I went to the bathroom and splashed cold water on my face and neck. *What the hell just happened? I can't believe I had a fight with Syd.* I cringed every time the exchange replayed in my head.

I didn't get all of the cases finished until well after midnight, but only because I found it hard to concentrate.

Chapter 24

"Beverly's a bitch." Jada sipped her wine.

"I know." I reviewed the menu. We were at a restaurant in Little Italy. Jada asked the waitress to bring us two glasses of merlot before we even got our menus. "At least I'm not in the office right now. Grateful to get out of there tonight."

On that night, unlike the night before, I was able to leave work by seven. I would have called Syd and tried one more time to meet up with him and his cousin, but I couldn't. We hadn't spoken or texted all day, and I feared it may have ended before it had really started. I tried to think of ways to fix it.

What can I possibly do though? Send him flowers?

"Have you heard from Syd today?"

"No." I shook my head, still studying the menu. "Oh look, they have *brasciole*. I never see that on a menu. Hmm. My grandfather used to call me his little *brasciole*."

"My little *brasciole*, I saw a penny this morning in the bodega. I was going to pick it up for you, but then I remembered your rule."

I closed the menu. "Thank you."

"To pennies and *brasciole*."

We toasted. Jada looked like a completely different person from the day before. Although she claimed not to have taken my suggestion of shopping or a spa treatment, she looked as though she had. She was in all black, her hair straight and sleek, her makeup brushed and blended to perfection. She took off of work again, which might have explained why she appeared so rested and put together.

I glanced out the window as the wine trickled down my throat. The summer night was hot and sticky, and the air conditioning was pumping in the restaurant. Through the window, I took in the row of stores across the street, all selling "I Heart NY" T-shirts and pins, along with Italian flags and "Italian Princess" baby T-shirts. *I love Little Italy.*

"I have news." Jada sat up straight.

I turned back from the window. *Oh no. Please don't tell me you're back with Todd. You've been broken up for one day, and I can't say this aloud, but I think it's for the best.*

"Oh? Good news, I hope." I forced a smile. *Maybe it's work-related. Maybe she got a raise.*

"Mark and I are back together." She swirled her wine and took a big gulp.

Huh?

"What's that face, Veronica?"

I shook my head. "Sorry. Wait, what?"

"Todd is selfish. And he's not ready for a relationship. Who knows if he'll ever be? But I realized, maybe I needed this time off from Mark to... to realize I really missed him."

Time off? What time? "Hold on, who did you miss?"

"Mark. We talked a lot last night, and I feel... he's so great, he's such a good guy. I don't know, I think I should try again. And we're going to just give it another shot."

"You dated for two years! Wasn't that enough time to figure out you were never in love with him? You know you were never in love with him. What's giving it another shot going to change? Appease your mother?"

I actually said that. Every word of it. It was all true, and I didn't want my friend wasting any more time and making a mistake.

Jada's eyes grew wide. "No," she said with unusual restraint, clearly trying not to sound too defensive. "My mother? No. I really do feel differently now. I want to see what happens."

Jada was going to be thirty next month, and I wondered if that might have something to do with it. "Are you sure it's not because you're afraid to be single and thirty?" I actually said that too. I'd come this far, after all, so I figured I might as well continue. "You're going to be thirty, and you have your mother breathing down your neck, saying the things she says to you. I'm not telling you what to do. I know how you feel, how you've felt for two years, and I know the pressure you feel. With your birthday. With your mom. With your sister already being married and having a kid. I just can't believe you would, I don't know, fold like this. One guy, Todd, disappoints you, and you run back to Mark? Why not try being single? Did you ever think of that?"

"I didn't *fold*," Jada said. "Be single? Like you? Go on Match? How is that working out? I'm sorry you're so miserable right now—you're unsure about your career, you're unsure about the guy—but can't you be happy for me?" Her face was red, and it wasn't from the wine.

"What is there to be happy about? That you're getting back together with someone you *cheated on*? And then Todd rejects you, and that's it? You just fold? Yes, fold." My voice was growing louder. "One stupid guy, and that's it? You gave yourself no time to be single. You're too impatient and afraid to give it any more time, so you're taking the easy way out. But it could be a *huge mistake*. Are we supposed to just marry whoever'll take us at the moment we're about to turn thirty? That's not how it's supposed to be!" I sensed the waitress walk over then quickly pivot away in the other direction.

"Thanks for throwing that back in my face." Jada threw her napkin on the table. "You were the only person I told about Todd and what I did, which I feel horrible about, and you keep taking it personally. I thought we moved past that? I thought I got an absolution from Sister Fucking Veronica."

I felt my blood course and my heart race as she practically spat the words out.

"You know what, Veronica? You can't be happy for me because you're so unhappy yourself."

Ouch.

She grabbed her bag and stormed out.

The waitress returned. "Do you ladies have any questions about the menu?" Maybe she assumed Jada was in the bathroom.

"My friend got sick and went home. I'm so sorry." I had to concentrate on getting those few words out as my heart punched my chest.

I sat there for a few moments, digesting what had just happened. Then, I paid for the wine and started walking home from Little Italy.

When I got to Fourteenth Street, I stood at the corner, waiting for the light to change, when I heard, "I love Paul Sorvino. Your dad reminds me of him."

"Really? I always thought my dad was more Danny Aiello," I heard a guy's voice respond.

I know that voice.

"No, he's Paul Sorvino." The young woman laughed loudly. "He is."

As we all crossed the street, I glanced over my shoulder. And there he was, Match.com Date #0001, the one who'd called his mother a bitch. He was holding hands with a very pretty brunette.

A lid for every pot?

When we got to the other side of the street, I pretended to look at the bottom of my shoe as if I'd stepped on something. I let them get ahead of me then I followed them for a few blocks. They held hands the entire time, laughing and talking as if they were the only ones on the street, or in the city, or in the world.

Definitely a lid and a pot. *Wow. Well, good for him. Is Syd my lid?*

I walked a couple of more blocks, trying to come up with more than one way to rhyme "Syd" and "lid." *He's my lid, Syd.*

Maybe I'll write him a funny poem to smooth things over? While I'm at it, I'll have to write one for Jada too. How about, "Roses are red, violets are blue. You're settling for Mark, you pathetic shrew?"

I sighed and hailed a cab. The poetry could wait a day. Or forever. What I needed at that moment was a good night's sleep.

Chapter 25

"I'M IN A FIGHT WITH Syd." I'd never talked about Syd to my grandparents, and I didn't know why. I looked for some sort of reaction to his name, but there was none, so I continued. "I'm in a fight with Jada now too. My boss is a bitch."

We were at the same restaurant I'd been at with Jada. "Oh, and I still have to finalize the written story about Selma. You know, in my spare time. Dave is losing his patience with me. For good reason. But I just can't bring myself to hit 'Send.'"

"All right, let's talk about the friend of yours." My grandmother cut her *brasciole*. "Ya know, the way you are, you think a lot. You've thought a lot about the fellas you've dated, what you wanted, what you didn't want, and this and that."

I felt a "but" coming.

"But that doesn't mean you know what's right for somebody else, for other people."

"Listen." I stabbed my *brasciole*. "Jada has always been so lukewarm about Mark. I know she wants passion and to be with someone who makes her laugh and who she feels crazy about. Getting back together with him makes no sense. I don't get it."

Grandpa Sal ripped off a piece of bread from the basket in front of us. "It's not for you to get."

"It's her journey, as they say, her things she's gotta learn," my grandmother said. "Her fears she has to get over."

"Jada's not afraid of anything. She tells off her boss. She'll tell anyone off. She's got—forgive me, Gram—serious balls. So, that's why—"

And that was when I saw Jada. She was at a table at the other end of the restaurant with a handsome, white-haired older man in a corduroy jacket and a regal-looking woman with jet-black hair in a sort of upsweep. The woman had just touched Jada's cheek, and Jada laughed but didn't look up from her meal.

I stood and waved, but my grandfather gently took my arm.

"She can't see you," he said.

"Why not?"

"Sit down, Veronica."

I sat.

"Sometimes, you can talk with other people, but not this time," my grandfather said. "Some visits are, what's the word, you can sorta mingle, ya know. You can interact with other people still living, but some visits are not open in that way." He motioned, palm out, in Jada's direction. "Those are her grandparents, both on her mother's side. Good people, right, Ant?"

"Oh, real nice," my grandmother said.

"No, that can't be right. She's never met her mother's parents."

My grandfather guffawed at this. "Oh yeah?"

"Yeah, I know that for a fact."

Grandma Ant stared at me for a moment and smiled. "Isn't that the beautiful thing about life on the other side? Someone can be looked after by someone they've never met. Jada's grandparents have known her for her whole life even if she doesn't realize it, even if when she's awake, she doesn't feel that she knows them at all. She does."

I was too distracted to absorb this, still peering in their direction. "I can't say hello?"

"Now, you make me sound like a broken record," Grandpa Sal said. "No. Not now. She can't see you this time."

"Why exactly not?"

"Who knows? They're probably talking about certain things," Grandma said.

"Yeah, I hope they're talking her out of getting back together with Mark," I said. I glanced over at my grandfather, who had finished his meal. He was taking a cannoli from a waitress who appeared to be serving *zeppole* in a basket.

"I can't just sit by and let this happen. She could be making a huge mistake." I stood and walked toward Jada and her grandparents.

"Where do you think you're going?" Grandpa Sal asked.

"I want a *zeppole* from that basket," I lied as I made a beeline for Jada.

Neither she nor her grandparents looked up as I approached the table. "Hi," I said with a wave.

They continued talking, but I couldn't hear the conversation. I waved my hand again. "Hello?"

Nothing.

I felt a hand on my shoulder.

"You're somethin' else, Veronica. Come on." My grandfather led me away. "You can't get through. I told you that." He shook his head. "Not your lesson, not your business." He stopped walking and turned to me, pointing a chubby finger. "Your lesson? Is to mind your own business. *Capisce?*"

Chapter 26

SELMA RENNER HAS LIVED NEXT *door to the Marches since—*
Selma Renner, the Marches' next door neighbor, believes—
I had finished the article and was about to hit the Send button to
Dave, but then, suddenly, there was this one sentence that felt completely
amateurish. *How could I have written such an atrocious sentence? What
was I thinking? People go to school for this. Did I really think I could do
this with no proper training?*

I wished I could call Syd. I would have sent him the latest version,
and he would have given me that one final vote of confidence.
Unfortunately, I hadn't heard from him at all. As I stared out my office
window, I decided if I didn't hear from him by the end of the day, I
would call and apologize. *Maybe I overreacted. But Beverly was being
extra beastly, and he couldn't understand.*

I refocused on my computer screen and hovered over the Send button
when my office door burst open. I should have known it was serious
because, for once, Beverly wasn't yelling my name. She was silent.

I looked up. I could hear myself swallow.

The door began to creep back. She took a step forward. "Trista
Hines."

Oh, shit.

"Let me see the file."

My heart was thumping in my ears as I stood and opened my filing
cabinet.

"Bring it to my office." She said the words in a voice so steady and
calm, it was terrifying.

Please don't fire me. Slaughter me any way you must, but please don't fire me.

I retrieved the file, walked into Beverly's office, shut the door behind me, and sat in the guest chair next to Kate. She was sitting smugly with one arm perched on the back of the chair.

How lovely. An audience for my torture.

Beverly spun around in her chair and folded her hands on her desk.

"I just received a very interesting email from the court in Schulster County." She spoke slowly. "A routine email in the Hines matter. Sending along a copy to our office of the docket. *Case dismissed.* I don't see an order to satisfy the judgment here." She said the last sentence as if they were all curse words.

"I can explain." I choked the words out of my mouth, which was getting drier and drier. *No, I can't.*

"You defied me." Beverly stared me down.

"What happened was"—my voice shook—"she showed up at court, then the client called. Well, I called him but—"

She bent forward and pointed her finger at her own chest. "I speak to the clients. Not you. I am the only one who speaks to our clients."

"I know. I just—"

"How are you going to fix this, Veronica?" I thought I caught a hint of a smile, a curl at the corners of her mouth, as though she were enjoying this.

"I don't know, but I'll—"

"How. Are. You. Going. To. Fix. This?" That was when the bubbles of spit at the corners of her mouth appeared as she spoke.

I could feel Kate's eyes on me. I could feel my chest, neck, and face burn.

"Go back to your office," she said. "I can't look at you right now. Kate and I will figure out how we're going to fix this, how we're going to save the client from having this drag on for who knows how long instead of getting the money he so justly deserves *now*. That's how we do things around here, Veronica." She yelled that last part. "My way. We do things my way!" She slammed her fist on the desk.

"I'm so sorry."

"And I'll decide what's going to happen with you. This is grounds for termination. But let me deal with one problem at a time. Go. Go back to your office."

I stood, and since I'd gone into her office with the Hines file, I had nothing in my hands. I clenched my fists and walked out with my head down.

I shut my office door and sat down at my desk. *What did I expect? That it would really never get back to her some way, somehow? I'm such a fucking idiot.*

My throat tightened, and I concentrated on swallowing, trying to push back the tears that welled up. It didn't work. Out of nervous habit, I shook my mouse. I saw I had a new email from my father. It read:

Here's another one of those vendor contracts. Mind taking a look?

I replied with shaking hands.

You never thanked me for reviewing the other one. I don't need this right now. Hire your own fucking lawyer.

Then, the tears flowed. Hard and furious. I put my head in my hands and let it out. My phone rang. It was an internal call. *Oh, fuck you, Beverly.*

I didn't look up. I just let it ring as I sobbed into my hands.

Then, I heard a knock on the door. *What the fuck?* "One second," I croaked out.

Silence. Then, another knock. *For once, she's not going to barge right in?*

"One second!" I screamed.

The door opened, and I looked up. It was John.

Chapter 27

"Uh, I guess that's Margaret?" John pointed his thumb toward the door. "She was calling you to let you know I was here, but... I don't know, she just said to come over here and knock, so I..."

If I could have opened my eyes any wider to make sure I was indeed seeing what I was actually seeing, I would have. But it was not possible. My eyelashes pressed against my brow bone.

John wore a perfectly tailored dark suit with a light-blue handkerchief in his breast pocket. "I know we haven't talked, and I probably should have called first." He stepped closer. "But I figured you wouldn't respond, and I'm just here for the day. I had a quick meeting, and I'm leaving for Paris tonight. Something told me that showing up was the only way this would work, the only way you would say yes."

"Say"—I cleared my throat—"yes?" I felt a roaring in my ears. *Is this real? And is he nervous? And what did he just say?*

"Yes," he repeated.

My eyes followed him as he walked past my desk, bent down, and gently swiveled my chair to face him. Then, he got down on one knee.

"Veronica, I have not stopped thinking about you. This time away has made me realize that you're the only girl who's ever made me laugh, you're the only girl who I can really talk to. I know I didn't say the things you wanted me to, but I'm saying them now. London is great, but it would be better with you. I miss you... I love you."

He reached into his pocket. "I should have done this before I left, but—" He gripped a small box with his right hand as he squeezed my left hand with his. "Veronica Buccino, will you marry me?"

I never technically uttered the word "yes." I actually mouthed "What?"

John kissed my forehead and helped me out of the chair. He hugged me hard and tight. I looked at the ceiling as he held me, and I let out a noise somewhere between a yelp and a wail as I tried to process what had just happened. All of it.

Only moments earlier, I had been humiliated at work for the millionth time. The one good thing I'd ever done on the job was about to be completely destroyed. I was in a fight with Jada. I was in a fight with Syd. I was done. I was done swinging. I wanted to be knocked out. I wanted to surrender.

Some people, like my grandparents or other older people, would probably say, "Surrender? Oh really, like you've had it so hard?" To which, in that moment, I would have responded, "Yes. For me, it's been hard. And now, I'm done."

When John released me, I looked him in the eye. "Is this really real? What's in the box?"

"Oh, yeah, I should have opened it." His hands appeared to tremble a bit as he lifted the box open. *Beautiful.* The ring, I would later learn, was a four-carat, cushion-cut diamond with small diamonds all along the band.

Let's do this. This is how my story should go, after all. Isn't this what I wanted? What I'd daydreamed about?

At that moment, Margaret appeared in the doorway with a concerned look. "I didn't know if you were laughing or crying," she said. "Is everything okay?"

John slipped the ring on my finger, and I showed Margaret.

"Oh, doll, it's beautiful. Congratulations, hon."

I stared at it while Margaret congratulated John and said she wished she had some emergency champagne in her desk.

"Well, I'll leave you two alone," she said. "Go celebrate!"

"Thank you, Margaret." I bit my lower lip as I stared at my left hand then back at John.

Is that sweat on his forehead? John doesn't sweat. But yeah, that's definitely sweat.

"There is something else," he said as he hastily shut the door.

I sat back down. "Oh God, there's more?"

"We're going to Paris for a few nights before I—we—go back to London. I have some business to take care of there. Nothing too time-consuming, but we have to leave tonight. I have a meeting tomorrow. But most of the time we're there, we'll celebrate. I promise. I just have to take care of a couple of things, go to a couple of meetings." He got back down on one knee so we were eye-level.

"Uh..." I laughed and shook my head. "Well, okay. I mean, I have some stuff to finish up here, and then—"

"Finish up here?"

"Well, I can't just leave." My heart skipped at the memory of having recently said those words to Syd.

Oh, Syd.

John reached for my left hand. "Yes. You can. Now you can. This is real, Veronica. You don't have to work here anymore. You're coming with me. I'm your knight in shining Armani." He smiled, pinching the collar of his suit. "It just took me a little longer than it should've. I'm sorry about that. But I'm here now. Let's go." He held out his arm, ready to escort me out of the dungeon.

"How much time do we have?" I asked.

"We have a couple of hours." He put his arm down. "I've got a driver downstairs. We'll get you home, and you can pack what you need for a few weeks, and you can come back next month to pack up your apartment."

I had never done anything impulsive in my life. I had never flown anywhere on a moment's notice. Hell, I'd never even skipped a class in college on the first sunny day of spring.

And where has it gotten me? I have the "right" job at the "right" firm in the "right" city, and none of it feels right. So in that moment, I gave myself a break. I mentally unlocked the chains holding me to my desk. I looked at the ring. My hands were shaking, and I impulsively reached for my grandmother's ring but felt the new one. I looked at John and said, "Yesterday, I saw an Audrey Hepburn quote: 'Paris is always a good idea.'"

"It's a sign," John said. John, who did not believe in signs.

My heart leapt. "Give me five minutes. I'll meet you in the lobby."

"I'll be in the black car out front."

After John left my office, I walked into Beverly's office.

"What do you want? Don't tell me you did some research. Come up with an answer, did you? Find a way to reverse this?" Beverly laughed as I stood in the doorway. "And what the hell was all that commotion?" She shook her head. "Don't waste my time. Do you think I have all the fucking time in the world?"

I moved slowly toward her. I knew I was being overly dramatic, but it felt good. "Yes, I do think you have all the time in the world." I spoke softly. "You have nothing else in your life. Nathan? Your husband? You love *this shit*. And for the record, I did the right thing by Trista Hines *and* our client. And I'd do it again. You might think you're a really good lawyer, but who cares? I'd rather be a nice person if I had to choose. And you, Beverly, are not a nice person. You have made me sick to my stomach for almost five years. You and your hacking cough, and now I'm coughing *you* up."

I was really proud of that last line in particular. *Maybe I am creative.*

Beverly always breathed heavily, but she was really taking in air at that moment. She stared at me as if I were holding a weapon. Then I turned to Kate, who was still sitting in the guest chair. Her eyes were wide, and it gave me such sweet satisfaction to finally see her be the one who was uncomfortable. I bent forward, close to her face.

"And *you*. You're right, Kate. These past few years, I did need to concentrate more, but it was just so hard when the work we do is so *fucking boring*. But it doesn't matter. It's perfect for you. Because you know what? Are you listening? Are you *concentrating*? You are a stone-cold bitch. You have no personality. This shit suits you."

I could have sworn I saw her shake. I straightened up and held my hands in surrender as I walked out of Beverly's office backward. "I'm out of your way now. You two can *concentrate* on suing all the people you want. Oooooh. Such exciting work. Have fun. All yours."

I actually said that. All of it. Every word.

Then as I raced toward my office, I thought I heard Margaret clapping. I picked up my tote bag and ran.

Chapter 28

"I HAVE TO USE THE bathroom," I said. John and I were waiting for our flight in the members' lounge at Newark Airport. John had his arm around me as we watched CNBC on one of the televisions perched on the wall.

I was only pretending to watch. I was actually reliving the past five hours in my head.

Did I just quit my job? No formal resignation? No two weeks' notice? Just like that? Did that really just happen? And I'm engaged? To John? And Syd. Oh, Syd.

John turned to me. "You have to go again?"

I shrugged. "Must be the shock and excitement."

"Must be." He winked and turned back to the television.

When I'd called Jada from my apartment as I was throwing dresses, sandals, and scarves into my suitcase, I'd started by saying, "Listen, I know things are weird with us right now, but I have to tell you something, and it's kind of major, and it just happened."

I could still hear her loudly repeating, "What? Are you fucking kidding me? What?" along with, "John? Really? John?" and "You're going where?" But she ended with, "Call me when you can, and... congratulations?"

Then, I quickly scrolled through my contacts and found Trista Hines's number. I got her voicemail. "Hi, Trista. This is Veronica Buccino. Listen, you may be getting a call from my office. I don't have time to explain, but whatever happens, you have a signed, enforceable Settlement Agreement in place. Remember that. I'm not your lawyer, and I'm not giving you legal advice. I'm just saying you've been making the payments under that Agreement. You haven't defaulted. Just... remember that. I have to go. Bye."

Before both of them, I had called my mother who, like Jada, kept repeating, "Paris? With John? Engaged? What about work?"

I held the phone to my ear as I opened my laptop and pulled up the most recent version of my Selma story. I attached "Selma_Story_Ver27" in an email to Dave, typed "Here you go," and hit Send.

Then, my mother had asked, "What about Syd?" which was when I told her I had to go because the car was waiting. I had only recently told her about Syd and how much I was enjoying getting to know him. She'd kept saying she liked everything she'd been hearing about him.

Syd was now the main reason I had just fibbed to John about having to go to the bathroom again. I made my way to one of the lounge's single-stall bathrooms. It was spacious and stocked with lotions, mouthwash, cotton balls, and white washcloths, which neatly lined the counter. I squatted down, resting my back against the wall, and balanced my laptop on my knees.

> Hi, Syd. I know I should be calling you with this, but it's easier for me to write it out so I can adequately express myself and say it the way I feel it.

I gulped at the thought of him even reading that first sentence. *He will probably assume I'm writing to apologize for our fight.* It took me a few moments and a few deep breaths before I could continue typing.

> Getting to know you has been truly special. You are a remarkable human being, and I knew that from our first meeting. It's clear to see right away. You're one of those people.

> Also, this has nothing to do with the stupid fight about work and Rachel and meeting up. I want to apologize for that. That is what my miserable job did to me. You are right about that. It makes no sense that I would be so

dedicated to such an awful situation. But like I said, that's not what this is about.

The thing is—this is about John. I spent two years with him, and I thought I was going to marry him. Two years is a lot of time. It's a real history. He has now come back into the picture. Quite suddenly, yes. And because of that history, I can't just push him away. I just feel that I have to give him a chance. So, I am.

I know this sounds like that fib I told before our first date, but believe me, this time, it's true. I even quit my job. Can't make this stuff up. Well, I can. But I'm not.

I'm extremely sorry. I can't even express in words how sorry I am and how the thought of hurting you is tearing me apart right now.

That was when I took a few moments to blubber into a wad of toilet paper while still squatting against the wall of the bathroom. I blew my nose and forced myself to continue.

I would do anything to make you not feel hurt or sad or ever be upset again in your life.

Writing that line required me to catch my breath before continuing.

You're too good for that. But I have to do this. It seems like the right thing to do right now. I am so sorry.

Love,
Veronica

It didn't feel right to mention the ring or Paris or the fact that I was probably moving to London, which I still hadn't wrapped my head around. As far as I was concerned, I was on vacation at the moment. I was going to say that maybe we could talk in person, but as I was trying to figure out how to explain that meeting in person couldn't happen for at least a few weeks, someone started knocking hard and loud on the bathroom door. I croaked out, "One minute," then scanned the email quickly, and hit Send.

When I opened the door, a short, gray-haired lady with sharp blue eyes stood there. I looked down and straightened my top as I excused myself to get past her. But we made eye contact long enough for me to see she had eyes like Grandma Ant's. All of her brothers and sisters had blue eyes too, which was so unusual for Italians.

Grandma and Grandpa—I held out my hand to study my engagement ring—*if you could see me now.*

I walked back to John, who was still watching CNBC. The market was up.

Chapter 29

WE SAT IN FIRST CLASS. After we'd been in the air for an hour, I took off my shoes and tucked my feet under me, resting my elbow on the armrest to watch John as he slept. He looked so peaceful, his chest moving slowly as he breathed.

I couldn't sleep at all, however. I kept reliving everything—John, the ring, Beverly, Kate, packing, calling Jada, calling my mother, sending that email to Syd. While frantically packing, I had spotted a journal Jada had given me in my nightstand and threw it in my carry-on. At various points in my life, I'd tried to keep a diary, but when I would go back and read what I had written months or years earlier, I would always be mortified and end up ripping out the pages and throwing them in the trash.

Someone had given Jada a beautiful gray paisley journal for her birthday last year, and she found it as she was cleaning out her desk a few weeks ago. When she gave it to me, she'd said, "What am I going to write in a journal? If I have something to say, I say it to people's faces, myself included. If mirrors could talk..."

I quietly stood up from my seat to retrieve the journal from the overhead compartment. As I did this, I thought how tired John must be because he didn't flinch, and he was the lightest sleeper in the world. When I sat back down, I opened the journal and read the first entry. I could have sworn the plane dipped a thousand feet.

Dear Antoinette (I'd named my diary after my grandmother),

I met a boy I really like. He's Jewish and bald. Well, he has a clean-shaven head, to be precise. I think about him all the time, and the funny things he says—he makes me pee my pants!

I rushed to the bathroom and ripped out the pages. I stuffed them down the small metal trash flap then grabbed some paper towels and pushed down again as far as I could for good measure. When the heat that had surged through my neck and face subsided, I patted my forehead with cold water and returned to my seat. I retrieved the pen from the loop on the side of the diary.

Dear Diary (I changed her name back),

I am on my way to Paris. Prince Charming himself appeared in my office doorway on a pretty awful day. He presented me with a glass slipper—aka a huge ring—and it fit like a glove. That reminds me, I have to ask him how he knew my ring size.

Anyway, then I told off the Big Bad Wolf and the Wicked Witch of the West Side, and now I'm flying off to Never Never Land. I can't believe it. We are on a magic carpet. I am free. I am happy. Fairy tales really do come true.

Looking forward to ever after.

I put the diary back and tried to get on Wi-Fi to check HumanInterestStories.net, but I couldn't get through. I didn't want to call the flight attendant over and risk waking John, so I pulled out my stack of magazines. By the time I finished the last article in the last magazine, we'd landed. It was the middle of the day by that point, and the sun was shining. A concierge picked up our bags while we sat in the car that was waiting for us. When we got to the hotel, John went to his business meeting, and I crashed on the large, soft bed.

The next night, after a full day of walking around and taking in the city, I pulled out the diary again while John was in the shower.

We ate lunch under the Eiffel Tower on a blanket I bought at a tourist shop, and we brought wine and sandwiches. Then, we walked around some more and ate dinner outside along the Seine, despite the July heat and humidity. John is in the shower now. He said something at lunch I can't stop thinking about, but I'm too tired to write it all out. Sorry.

I was telling him about my class, Selma, the video story, the written story, and the upcoming trial.

He'd said, "Well, the good thing is you don't have to worry about any of that now. You can relax. If anyone was born to be a housewife... and a mom, it's you. You're going to be a great mom, Veronica."

I was suddenly hit with a pang of depression. It was really more like a stab. I didn't want to stop talking about the case or "worrying" about it. It was interesting to me, and I was proud I'd done the video story and the written piece too, no matter how they were going to be received, which I was actually not worrying about at the moment.

I will end with this though. Last night at dinner, John ordered dessert while I was in the "toilette." Berries and whipped cream! My go-to dessert at restaurants because they never have cupcakes. He always used to say, "Why the hell do you get fruit for dessert? Fruit is not dessert." But he didn't say that tonight and even had a bite. It was sweet.

Another thing I didn't note in my diary was that John and I might be the only couple in history not to have sex while in Paris. First, I'd said I was tired from the flight. Then, I'd said my stomach hurt from the rich food. *How romantic.* On the third night, I fell asleep while he was still in the shower. It was true, though, that I was tired, and my stomach did hurt a little. But it wasn't because of the long flight or the rich food.

"I remembered your father's pinky ring," John said.

I cringed at the fact that my father wore a pinky ring with a cross on it.

John and I were at an outdoor café, enjoying a bottle of champagne before dinner. It was another hot day, and I was sweating profusely. The champagne didn't help. I kept pulling up my black strapless dress and readjusting it to relieve my damp skin. I looked at John, who appeared clean, crisp, and dry.

"I was joking with him about it at one of the holidays or one of your cousin's birthdays or something, and he took it off to let me try it on. It was big on my pinky but went up to my knuckle on my ring finger. You tried it on, and it fit your ring finger perfectly. I knew your engagement ring would have to go up to here on this finger." He held out his ring finger.

Wow. I was impressed with John's ingenuity and his memory. Then, I thought about how happy my father must be about my engagement. I hadn't called him, but I'd told my mother to tell him and Aunt Marie.

Is he going to walk me down the aisle? I guess that's how it works.

I gulped my champagne and promptly changed the subject. "Did Van Gogh really cut his ear off?"

John was sipping some champagne and turned red.

I sat up. "Are you okay?"

After a few hearty coughs, he managed to say in a throaty whisper, "Wrong pipe."

I sat back and suddenly remembered a story Syd had told me about being on a first date with a girl who he'd made laugh so hard that water shot out of her nose. When I thought of this, I couldn't stop laughing. Before I knew it, I was laughing so hard, I couldn't talk.

"Do you think it's funny that I almost choked?" John asked, clearing his throat.

My laugh stopped then. "No, no, no." I tried to explain the story, saying it happened to a friend. He wasn't amused.

Afterward, as we walked down the street, I spotted a penny on the sidewalk. *An American penny!*

I wanted to point it out to John but remembered his feelings about it, so I just kept walking.

Later, when John stopped in a café to use the bathroom, I quickly checked my phone. The connection was slow. "Come on!" I wanted to scream. A few moments later, I finally got into my email.

No response from Syd. No response from my father. One email from Jada:

> Hey, I made a list of things we need to reenact when you get home. 1. The resignation where I hope you told Beverly and Kate to fuck off. 2. The proposal. 3. The resignation where I hope you told Beverly and Kate to fuck off. Yes, 1 and 3 are the same because I need to relive that again and again. Hope you're having fun. If you get this, just reply "yes" or "no": Did you tell Beverly and/or Kate to fuck off? Did Kate's hair turn white from shock? Are she and Beverly the Warhol twins now?

I guessed that meant Jada and I were back to normal. It was done, Jada-style, of course, with no apology or discussion of what had happened. *Well, at least I have a maid of honor.*

Chapter 30

A LOUD KNOCK ON THE door woke me up at three o'clock in the morning. I peeked over at John. It didn't wake him.

Thank God.

I thought I should put on a robe before answering the door because I was wearing a lace top-and-bottom set that John had purchased for me from an elegant lingerie shop on the Champs-Elysees. But in my grogginess, I didn't.

When I opened the door, my grandfather put his palm out as if the sun were blinding him and looked away. "Oh, for the love-a-God," he said.

My grandmother handed me a plush black robe. "Put this on, dear."

Ah, I got it now. I'm sleeping. This is a visit. No wonder John didn't wake up.

I slipped on the long, soft robe and tied it at the waist as my grandmother handed me a beautiful pair of pink silk peep-toe slippers with kitten heels. My grandfather waited with his hands on his hips.

I slid into the slippers. "These are cute."

"Come on," Grandpa Sal said as he marched down the hallway.

"Where are we going?"

"You'll see," he called over his shoulder.

Grandma Ant linked her arm through mine as we walked. Grandpa Sal finally stopped at the end of the hallway and turned around.

But my grandmother was the one who spoke first. "Veronica, we're going to take you somewhere... well, more than one place. There are things you need to see."

"Huh?" was all I could utter.

My grandfather was making a circular motion with his hand near his temple as though he was attempting to jostle a memory free. "You know that blond actress?"

"Oh, her?" I laughed. "Can you be more specific?"

"The movie star. What's her name?" he asked. His palm was up in front of him as if he were twirling pizza dough with one hand, still trying to retrieve the memory.

"Jean Harlow? Mae West? Fay Wray?" All of my suggestions were met with head shakes.

"More recent."

"Grace Kelly?"

Grandpa Sal gave another head shake. "Gwendolyn!" he shouted. "That Gwendolyn Paltrow!"

"Gwyneth Paltrow?" *Where the hell could this be going?*

"We know you saw her on TV when they were showing an old interview. She was saying that thing about her father and Paris," Grandpa Sal said. "About how her father took her to Paris when she was a young girl. He told her that she should see Paris for the first time with a man who truly loves her."

I quickly unlinked my arm from my grandmother's and raced back toward my room as I shook my head. *No, no, no. I don't care what you think of him. I'm here now. I'm in this now.*

"Ya just gonna run away?" my grandfather called out.

I couldn't find the room. *What room number was it? Crap. Isn't it 707?*

I scanned the room numbers one by one but couldn't find it. *Come on already. Chambre sept cents et sept... but where is it?*

"We have to do this, Veronica. Come on now." My grandmother's voice was calm. I could feel her close behind me now.

"Listen." I turned to face them. "I just have a feeling that I know what you're trying to do, and it's not going to work. I've taken your advice. And while I love you both, where has your advice gotten me? Really? So please, listen to me and try to understand. I know what I'm doing." I placed my hand over my heart. "I know what's best for me, and this is best for me. I will have a great life with John. I will have a comfortable life. Isn't that what you want for your granddaughter? I'll have a happy and comfortable life. I was struggling. I couldn't do it anymore. Couldn't you *see* that? I was swimming against the tide and had been for so long. I'm done. I'll be happy with John. I will!"

They stared at me, expressionless.

I continued. "We will be very happy together. So stop. Just stop. Listen to me. I'm happy. I'm very happy."

My grandmother moved in closer and touched my arm. "Then why are you crying, dear?"

I instinctively touched my cheek and wiped away a tear. "I'm, I don't know, I'm confused."

"It's confusing when the things you think will make you happy and the things that will actually make you happy are very different," my grandmother said.

She handed me a tissue and linked her arm through mine again. "Come on."

"Grandpa, Gram, I don't think we're in Paris anymore." I stood on the street before a blue split-level house in the suburbs. I couldn't tell where we were. It looked as if we were in America, but everything looked dated. A maroon Chrysler LeBaron sat in the driveway, and a blue Big Wheel was parked on the front lawn. I knew kids didn't have Big Wheels anymore. My cousin's five-year-old twins had motorized cars.

And it was cold. I didn't feel cold, but I could see my breath in the air when I spoke. Christmas lights outlined the windows of the house, and a wreath hung on the door. "Where are we?"

"New Jersey," My grandmother said.

"Go in." My grandfather motioned toward the house. "It's all right. They won't notice. We're right behind ya."

"Just go in this strange house?"

"Just go right in," my grandfather said. "They can't see you. Don't worry."

I wanted to ask who couldn't see me, but I just did as my grandparents said, staring at my pink slippers as I walked toward the house. I assumed

I wasn't supposed to ring the doorbell, so I opened the screen door, then the front door with the wreath on it, and entered.

A boy came running out from behind a tall Christmas tree in the corner, carrying a toy gun while another boy ripped the wrapping paper off of a large box. It was obviously Christmas morning. It was also clearly a few decades ago. A bulky TV with a big cable box stood in the other corner.

The children were really cute. Two little dark-haired kids. One must have been about six or seven and was wearing Batman pajamas. The other little boy wore Superman pajamas. He had dark eyes and thick eyelashes and was concentrating hard as he pointed his plastic toy gun out the window. He must have been eight or nine. I inched closer to get a better look.

"John, get over here," a woman yelled from the kitchen.

My heart fell. *John.*

"You each opened one gift." His mother was standing in the doorway. "Now, that's enough. We have to have breakfast."

John and his brother Jason groaned. "Can't we eat breakfast after we open all our gifts?"

"No." John's mother walked back into the kitchen. She was wearing a long gray robe, and her curly black hair was shooting out in all directions.

"Louise! What is wrong with you?" I saw his father then, sitting in a recliner in the corner of the living room. He appeared healthy, but he had a smoker's voice like Beverly's. "It's Christmas. You're gonna tell these kids they have to wait to open the rest of their gifts?"

His mother walked out of the kitchen, holding a wooden spoon in one hand and the other on her hip. "Yes, that is exactly what I'm saying. Breakfast doesn't take that long. It's already eight o'clock. By the time they finish opening gifts, it will be who knows what time. They'll be off their schedule."

"Your fucking schedule!" His father threw his hands in the air and marched off to the basement, slamming the door behind him.

His mother calmly returned to the stove where she stirred something vigorously. "Get in here," she yelled.

"Why?" Jason yelled back.

His mother, still stirring, yelled back, "Because I said so! Get in here right now!"

John put his toy gun back under the tree and walked into the kitchen. John's family had moved to South Jersey when he was in college, which was why I didn't recognize this house. This must have been their house in North Jersey.

Every time we'd visited, which was only a handful of times, they had been nothing but gracious to me, but not so much to each other.

"One more damn fumble from you. Just what I need," his mother would call out if John or his brother or father dropped or spilled something.

I was always extra careful not to be my usual klutzy self at their house. I had to actually *concentrate* whenever I was asked to pass the salt or bread basket.

My grandparents were beside me as we moved into the kitchen. Jason sat with his elbows on the kitchen table, his hands holding up his face. John ignored him and poured milk into his cereal. His mother picked up the cereal box from the table. "You finished with this?"

John said yes, that he wanted only one bowl.

"Were you just going to leave it out?" she asked.

John shook his head.

His mother turned to his brother and knelt down approximately two inches from his face. She pointed to the living room. "If you don't eat something, I will throw every one of those gifts in there away. Do you hear me? All your damn new toys. In the garbage!"

His brother started to cry and put his head in his hands.

I wanted to whisper, "Jay, just eat something, kid," but I was frozen as I observed the scene. And I knew he couldn't hear me anyway.

Their mother marched toward the cabinet to put the cereal away. "I won't have my kids eating breakfast at noon, in their pajamas all day, living like animals. We eat. We brush our teeth. Wash our faces. And change. Like civilized people. I don't care what day it is."

Then she walked back toward Jason, who was sobbing into his arms. John's mother grabbed one arm, yanked her son off the kitchen chair, and spanked him on his behind as she yelled, "Go to your room. You're a crybaby."

Jason ran off, wailing. John continued to munch on his cereal, reading the milk carton.

"And you." John's mother pointed a spoon in John's direction. "If you even think of going upstairs to talk to that crybaby or talk to your damn useless father downstairs, I'll throw every one of your toys away and keep Jason's. Do you understand me? That's called loyalty. Don't you dare defy me."

John stared at her, motionless, his mouth full of cereal. She went back to stirring the pot on the stove. He went back to eating his cereal.

My grandparents and I were all watching John.

Then, my grandfather whispered in my ear, "Merry Christmas."

I said nothing.

I wanted to talk to my grandparents about why we were there, but before I knew it, we were leaving. "Where are we going now?"

When we got to the street, I turned around to take in the house again, but it was gone, and we were in front of another house. This one, I recognized. It was my Aunt Marie's.

It was still Christmas. My aunt had a single candle in each of the windows. And it was the current decade. I recognized John's black Jaguar in the driveway. My father always insisted that John be allowed to park in Aunt Marie's driveway. "A car like that you can't park on the street."

I thought of that and rolled my eyes.

Grandpa Sal motioned to the house as if he were ushering a group of schoolchildren through a doorway. "Come on, let's go. No pushin'. No shovin'. Let's move it."

I'd always spent Christmas Eve with my father's family and Christmas Day with my mom and grandparents and, most recently, Mom and Don. I used to wish I could also spend Christmas Eve with Grandma Ant and Grandpa Sal. I would hear all about the seven different kinds of fish they would make. But Aunt Marie was a great cook, even though she only made shrimp and linguini on Christmas Eve. When I saw the scene before me, I knew it was two Christmases ago and my first holiday with John. I spotted The Perm and turned to my grandparents. "You know who that is, right?"

"We've met her," Grandma Ant said.

The Perm was adjusting some candy canes that had fallen off the

Christmas tree. My father sat on the couch with my Uncle Al and cousins Paul and Christopher. John was on the recliner but wasn't reclining. My Aunt Marie, Paul's wife Kara, and I were in front of the fireplace, playing Ring Around the Rosie with Paul and Kara's twins, Jake and Hadley.

I froze for a moment, examining myself as I twirled and laughed with the twins.

My grandfather stood next to me. "It's a little different than looking in the mirror, isn't it?"

I nodded. *Hey, I'm not that short. And I always think I could lose five pounds if I had more time to go to the gym, but I look okay. Really okay.*

As I surveyed the scene, I froze on John too. Even though he was back in my life, it was strange to see him again in my environment, in my aunt's home. And even though it was only about a year and a half ago, he looked younger. His skin was a little smoother, and his hair a little thicker and blacker.

I stood against the doorway of the living room. My cousin's twins were now singing a song for everyone—something about Jesus in a manger. We all clapped when they finished, except for John. He pecked away on his phone.

"Who are you emailing on Christmas Eve?" I watched myself whisper to him as I sat next to him on the couch near the recliner.

"It's still just a Wednesday to some people, Veronica." He didn't glance up from whatever he was typing.

I remembered thinking that I'd hoped my aunt and uncle didn't think John was rude. I knew, in my father's eyes, John could do no wrong, and I didn't care what The Perm thought.

Now, I saw Hadley handing out candy canes. When she got to my father, he took the candy cane and said "Grazie" in a very bad Italian accent. When she got to John, he didn't look up.

"Thank you, Hadley," I said loudly and a little too demonstratively. "Can I take one for him, the author?" I cocked my head toward John. "He's writing a book there."

John smiled as he continued typing.

"No!" Hadley said emphatically before moving on to Uncle Al.

John smiled again, head still down, focused on his phone.

I turned back toward the dining room and sat down at the table with my grandparents. "I used to like that he was so dedicated to work. I thought it was sexy or something."

I picked up an orange and squeezed it as if it were a stress ball. I remembered my grandmother telling me that she and her brothers and sisters used to get fruit for Christmas when they were young. I remembered thinking that was strange—to get only oranges and grapefruits as a gift from your parents. Whenever I would ask her about it, she would always say, "Veronica, we were poor. It wasn't like it is today. We went without, and that was how it was. We were happy to get fruit. That was a treat."

"What do you think is sexy now?" Grandma Ant asked as she used a nut cracker to open a walnut.

I put the orange back. "I don't know." I shrugged, but I thought of Syd, talking about his work, how he came up with ideas for ads and presented them to clients. Anyone could have seen he loved what he did and was passionate about it, which was sexy. I rested both elbows on the table, staring at my grandmother as she cracked another nut and handed it to my grandfather.

The doorbell rang, and Aunt Clem walked in. She was my grandmother's sister, my dad's mom, the one who never left Florida. Aunt Clem was about four foot ten, her dyed black hair in a large, stiff bouffant. She wore red lipstick and tornado-shaped, rhinestone clip-on earrings. Her black pants and red sweater were accented with a thick gold belt.

"Merry Christmas, everybody!! *Buon Natale! Buon Natale!*"

I saw myself get up and kiss Aunt Clem hello.

"Oh, V, honey, look at you. Beautiful." She stood on her toes to kiss me.

I always thought it was cute that she called me "V."

She handed my Aunt Marie a pastry box, took off her coat, and rested her large black purse on the floor before sitting on the couch. "So, V, my grandniece got married two weeks ago. I was thinking, how can you have a wedding so close to Christmas, but it was fun. Really fun."

"That's nice. Where was it?" I saw myself ask.

Aunt Clem, a heavy smoker, coughed—a deep, hard smoker's cough—before answering. I didn't want to see the look on John's face. He had such a disdain for cigarettes and smokers, especially people who smelled like ashtrays and had the "death cough."

Aunt Clem was covering her mouth with her chubby, yellow-stained fingers, which were accented with brightly painted red nails. "In Staten Island. She's a *manicure* girl, and he's a fireman. Nice kids. Beautiful couple. And oh, what an affair. The food, the music, everything. Let me tell ya. And how cute is this? Listen to this." Aunt Clem patted the couch as she talked. "So, you know how they announce the party? The bridal party? And then everybody comes out with their partners? Right? So they announce the groom's parents. He actually has a stepfather and a stepmother, and so they announce those couples, and then they announce the bride's parents, and then it's time for the bridal party. And they all come out at once. Oh, V, how cute is this? All at the same time, they come out, and they're all wearing sunglasses."

Aunt Clem's mouth was wide open as The Perm and I said, "how funny" and "that's really cute."

As Aunt Clem turned back to talk to Uncle Al, John whispered to me, "Really cute? Really Staten Island, no?"

I shrugged and looked away, but I knew I felt a pang at that moment. A pang I'd ignored then. But now, I acknowledged it. *She's in her nineties. Don't be a jerk. And don't be such a snob.*

"All right, let's get moving. There's more." Grandpa Sal popped a nut in his mouth and wiped the table with his hand to collect the walnut shells in a pile.

I felt a pit in my stomach and closed my eyes.

"I don't want to see the future," I said and buried my head in my arms on the table. "Haven't I seen enough?"

"*You* don't want to know the future?" Grandpa asked.

Then, it occurred me. "Hey, wait. I thought you couldn't predict the future?"

"We can't," my grandfather said. "But we can see more than you, ya know, be in places you can't unless you were invisible. We see things, we hear things, we know things. And now we can show you, based on what we know, ya know, what it will look like."

I rubbed my eyes and reluctantly stood up from Aunt Marie's dining room table.

"This way, my little *brasciole*." My grandfather stepped back and swept his palm toward the door.

"I'm going. I'm going," I said.

As I walked through the living room toward the front door, I took in the scene one last time—Hadley on my lap, John typing on his phone, my father pulling a cigar out of his shirt pocket and examining it, Aunt Clem eating chunks of provolone gathered in her hand, Uncle Al asking if anyone wanted a refill of their drink, Aunt Marie and The Perm clearing the dining room table, Paul, Christopher, and Kara playing a video game with Jake.

My grandmother gently touched my back. Suddenly, I was on a circular driveway. We were in front of a massive, white brick house. The front door was actually two brown, carved wood doors with gold fixtures. There was a large window above the front entrance with a massive chandelier showing through.

"Wow," I whispered to myself. I moved slowly toward the house and walked up the three front steps made of stone. The only Christmas decorations were two large poinsettia plants on either side of the front entryway.

I turned the massive doorknob and entered. The foyer was marble. To the left was a curved marble staircase that was at least six feet wide. The living room looked like Versailles, with cream-colored couches and gold coffee tables. It was so big that there was more than one couch as well as several coffee tables and small tables. It was beautiful and cold-looking—clearly a living room that wasn't lived in. At one point in my life, it was the type of house I'd dreamed of having someday.

Is anyone home?

I walked through the living room into a kitchen with stainless steel appliances and more marble. In the center was a granite-top island with copper pots hanging above it. There was a breakfast nook, enclosed on three sides by large windows, and I could see into the big backyard. What seemed like acres of grass was spotted with patches of snow.

As I moved my hand over the cold granite countertops, I heard voices coming from a room off the kitchen. I slowly entered what was clearly a family room with a large sectional couch, huge entertainment center, pool table, and a Christmas tree.

And me. There I was. Older me. Not much older, but older. I appeared a little thicker around my hips, but other than that, I looked pretty much as I did now, except a lot more tired.

I was standing by the corner of the couch in a cranberry-colored robe with my hair in a ponytail and a cup of coffee in my hand. With the other hand, I was gently rubbing the back of a dark-haired boy who was crying. He wasn't bawling, but tears were streaming as he stared out the window. He must have been nine or ten.

Then I saw John, sitting on the other end of the couch, watching two other children, a boy and girl, unwrap gifts. They were ripping open the wrapping paper and squealing with excitement. No one appeared to be paying much attention to me or the crying boy.

"I wanted this my whole life!" the other little boy screamed, holding up what looked like some military-type figure toy in a box. He must have been six or seven and had large brown eyes, brown hair, and a round cherub face. I couldn't help but marvel at his beautiful little face.

From across the room, I laughed and said, "Your whole life, Anthony? All seven years?"

John laughed. He was sitting back on the couch with his elbow resting on the armrest. His hairline was farther back, and what was left was sprinkled with gray, but he looked virtually the same.

The crying boy stood and hurried to the kitchen. I watched the older me follow him into a bathroom off the kitchen. The boy grabbed a tissue and blew his nose as I pushed back his short black hair.

"I didn't mean to knock it over," he said, sniffling. "It was an accident." The tears started again. He cried heavily into his hands.

"It's okay," I said emphatically, my arms spread out. "Accidents happen, John. Don't worry about it. You know how long I've had that vase? It was one of the first things I bought when I moved into the city, before I even met your dad. And honestly, it's dated now. I've been trying to figure out how to get rid of it."

He laughed a little and blew his nose again.

"Don't worry about it. It's Christmas. You have more gifts to open. Come on."

"I hate him," the boy said, his voice muffled by the tissue under his nose.

"Don't say that." I sounded stern but also as though I'd heard it before. "Daddy means well. He just wants you to be more careful."

"He called me Hurricane Junior. He says that all the time. He said it when I missed the free throw shot the other day, in front of everyone."

I hugged him. "He's going to stop that. I'll talk to him. I don't like when he says that either. He thinks he's just teasing, but it's not funny."

Oh, that jerk. This poor kid.

The boy wiped his nose and threw the tissue in the garbage while I sipped the coffee I was still holding. We went back into the family room, where John Jr. walked toward the tree and started quietly unwrapping the rest of his gifts. The other boy—Anthony—was on his hands and knees rolling a miniature tank along the floor and making *vroom* sounds. The little girl was brushing a doll's hair. I sat down next to John.

"How's the crybaby?" John asked.

"I need to talk to you later."

"About what?" he asked, glaring at me defensively. "Let's talk right now."

We went into the same bathroom off the kitchen.

"You've got to stop calling him 'Hurricane Junior.' You've said it in front of his friends. You've embarrassed him. Do you know what this is doing to his self-esteem? Please stop it."

"Listen, that kid's got to learn. He's a disaster. He *is* Hurricane Junior. What kind of man is he going to be? I've got to straighten him out now before it's too late."

"He doesn't need to be straightened out. If you constantly harp on him and call him names and embarrass him, what do you think that is going to do to him?"

"It'll help him!"

"Help him? How? You're too hard on him. On all of them. On me too. You can't expect people to be perfect. You're not perfect. You have to stop. So please, stop it."

"Veronica, you need your head examined. You were a lawyer once. You make no sense sometimes. I never said I was perfect, but I need people to try a little. I give you a great life, this house, your car, your vacations. You don't have to work, and what do I get? I get one son who's a sissy. He can't make a fucking basket to save his life. He trips and breaks vases while unwrapping Christmas gifts with, let's be honest, a little too much excitement. I get a middle son who's fat. We're going to have to put Anthony on a diet. What the hell are you feeding him? And our daughter, let's face it, she's not the brightest. John Jr. was doing everything she does when he was half her age. You better start working with her instead of getting your nails done and your hair done all the fucking time."

I shook my head.

You're just going to stand there and shake your head? Fight back!

Then, the bathroom door swung open. It was my grandparents. My grandfather clapped his hands once and said, "Seen enough?"

But I shooed them away. I had to see more. I saw my arms were crossed and I was staring at the floor, but then I looked up and said, "What kind of father calls his children these things? A *sissy*? Really? And fat and stupid?"

Yeah! Tell him!

"Are you kidding me?" John practically spat the words out. "Like you know what a good father is? I grew up in a normal household with two parents. I know what I'm doing, Veronica. I know I've got three kids who need straightening out."

"There's no talking to you. No reasoning."

"Reasoning? What do we have to reason? It is what it is."

I looked down again. Defeated. Pathetic.

Lift your head! Tell him off!

I saw myself grab my coffee cup on the edge of the sink and walk out of the bathroom, up a back stairway off the kitchen. John went back into the family room.

Upstairs, there was yet more marble. I followed myself down a marble hallway through French doors and into a large bedroom. My grandparents followed current me and older me up there.

I saw myself open another set of French doors that led into a large walk-in closet. It wasn't even a closet. It was a room, really. In the center of the room was an island with drawers.

I got on my knees in front of the island and opened a bottom drawer.

Socks. I reached to the back of the drawer and pulled out a sock that had something in it.

Pills? They weren't even in a prescription bottle. Just loose pills.

I swallowed a handful of them. It seemed they were hard to swallow, and I reached for my coffee cup. I squinted and swallowed again. I put the sock back, shut the drawer, and rested my back against the island. I slowly closed my eyes.

"Oh God. Oh no. I don't die, do I?" I looked at my grandparents, who were looking at me on the floor.

They said nothing.

"What am I doing?" I said louder, knowing "I" couldn't hear me.

They said nothing, just stood with their arms crossed, still staring at me on the floor.

"Oh God, what are you showing me?" My heart beat faster. "Do I die?"

"No," Grandpa Sal said calmly.

"I don't die?"

"No." Grandma Ant shook her head. "You take these pills to... I don't know, calm you down, make you feel better? I really don't know. But no, you don't die. That's not what this is. This isn't how you die."

I breathed a sigh of relief.

Then, Grandpa Sal moved closer to me and motioned toward the floor, palm up. "But would ya call this living?"

Chapter 31

My eyes flashed open. The room was almost completely dark except for a dim ray of light from the street lamps coming in through a gap in the curtains. I checked the clock. 3:04 a.m.

I placed my hand on my chest and peeked over at John. He was still sleeping soundly. *Thank God.*

I quietly lowered my left leg to the floor for leverage as I reached for my tote bag and grabbed my diary. Then, I pulled my hair back, wiped the sweat from my forehead, and wrote with the help of the crack of light coming through the window.

The World According to John:

1. Pants should never be folded and stuck in a drawer. They should be hung in the closet on all the same type of hanger. Plastic. White. From left to right, darkest to lightest.

2. Did you wash that apple? You're supposed to use a dime-sized amount of liquid dish cleanser. Did you know that? You never heard that? Do you live under a rock? I don't care what you do. Eat pesticides then. That's what you're doing. Don't complain to me if you get sick.

I always wanted to say, "No, I don't want to eat pesticides, but I don't want to ingest liquid dish cleanser either." But I never did.

3. Your wallet is so disorganized. Look at mine. Bills face the same direction and in denominational order, smallest bill facing outward. No wonder you're always fumbling around whenever you're checking out of a store.

4. When you pay the bill at a restaurant with your credit card, put in a tip amount that results in a total amount with zero cents. It looks cleaner on your credit card bill.

I always wanted to say, "Who gives a crap how clean your credit card bill looks?" But I never did.

5. Didn't anyone ever teach you how to put coffee cups and bowls away in a cabinet? Don't stack them on top of each other like that. There's enough room to line them up in rows.

6. When you have a cold, don't blow your nose so much. It irritates your sinuses.

I always wanted to ask "What about all of the snot up there? Where's it going to go?" But I never did.

7. You're doing it wrong. Everyone does everything wrong— the bank teller, the guy at the deli counter, the cab driver, the waitress, the bartender, the doorman, the flight attendant, the concierge, the tailor, the dry cleaner, the cashier, the masseuse, the hostess, the receptionist, the doctor, the chiropractor, the mailman, the guy on TV making little pastries. Everyone. No one takes pride in their job anymore. No one.

I finally looked up from the page after I came up with forty-seven Johnisms. I craned my neck to peek at him. Still sleeping.

Jerk.

I placed my hand over my heart again. Although it had slowed while I wrote, it fired up again, angrier after I read each Johnism back to myself. I had planned to lay there until the sun came up as I figured out what I wanted to do next. But somehow, I ended up falling back to sleep.

I was drinking coffee in Syd's kitchen while eating a bagel with cream cheese and jam. *Bridget Jones's Diary* was on television. I looked up from my phone to watch my favorite part—when Bridget's friends are sitting around her dining room table, and they toast her with, "To Bridget, just as she is."

Syd walked out in a towel. His broad chest was still wet from his shower. I stood to refill my coffee and kissed him on the lips.

"What are you smiling at?" he asked.

"Nothing." As I poured milk in my coffee, it overflowed.

Syd leaned over to kiss me. "Merry Christmas."

"Thank you."

"What time's the bus?"

"Uh, I think it's at 11:14. I have to check. My mother will pick us up at the station."

"What's on your shirt?"

I looked down. "Strawberry jam."

"Oh, I was afraid it was blood." He sniffed my shirt.

I laughed. He took a sip of my coffee then headed back to the bathroom.

There was a fly in the room, in December. I started to swat it away, but my attention was brought back to *Bridget*. She couldn't cook, but they loved her anyway.

I woke up suddenly and sat up in bed. I checked the clock. 7:14 a.m.

John was awake, leaning against the headboard with a newspaper spread out in front of him. "You breathe so loudly, especially in your sleep." He shook his head. "The shortest, choppiest, loudest breaths."

I rubbed my eyes.

He didn't look away from the paper but continued to talk. "You breathe like a baby. It's because you weren't an athlete growing up. You've got no lung capacity."

I got up slowly from the bed, not bothering to adjust my pajama bottom that was twisted to the left. I stared at him as I took off the ring and walked around to his side of the bed. I placed it on the end table next to him. It made a high-pitched clink sound as it hit the glass.

He glanced up from his paper, rolled his eyes, and went back to reading.

That was when I started moving quickly. I gathered my clothes off the floor. I went through every drawer. I pulled my suitcase out of the closet and filled it. Clothes, shoes, makeup. *What am I forgetting?* I went to the bathroom and changed into what I'd worn on the plane, my work clothes. That day seemed so long ago.

"Cut the fucking charade, please," John said. "Are you always going to be this sensitive? We have to work on that."

When I finally zipped my suitcase and realized there was nothing left in the room I wanted—nothing at all—I said, "Merry Christmas."

"What?" He looked up from the paper, incredulous. The headline read, "Longue vie a la France." It was July fourteenth, Bastille Day.

I lifted my suitcase off of the chaise, grabbed my tote bag, and headed toward the door.

John got out of bed. His white V-neck T-shirt that fit him perfectly looked a little too white in the artificial hotel light. His silk boxers also appeared to be reflecting light as he moved toward me. "What the hell has gotten into you, Veronica?"

"Merry Christmas!" I repeated, louder. As I opened the door, I felt a rush of giddiness.

"What the fuck are you talking about?" he yelled.

I rushed into the hallway. I couldn't believe how fast I was moving, considering how heavy my suitcase and tote bag were. A bellboy nodded as I rushed past him in the hallway.

"Merry Christmas!" I called out.

He nodded again and smiled.

Then I saw a middle-aged woman setting her room service tray outside her door. I pointed to her. "And a Merry Christmas to you!" I didn't have time to see her expression, and I almost didn't recognize my own voice, which held shaky excitement.

When I heard John in the distance—"Where the fuck are you going?"—I started running. I glanced down at my feet. The gold triangles along the burgundy carpet in the hallway whizzed past. I didn't trip once. When I made it to the elevator, I caught my breath as a couple stepped off.

"And a Merry, Merry Christmas to the both of you!" I was out of breath. "Merry, Merry Christmas!" I stepped onto the elevator and pressed the lobby floor. The couple turned back and stared at me with wide-eyed confusion as the elevator doors closed.

Chapter 32

"ONE WAY?"

I grinned. "Yes, please." *I'm the only person in history to be ecstatic to leave Paris.*

The woman behind the counter was skinny with jet-black hair and sharp features. She spoke English with a barely discernable French accent. "The next flight is not for another five hours."

"That's fine." That would give me about eleven hours, including flight time, to prepare my speech. I didn't wish the woman a Merry Christmas. When she handed me my boarding pass, I wished her a "Happy Bastille Day."

She didn't respond or smile or even nod. *Is she Kate's long-lost French cousin?* I brushed the thought of Kate out of my mind and practically skipped away from the counter, boarding pass in hand, humming Jingle Bells.

Syd, hi. Listen, I know you might feel like you're seeing a ghost right now. After all, I'm the girl who took off in a whirlwind with her ex-boyfriend... but surprise! I'm back. Ha ha. This is going to sound completely crazy, and I don't blame you for thinking I'm a flake or worse, but you have to know that this is not typical of me. I'm more grounded than this. I think you can tell that. I just kind of went temporarily insane. A buildup of things. I don't know. Anyway, I have come to my senses.

I envisioned he would then cut me off and kiss me passionately as I tried to tell him about Paris and what happened, how John was not the one for me, and that I realized that now. Then, we would hug and hold each other. We would probably laugh at what a nut I was and wonder what I'd been thinking, then we would pick up right where we'd left off.

At least, that was what I kept envisioning… and prayed for over the next eleven hours.

I didn't sleep on the plane. I arrived at LaGuardia with dark circles under my eyes, and I was pretty sure I didn't smell like roses. But I wasn't particularly tired. I was no longer humming Jingle Bells, but I was still excited. And anxious.

As I waited in the cab line for forty-five minutes, I reviewed my emails and texts. There were several from Dave that were increasingly frantic in only the past few hours.

Selma Renner is blowing up the Internet. Have you seen how many Facebook likes and tweets your story has gotten?

Is Selma in Florida? How can she be reached?

Where are you? What's your Twitter handle?

I left you a voicemail and tried you at work. Someone named Margaret said you're out of the country? Your work email is disabled? Do you know how many other news outlets are picking up your story? You and Selma are hot right now, and I'm pretty sure neither of you know it. CALL ME. Class may be over, but you're getting extra credit, girl.

Wow, people are reading my article? Someone other than my mother was watching my story? I felt giddy again for a moment. I typed a reply to Dave as I moved up in the taxi line.

Hey Dave, that is awesome! I'm so happy to hear that the story is so popular. And I'm so sorry for the lack of response. Yes, I've been out of the country. It's a long story. I'll try you later.

One explanation at a time. Syd first.

I wondered if I should make sure that Syd was home before I just showed up. But I decided that arriving unexpectedly was more romantic and would have more of an impact.

What if he's not home? Should I shower first? No, I couldn't wait any longer.

When I opened the cab door, there was a shiny penny on the seat.

"Where to?" the cab driver shouted.

"Uh, yes." I got in. "West Broadway and Houston, please."

I moved the penny to the other side of the seat. *Thank you, Gram. Thank you, Grandpa. Syd will be home. He won't mind that I'm a little smelly right now. And he won't mind that I left for a little while... because I'm back now.*

Half an hour later, I rested my suitcase against the wall in Syd's hallway and pushed my hair back before knocking.

He opened the door, and I felt instantly at ease. He looked relaxed and comfortable in a gray T-shirt and jeans.

"Hi," I chirped.

"Hi." Syd's brow furrowed. He was clearly stunned.

"The doorman wasn't there," I explained. "Some guy was leaving just as I was entering, and he let me in, even helped me with my suitcase when the wheel got stuck in the doorway. You have nice neighbors."

Not exactly the intro I'd planned. My nerves got the best of me, and my voice started to shake. "Um, I know this is weird... Can I come in?"

Syd looked down. "Now is actually not a good time."

"Listen, it's a bit of a long story." I swallowed. "And I'll explain, but can I come in?" I thought about just blurting out my speech, but it didn't feel right. I had to get comfortable first.

Then, I noticed the sound of the television. A movie was on. And that was when I heard the flush from the bathroom. "Is someone here?"

"Veronica, listen, do you want to call me later?"

"Is there a girl here?"

At that moment, a woman about my age with long, curly brown hair came out of the bathroom, wearing short shorts and a tank top. She glanced quickly toward the door as she moved into the living room.

My mouth dropped; I couldn't help it. I pushed past Syd and

marched into the living room. The girl was tiny and familiar-looking, in a way that made me think I may have gone to college with her.

"Hi. Who are you?" My nervousness had turned to fury.

The girl's eyes opened wide. "Rachel?" She said her name as though it were a question and looked at Syd.

My God, this can't be happening. I suppose I deserve it. But no, he's mine. He's the only one for me.

Syd walked toward the couch. "Rachel, this is Veronica. Veronica, Rachel... my cousin."

I didn't audibly gasp, but my hand reflexively rose to cover my mouth. *Oh my God. Rachel. Cousin Rachel. The cousin I wanted help from. The cousin I canceled on. The cousin I want to like me because I want to be with her cousin.*

"Oh. I'm so sorry," I mumbled. "Oh, God. I'm... I'm so out of it. I barged in. I, I don't know. I'm so sorry."

They were both looking at me as if they couldn't take their eyes off the disaster. I felt my whole body tingle with horror and shame. I hurried toward the door, shaking my head and still babbling, "Sorry" and, "I just got off a long flight." Then, I pivoted back around quickly and blurted out, "Nice to finally meet you."

Rachel gave me a sympathetic smile and a one-shoulder shrug.

Syd followed me out the door. I yanked my suitcase, swung it around, and was ready to bolt.

"Hey." Syd shut the door and came out into the hallway in his socks. No shoes.

John would be so grossed out. I love it. I love Syd.

"Syd," I almost choked as I tried to explain, "I went to Paris, I quit my job, and then I left Paris, and I left John. I just knew I had to come back to you. I knew I couldn't marry him. I just want to be with you." I started to cry an ugly cry, but I couldn't help it. "I made a huge mistake. I'm sorry. And now, I feel so stupid. I was rude to your cousin." And soon I was blubbering. "I'm so sorry. I feel so stupid."

Then my nose started to run, which I tried to shield with the back of my hand. *How attractive.*

"Hey, it's okay." Syd put his hand on my shoulder. "You were in Paris? Did you say you quit your job?"

"Yes," I wailed as I wiped my eye with my other hand.

He looked at my suitcase. "Did you come from the airport?"

I nodded. "I came back for you." I sniffled as I fished in my bag for a cocktail napkin from the plane.

"Let me get you a tissue," he said.

But I'd found it and practically shouted, "I got one."

We stood in silence while I tried to maintain some dignity, wiping my nose with the napkin. "I made a mistake." My voice was hoarse.

He stared at the floor.

"Say something."

He took a deep breath. "No."

"What?"

"No." He shook his head. "Veronica, listen, after what happened, how could I ever trust you? I can't. I just can't."

"But you don't understand. It was—"

"You didn't even call me." He looked me straight in the eye. "Wasn't I owed at least a phone call if not in person? I got an email. Really? An email?"

I lowered my head.

"And you quit your job?" His voice was louder. "Wasn't that what I suggested the night before? But you didn't run off to Paris with me. You got pissed. It makes no sense."

"I know. I was wrong. But I realize now. And I came here for you." I was a blubbering fool again. "Right from the airport. And there was a penny on the seat in the cab. You know what that means? It was all supposed to be okay."

I sobbed. Syd reached for me, and I let him hug me. I cried into his shirt for what seemed like a long while, then I hugged him back. I nestled into his broad chest. I didn't want to let go.

He adjusted the collar of his shirt. "Let me get you another tissue."

Could this get any worse?

"I have to go." I grabbed my suitcase and raced to the elevator.

Here I am again, running with my suitcase down a hallway. Only this time, it doesn't feel like a brand-new day. It doesn't feel like Christmas.

Chapter 33

"WHAT AM I GOING TO do?" I was wrapped in a blanket on Jada's couch with a cup of hot tea in my hands.

"We'll figure it out," she said.

Jada was the first person I called when I'd left Syd's apartment. I thought about how I'd sat in the same spot on her big, comfortable couch the night after I thought John was going to propose. That felt like a century ago.

"Why 'Merry Christmas?'"

"I don't know. It felt like a brand-new day. Like a gift. I can't explain it."

"How can you? That's just weird." Jada leaned back in the chair next to the couch. "Has John called?"

"He left a 'Where the fuck are you?' message on my voicemail, and that was it. That chapter is officially closed. I went temporarily insane. I can't explain it."

"How can you? That was just weird," Jada repeated. We both laughed.

Then, we sat in silence for a few moments. I wouldn't blame her if she brought up my criticism of her getting back with Mark after I'd gotten back with John. But true to form, she didn't bring up our fight. And for that, I was grateful.

"Listen," she said. "There's another guy out there for you. It's not something you want to think about right now, but when the time is right, you can pick yourself up and be ready to meet a great guy. Forget John. And forget Syd too. You'll find a combination. You'll find... Sohn. Or Jyd."

I smiled at her effort.

"I mean, did Syd even have your 'four requirements?'"

I wrapped the blanket tighter around me. "More. There were so many things about him I never knew I wanted, never even thought about or thought would be important."

"Like what?"

"Well, for one, he's so relaxed. He's so chill. And he loves me just as I am."

"Have you been watching *Bridget Jones*?"

We both loved that movie. "It's true though. It's so important. He's not judgmental. I feel I can take him home to my family—some of my more cliché family members too—you know, the real *boombozz* Italian Jersey types—and he'd get along with everyone, with anyone. He's amazing." I rested my head on a fancy throw pillow.

"Hey, your story, the one about the trial of that doctor, the old lady, it's everywhere. You were awesome too. Maybe this is your chance to become the next Rosanna Zotto?"

"Thanks." I slowly lifted my head. "But I need money. Seriously, my savings is pitiful. Like almost in the red pitiful. And with rent and loan payments and credit card bills, especially after that plane ticket, I don't know how I'll make it in between jobs right now, and I definitely can't switch to a far less-paying job." I felt my throat tighten. "What am I going to do? I can't believe what I've done."

"Okay, listen." Jada set her tea on the coffee table. "You have to call Grace Black."

"Who?"

"She's a legal headhunter. I've heard she's awesome."

"I've worked with headhunters before. They're no help."

"Way to look on the bright side. And do you have a choice?"

"Text me her number." I sighed. "What about when she asks about prior employment? I guess I should leave out that I told my boss to fuck off?"

"That might be a good idea."

"What about when they ask for references? I'll never get one from Beverly." I put my head in my hands. "That's five years down the drain."

"Just call her. What else can you do?"

Jada told me I could stay on her couch as long as I wanted. But I eventually picked myself up, suitcase in tow, still wearing the work clothes I'd quit my job in, run off to Paris in, ran back to Syd in, and now, made my way home in. As I waited for a cab in front of Jada's building, it started to rain. I didn't have an umbrella, and I didn't care. I let the fat raindrops hit me.

One week ago, I was a gainfully employed, miserable lawyer in a budding relationship. Now, I'm a heartbroken, unemployed lawyer. A lot can happen in a matter of days.

Chapter 34

I STARED AT THE CEILING, the covers up to my chin. My grandmother sat at the edge of my bed while my grandfather stood against the window.

"How did this happen?" I asked.

"It had to happen," my grandmother said.

"Please don't give me that. That's not what I want to hear."

"Well, it's the truth," she said.

"You're going to be all right, *brasciole*," Grandpa Sal said.

"Really? Syd won't have me back. I'm unemployed. And I'm broke on top of it. Tell me, how exactly am I going to be all right?"

"You'll see. You'll do it." Grandma Ant patted my leg through the covers. "You'll surprise yourself. You've got more courage than you think, Veronica. You can take it from here."

"What the hell are you talking about?" I sat up. "I had more courage than I ever had when I finally told off Beverly and quit my job in a blaze of friggin' glory, and now where am I?"

Grandpa Sal stepped forward, sat on the other end of my bed, and looked me straight in the eye. "No, that wasn't courage. That was escaping. Ya thought you were *rescued*. Courage, Veronica"—he put his pointer finger in the air—"is what you'll do next."

"Beg for my job back?"

"Ha!" Grandma Ant laughed. "You'll see."

"No 'You'll see!' See what? Oh, and I also had the courage to go to Syd's, and you saw how that turned out, right? You see everything, don't you?"

They didn't react. We sat in silence for a few more moments.

Then, my grandparents glanced at each other before my grandmother patted my leg again. "All right, we need to get going now. Veronica, listen, our visits are going to stop here for a little while."

"What? Why? Am I that much of a pain in the ass? Or a hopeless cause? I'm sorry. It's just—it's a hard time."

"No, no, dear. Listen, it's Mary's great-grandson," Grandma Ant said. "He's in college, and he's doing a lot of stuff he shouldn't be doing. And she's trying to help him, but they need more... energy."

"A lot more energy," Grandpa Sal said. "She's calling on everyone. We've got to go do what we can. But Veronica, we've gotten ya this far, haven't we?" He held his arms out wide.

"This far? I've never been worse off!"

"And the rest," he continued, "well, the rest ya gotta do on your own. And you can. You've got the power."

"What are you, Glinda the Good Witch? I've had the power all along? I just needed to click my ruby slippers? Is that what you're telling me?"

Grandpa Sal laughed loudly. "Oh, believe me, no. You have not had the power all along. You needed us. Boy, did you need us. But now, you can take it from here."

"Wait. Hold on." I looked back and forth at each of them as they both got up from my bed. "When are you coming back?"

My grandmother leaned in and kissed my forehead.

"I don't understand." I pushed the covers off with my feet and sat up, tucking my knees under me. "I need you now more than ever."

"We're just going to help Mary. We'll be back," my grandmother said.

"I can't believe you have to go now." I followed them to the door, my voice rising with each step. "Of all times. Now? Really?"

"By the way, about Grandma's ring?" Grandpa Sal said over his shoulder.

I stood still. *I forgot about that. Funny how some things used to be so important.*

"St. Anthony always comes through, by the way," Grandma Ant said. "But we had to, well, *intervene* this time. You understand."

"It's in your underwear drawer," Grandpa Sal said.

My underwear drawer? How did that happen? Then it hit me. *Yes! Granny panties!*

I turned to stare at my dresser as it all came back to me. Two days before I thought John was going to propose, I'd worn pants to work—no underwear, just pants. That was how I prevented panty lines. But I brought a pair of granny panties in my tote bag because during lunch, I wanted to try on a pair of pinstripe pants I'd seen in the window at Barneys. I didn't want to try them on with no underwear—ew!—so I had to bring underwear. I just grabbed an old pair from my drawer and threw them in my bag. But I never had time to go during lunch. For two days, I'd carried around granny panties in my tote bag. On the day I thought John was going to propose, when I assumed I shouldn't wear any rings because I thought I was getting an engagement ring that night, I'd put Grandma's ring in my tote bag *wrapped in the granny panties* for safekeeping, I figured at the time. But obviously, I didn't do it with enough conscious recognition to sear it into my brain, probably because I had Beverly screaming my name at that moment, or visions of a big, fat engagement ring dancing in my head, or both. It made sense that, a day later, still reeling from the non-proposal and London and "it's up to you," I'd put the bunched-up undies—and apparently the ring I'd completely forgotten I'd bunched up in them—in my underwear drawer.

Wow, I really am Hurricane Veronica. Is anything safe in my path?

When I turned around, my grandparents were gone.

Chapter 35

THE NEXT MORNING, I SHOT out of bed. *Old lady underwear.*

That's what I did with it! Pinstripe pants. Lunch break I couldn't take. Wrapped in undies for safekeeping. Implosion of relationship. Of course, the perfect storm, or Hurricane Veronica.

I jumped up and ran to my dresser. I pawed through it until I found them. Tucked in a corner, crumpled in a ball. I uncrumpled the undie ball, and the little circle that I had learned to no longer depend on to get me through uncomfortable moments fell out on top of my dresser. Clink. Like the sound that other ring had made when I'd placed it on the end table in Paris.

Well, hello there. I slipped it on my finger. *I made it through some nerve-wracking times without you.* I held my hand out to admire it. *But I'm glad we've reconnected. I may no longer need you, but I still want you around. You are a pretty little thing.*

Then, I pulled out my laptop and sent my résumé to Grace Black.

Grace Black laughed in my face—well, not literally in my face, but over the phone—when she said she'd checked my references. I had no choice but to provide the contact information of my former boss for the only full-time job I'd had since law school. She said, "I'm sorry, Veronica. That Beverly is a hoot though, isn't she? But I'm afraid there's nothing I can do for you."

After a few more similar responses from other recruiters and a dwindling bank account, I had no other choice but to move home with my mother. I was almost thirty, single, unemployed, and living with Mommy. *Pathetic, yes, but I was grateful I at least had that option.*

Jada was taking my martini glasses one by one from my kitchen cabinet and wrapping them in newspaper. "These are nice." She twirled one in her fingers. "You and Connie can watch *Sex and the City* together and drink cosmos."

"You can have them," I said as I lifted a box of sweaters off the counter and dropped it in the corner. "I don't think my mother and I are going to be getting tipsy together."

My mother, who was emptying my sock drawer into a shopping bag, looked up. "I get tipsy. Sometimes, Don and I finish a whole bottle of wine."

I looked over at my mother. Her jet-black hair was sprayed into "piece-y layers," as she called it.

Thank God for you, I thought. *Thank God you're the type of mom to say, "Of course" when I asked to move back home. Where else would I live? Who else would help me move?*

"Ma, you dropped a sock." I pointed to the floor.

"Should we order a pizza?" my mother asked as she picked up the sock.

"Yes, we should," Jada said, then patted the newspaper-wrapped martini glasses that were now in a box. "And we should wash it down with a bottle of wine. A whole bottle. Let's get crazy."

I scanned my apartment. I expected it to look bigger as everything was getting cleared out, but it felt like the place was shrinking. I stared at my couch and touched it.

This beige three-cushion couch is where I logged onto Match. It's where Syd told me the story of how he did the conga, holding onto the hips of a sexy blond band singer at his bar mitzvah. It's where I told him about winning tickets to be on Sesame Street when I was five, and how I walked in a parade past Mr. Hooper's store with Big Bird and fifty other kids. It's where I researched and wrote some of my Selma story.

"What are you staring at? They'll still take your couch even if it has a couple of stains. Goodwill is good like that." Jada moved on to my bookcase. "Can we order food already before I faint?" Jada was one of those friends who never feigned being extra nice to someone in front of her mother.

A few hours later, after my mom and Jada had left, I finished packing some more boxes, including the contents of the end table next to my bed, which was when I found the diary. I hadn't written in it since Paris. I took a deep breath and peeked with one eye. When I saw the words "Magic carpet," I became nauseated. I ripped out all the pages I'd written on and stuffed them down the trash with the pizza box and empty wine bottle.

After that, I crawled into my bed. With all the boxes surrounding me, I felt as if I were in a cardboard igloo. It would be the last time I would crawl into bed in my Manhattan apartment.

My mom and Don insisted on driving into the city to make sure the movers got everything into the van without a problem. I insisted that it was completely unnecessary for them to fight traffic all the way into the city just to keep an eye on the movers, but they wouldn't listen.

As it turned out, the movers didn't need to be watched as they were packing the van. It was when they got to my mother's house that we had a problem.

They showed up almost two hours after us. Don had to leave for work an hour before that, so it was just my mom and me, sitting on the front steps when they finally showed up.

I had been calling the leader of the group—who went by "Dito"— but he hadn't picked up. There were two others with him, but I hadn't learned their names; they could have been his brothers. They looked like triplets. The three of them were between five-eight and five-nine and couldn't have weighed more than a hundred thirty pounds each, but they were strong... really strong. The men had handed each other some of my heaviest boxes as if they'd been throw pillows.

When the van finally pulled up and parked in front of the house, Dito exited and stomped his cigarette out on the sidewalk, grinding it on the ground in front of my mother's house.

I stood up. "Did you get lost?"

"We got a teeket," Dito said. "A speeding teeket, coming out of the tunnel. Thousand dollars."

"I'm so sorry! That's horrible." *A thousand dollars? Clearly, he is mistaken, but that would explain the delay.*

My mother also apologized. "How awful," she said. "Can I get you some water? Lemonade?"

Dito didn't respond as he and the other two immediately opened the back of the van and got to work. After about forty-five minutes, my mother's living room was full, and the van was still only half-emptied. My mother and I started to move boxes from the living room to the dining room in order to make more space when, both drenched in sweat, we realized no one had been back in the house for several minutes.

When I opened the front door, Dito and his brothers were in a hushed conversation in front of the van. Dito was doing most of the talking, and although I couldn't hear him, it seemed as though he was giving them directions.

"Hi." I walked toward them. "Is there much left?"

Dito turned to me with a serious expression. "Yeah, you know, with this teeket, you see, we can't finish, you know, unless it's paid. The teeket, you see, thousand dollars. You have to pay."

"I have to pay for your speeding ticket?"

"Yeah, we got it coming to New Jersey. We can't add it to the bill. You have to pay separately."

"Excuse me? First of all, your ticket was not for a thousand dollars, and secondly, I don't have to pay it." I gave him my most skeptical look that I hoped said, "Just stop now. This isn't going to work on me."

My mother started walking down the front steps. "Is there a lot more left?"

"They're saying I have to pay their speeding ticket."

Eyebrows raised, she said, "Oh, okay, in cash?" which only made my blood go from racing to boiling. I gave her a look that I hoped said, "Are you kidding me?"

Dito continued. "Well, you have to pay it because we got it coming to New Jersey, and you know, you have to pay it."

"I'm not paying your fucking speeding ticket. You're holding my stuff hostage. Can you please finish emptying the truck?"

My mother was nervous, licking her lips, her hands in prayer position.

"We can't finish until you pay." Dito started to raise his voice.

I didn't know for sure what was in the rest of the boxes, but I knew it was half of my stuff. I had sudden visions of losing my favorite things—my favorite shoes, clothes, handbags, coats. Whatever it was, it was my stuff, my belongings, my possessions. The things I'd worked for were being held hostage by this creep and his two sleazy brothers. And worst of all, I couldn't afford the thousand-dollar ransom.

I held out my cell phone, then Googled, tapped, and scrolled until I found the number of the police station as Dito, his brothers, and my mother all watched me. "Hi. This is Veronica Buccino. I am at 421 Milton Street. I have movers here from White Grove Moving who are telling me I have to give them an extra *thousand* dollars or they'll drive away with my personal belongings. It's been a few years since I took the bar exam, but I believe... um... that's theft. Isn't that grand larceny? Or grand theft? Or something, I know. I don't practice criminal law. But I know it's not right. I need someone here as soon as possible, and I want all three of them arrested... please."

I stared Dito in the eye as I repeated the address.

Out of the corner of my eye, I could see his two brothers, shaking their hands wildly in the air and saying, "No, no, no." Dito got into the passenger seat of the van and slammed the door shut while his brothers went back to work.

A police car arrived ten minutes later. The two cops who emerged from the vehicle were so good-looking that if I hadn't known better, I would have thought they were going to fake handcuff me, play music from a boom box, and strip.

They were both about six feet tall with broad shoulders and dark hair. As they sauntered toward the house, their radars and radios beeping, I smiled apologetically.

"I'm so sorry," I said. "They're emptying the van now. Well, two of them are. I didn't know what else to do."

"Not a problem," one of them said. His name tag read Perez. "We'll just make ourselves comfortable while they finish the job."

Please do so. I had to consciously stop smiling.

"Thank you," my mother said with an exhale.

"Can I get you guys anything to drink?" I offered.

"Water would be great," the other officer said.

"Alvino?" My mother read his name tag. Alvino was my mother's maiden name. She and I exchanged a glance before I went inside to retrieve two glasses of water.

As it turned out, Officer Alvino was not related, but my mother, like me, found coincidences comforting.

We enjoyed chatting with the officers so much that we barely noticed the last of my wardrobe boxes being brought into the house.

"Looks like the boys are finished." Officer Perez jutted his chin toward the van. Dito hadn't moved from the passenger's seat, but the two brothers had worked fast.

My mother, the cops, and I looked inside the van to make sure everything had been moved. One of the brothers gave me the credit card slip to sign, which I did, making sure to circle the original flat rate. Twice, for good measure.

He then thanked me profusely and glanced nervously at the cops, who were standing back with their arms crossed.

As they pulled away, Officer Alvino shook our hands. "All right, my long-lost cousins, maybe I'll see ya around."

I shut the front door behind me, leaned against it, and slid to the floor.

"That could have been very bad," my mother said. "They could have taken off with half your stuff! I think they'd have done it too. What would we have—"

"Ma. Please. I don't want to talk about it," I said. "It's over. I want to shower and go to bed... and not talk about it."

After a few moments of resting against the door, I walked upstairs to my old bedroom, fell back on my twin bed, and stared at the ceiling. A year ago, I would have called John and asked him if I should write a check for the extra thousand or give them cash.

I rolled onto my side and pulled one of my stuffed animals closer for a better look. "Yup, things have changed," I professed to a stuffed panda bear I'd won on the boardwalk twenty years before. "Things are definitely different." I started to pet him and noticed how sparkly my grandmother's ring looked against his black-and-white hair.

Within a week, my mother and I had established a routine. We would both wake up before seven a.m., sip coffee out of her 'Thank you for your donation to the Red Cross' mugs, and watch the morning shows before she went to work and I searched the legal job boards. Then, she would come home, and we would eat dinner, usually soup or salad, and watch the entertainment news shows, true crime shows, and *Sex and the City* reruns while drinking after-dinner martinis. Luckily, the reruns cut out most of the sex scenes because at any age, those scenes were still mortifying to watch with my mother. And as it turned out, I made a delicious cucumber martini with vodka and Diet Sprite.

In between morning coffee, dinner, drinks, and our favorite shows, I would panic about my job prospects, and if I'd gone heavy on the vodka, my romantic prospects too. My mother tried to be as comforting as possible, always saying, "Something will come up."

I wanted to believe her, but with each passing day, my panic level rose. Finally, one afternoon, I received an email from Dave. I had emailed him a long explanation, in perhaps too much detail, about everything that had transpired around the same time the Selma story was blowing up. I had hoped it clarified that while I was thrilled to hear the story was so popular, the timing was a little unfortunate for me to truly absorb it and appreciate it, considering the personal and professional events occurring at that time in my life. He'd seemed to understand, replying: *Wow. Sounds like a whirlwind. I'm sorry. Hope it all works out. Let me know if there's anything I can do.*

Dave had also noted that I'd won the "hits contest" for our class—the contest in which the person who received the most hits on their story would be automatically eligible for freelance assignments from NewYork3News.com. However, he was aware that I was trying to find a legal job while also settling into my mom's house in New Jersey, so he said he wouldn't bother me if any assignments came up in the near future, but that he would reach out to Elena.

That felt like a knife in my heart even though I knew a slew of freelance assignments still wouldn't pay my school loans and other bills. I thanked Dave again for the experience and sent a congratulatory message to Elena.

I then went back to scouring the legal jobs section of every career website I could find.

A week later as I refilled my coffee cup in my mother's kitchen, I was about to sit down and send out another round of résumés when I received a message from Dave: "Hey, how have you been holding up? Any job prospects? Listen, I know you're a lawyer, and this may be of no interest to you, but our board just signed the budget for the next fiscal year, and it includes the salary for a new reporter. Would you happen to be interested? Call me, if so. Either way, hope you're doing okay."

I walked into the reception area and was reminded of the last time I'd been there, on the day we set out to interview Selma. I rang the doorbell since there was no reception desk and wiped my palms on my skirt.

Through the glass, I saw a tall woman in her forties with long, red hair and a slightly awkward gait, heading toward the door. She was dressed in a navy blazer, jeans, and sandals. "You must be Veronica. Come on in. I'm Sara."

Her office was small and cluttered with one wall covered in news clippings and the other with a whiteboard that said, "MOMA event/ Mayor's press conference/Javits at 2PM for tasting." I assumed those were stories that needed to be covered.

"So, first, I just have to say," Sara sat down behind her desk, "thank you for your Selma Renner piece. The number of hits to our crimes and courts page was the most we'd ever seen. So, we appreciated that."

"Oh, good." I tried to make myself comfortable across from her in what looked like a kitchen chair from IKEA. "She was funny... and she had a lot to say. It was so much fun to do... so much more fun than being a lawyer."

"Yeah, so tell me, why would you want to go from law to this? After all of that schooling, enduring the bar exam, not to mention the money."

"I will never regret going to law school. It's a great background for anything. But after almost five years of practicing, I've learned a lot more about myself, including that while some people might find filing complaints and motions and researching statutes fulfilling and fascinating, I don't. I'm thrilled for the people who love it. That's wonderful for them. Or they're just better fakers than me."

She laughed.

I continued, "But I'm not one of those people, I've come to realize, and that's all right. What fulfills me, what fascinates me, are stories. I want to tell stories about people and their lives, human interest stories, and I can't care what people in this business, this business of journalism, think of that. People might not think human interest stories are where... it's *at,* but—that's what interests me. And if I don't do this now, if I don't go for it, if I don't really try to do what I love, I'll regret it forever. So here I am."

She nodded.

Does she know I'm currently unemployed? I wonder if she thinks I'm desperate. Yes, I do need a job, but from what I've learned, this doesn't pay enough for me to move back into the city. Still, this opportunity has come to me for a reason, and I want it. What I just explained is the truth. The whole truth. Nothing but the truth.

"Good," she said. "Now, I think Dave had you come up with two story ideas. Let me see what you've got."

I pulled out the binder I'd spent the last week creating and rearranging and using to practice my pitches to my mother. I put it on Sara's desk and pulled back the first tab. I then took a deep breath and pitched two stories to her.

"One. A day in the Life of Jackie O, the editor — In 1979, Gloria Steinem put Jackie O on the cover of Ms. Magazine with the headline 'Why does this woman work?' The story will retrace the steps of Jackie, the working girl, by interviewing former authors, former coworkers, former bosses—any of them who are still alive and willing to talk—and uncovering why someone who had significant financial resources, and consequently, the freedom to never work another day in her life, would choose to go to an office every day and do just that. What do former authors, coworkers, and bosses recall about what made the job worth it for her? Why do they think it was so fulfilling for her?"

I glanced up at Sara to make sure she was still listening.

"Two. A Day in the Life of a Matchmaker — Interview the woman who teaches "How To Find A Man" at The Learning Center and follow her on a date. Follow her at one of her speed-dating events too. What are her tips for online dating? How did she become an expert? Why isn't she married? What's the best date she's ever experienced and/or set up? And the worst? Names will be withheld to protect the guilty. If she had four requirements for a mate, what would they be?"

Though Sara appeared to be listening and never took her eyes off of me, she didn't ask any questions or say much throughout my pitches. I was about to suggest we review one of my backup stories when she said, "These are great."

Oh, thank God!

"They're both day-in-the-life kind of pieces, but—"

Oh no.

"They're evergreen, and that's good. You know, stories that can stay on the site for a very long time and still be of interest to our readers? Well, you'd have to get to the Jackie one quickly before there is no one left, but you know what I mean. We like evergreen stories here. Now, I have to tell you, while I saw you on the Selma story, of course, that's just one story, so I had to watch your demo reel."

I cringed.

"And it was obviously done in a classroom. Dave is a great teacher, but it's still a demo reel."

Here it comes. I knew it was too good to be true.

"But I could see that you've got a presence. You definitely have potential."

I grinned. "Thank you." *She thinks I've got potential?*

"You're welcome. Have you shown your reel to anyone else?"

"God, no." I didn't mean for it to come out like that.

"You should. Show your friends and family. It's not bad."

"Thank you."

"All right, let me find Dave for you."

That's it? Not so fast. "So, what's the next step?" I asked.

She slowly looked up from her phone.

I wasn't leaving without some idea of where we went from there. I wanted the job, and I wanted her to know it.

"Uh, well," she said, folding her hands. "We have a few more interviews, a few more people coming in today and tomorrow. And I have to be honest, we have some journalism majors and one individual who actually has her master's in journalism. So, it's competitive. But as far as next steps, once I conduct all of the interviews and submit a report to the board of directors, we can hire someone."

"How many lawyers do you have interviewing?"

"You're the only one, I believe."

"How many interviewees had a story go viral on your website?" I refused to break eye contact. "I really want to work here. I love what you're doing, and I know this is what I'm meant to do. I just want you to know that."

"Thank you, Veronica. I can see that."

Good.

She called Dave then walked me over to his office. He and I chatted for a long time, but he couldn't reveal anything about my chances.

By the time I left the NewYork3News offices, it was dusk. I decided to walk a few blocks before getting on the subway and heading back to the port authority to take the bus back to New Jersey.

On the way home, I received an email from my father, asking me to review another vendor contract. He made no mention of my last reply right before I'd left for Paris, when I told him to hire "his own fucking lawyer."

I tapped out a response as the bus passed from New York to New Jersey.

Sure. Why not? I've got nothing else to do these days. But I've got a request for you too.

Dave had remembered that my father owned a restaurant. When we'd chatted earlier, he mentioned that his partner needed about a hundred aluminum catering trays for an art project at the elementary school where he taught. Clean and unused. A true donation, not garbage.

Quid pro quo, Dad.

I ended the email.

That's a legal term.

Chapter 36

"Do you need to see my passport?" I asked the NewYork3News.com human resources professional, a friendly young woman named Ginger, who had a sleeve tattoo and a nose ring. "For the proof of citizenship form?"

"Oh yeah, thanks." She bounced back toward me as I sat at a long folding table in the middle of the room. All of the junior reporters, editors, and producers sat in an open area that, many years ago, I imagined, would have been buzzing with phones ringing off the hook and cigarette smoke wafting through the air. Now, it was filled with the relative quiet of laptops, smartphones, and energy drinks being sipped.

"I suppose I'm getting trained today? How many days is it usually? A week?" I asked Vince, who was sitting next to me.

He laughed, never taking his eyes off his laptop as he pecked away. "Training? What training?"

Friendly but flaky HR staff. No office of my own. No training. I wanted to turn to an invisible dog and say, "Toto, we're not at a law firm anymore... but it's all good."

Only a week earlier, I had been sitting with my mother on the couch in front of the television, watching Carrie walk out of the hospital after Natasha gashed her teeth and lamenting that I'd added too much Diet Sprite to the cucumber martinis we were drinking, when I received a text from Dave.

"Start practicing 'This is Veronica Buccino for NewYork3News.'"

I replied "Shut up!" *So professional.*

"You'll be getting an official email tomorrow morning, but I've been given permission to let you know informally."

Then, my mother and I jumped up and down, and when I cried, so did she.

"Veronica!"

My stomach flipped. *Like Pavlov's dog.*

I spun around to see Dave and was reminded of our first awkward meeting. I smiled as he pulled a chair out and flipped it around, straddling it so the back was facing me, and I thought, so his nether region was guarded.

We talked about two stories for me to research—one about a discrimination lawsuit filed against the city by a former police officer and one about an auction of Princess Diana's handbags. We also discussed the upcoming March trial and my follow-up questions for Selma after the verdict. Before I knew it, it was time for lunch, which consisted of a bag of pretzels from the bodega downstairs. Then, again before I knew it, it was time to take the bus back home to Jersey. That had never happened at the law firm. At the law firm, I would look at the clock all morning, anticipating lunch, the "only enjoyable part of my day," as I'd called it. Then, the hours between one and seven p.m. would feel like an eternity. My law firm days never whizzed by.

That was how it was every day of that first week. I knew that every day at NewYork3News wouldn't be like that, but I liked how I felt when it was time to go home—exhausted, happy, intrigued—and it made up for the lack of privacy in the open-space newsroom.

I was beginning to realize that happiness to me didn't mean money. Happiness, for me, was defined by how I spent my time. Spending my time engaged in material that was genuinely interesting to me made up for the lower paycheck too. So I stopped shopping at department stores and started buying clothes at the mall that I could wear on camera. The mall. I was now officially a Jersey girl again.

The courthouse was packed, and cameras weren't allowed inside. So I sat in the courtroom for the actual reading of Dr. March's verdict, monitoring reactions to include in my written piece later on, and Vince waited outside to capture reactions from the people leaving. Selma had called me earlier that day. She was back from another trip to Florida, and although she'd just joined a "salsa league" and hurt her hip, she didn't want to miss this day, she'd said.

"A salsa league?" I felt a pang of sadness as I thought about how funny Syd would have found that.

Dr. March was found guilty on two of the three counts of conspiracy to commit murder. Filamina shook her head but had no tears. Throughout the trial, she'd played the part of dutiful wife and never wavered. Maybe Dr. March wasn't holding her own indiscretions over her head in exchange for her support. It made me wonder if despite everything, despite what he'd done, despite what she'd done, maybe she really believed him in this situation, that he would never actually go so far as to try to have her killed. Maybe it wasn't entirely black and white. I'd learned people could be complicated.

As Filamina walked out of the courtroom with defense attorneys, throngs of reporters pushed and shoved with microphones held out. I was one of them. Filamina said nothing. But she saw me. We made eye contact. And in that moment, I didn't feel proud.

Selma, on the other hand, was ready for another moment in the spotlight. Her accusations had received a lot of attention, including the attention of prosecutors who'd called her as a witness earlier that month. She was as colorful on the stand as she had been in our interview. She was again courted by all of the news outlets, but she never forgot who'd found her.

"Veronica, dear!" She waved her hand wildly in my direction and hobbled over before speaking directly to the camera. "Of course he's guilty. These people are not the most upstanding citizens even with their perfect hair and their perfect smiles. They cheat. They lie. They record each other on the camera. They don't like dogs. I could go on and on. And I coulda called this from a mile away. Guilty as sin. The wife too. She's no saint, that one. I'm glad I told the truth. But don't get me wrong, I'm glad she wasn't murdered. Thankfully, the good doctor and his dippy mistress didn't succeed on that front. Even tramps deserve to live. Alrighty, well, I gotta go to bridge now! Bye!"

Later that night, I talked about it all with my mother over martinis and minestrone. I concluded that I'd felt most proud when I helped Trista Hines, and that was at the job in which ninety-nine percent of the time I'd felt shame, boredom, and angst.

Now, I was at a job where ninety-nine percent of the time, I felt proud of what I did—proud and fulfilled—except when it came to that one case that had put me on the map at NewYork3News, as Dave had put it. It was sad and ironic at the same time.

The next day, I knocked on Dave's office door. "I have an idea. It will be extra work for me, but I don't mind," I said.

"Yeah? What's that?" He was shooting a spongy basketball into a small hoop that hung from the edge of his desk.

"I will cover any story you want me to, but if possible, I'd like to do a page called 'NewYork3News Heroes' where we cover stories that are inspiring and redeeming."

Silence. Part of me expected a response along the lines of, "We're a newsroom, Veronica, not a bouncy house," but then I remembered I didn't work for Beverly anymore.

Dave made the shot and then said, "Sounds cool. Let's do it."

There was nothing to like about Sebastian Gilbert. One morning when Doug finished logging the tape from the morning's shoot, Sebastian said, "Vanessa. I mean, Veronica. Whatever. If you don't start talking from the back of your throat and sounding less like you're from Joisey, you won't last here very long."

He resembled a cartoon bug. His eyes were two enormous globes on his narrow head. His hair was jet black and slicked back with so much goo, it looked like the roof of a car that had been waxed to perfection. He was about six feet tall and weighed about a hundred and six pounds. He wore black T-shirts every day, tucked into black pants with a belt buckle shaped like the state of Texas.

Since he was the co-producer with Dave Kennedy, he was my boss, so he saw almost every story before it went up on the site.

"Sebastian Gilbert, I know *your* name. And yes, I am from New Jersey, but this is not Illinois3News after all. Still, I'm working on my accent, but I'll need you to work with me. We're not live, so when you're watching a taping, just stop me if it gets too bad, and I'll do it again. Okay?"

I actually said that.

Then he said, "It's always bad," and stalked off.

As I turned back around, I caught Vince's eye, and he winked.

Dealing with Sebastian was another small price to pay for finally doing something I loved. *I'll take it. And I'll stick up for myself. You can't change people. You can only change yourself.* That, I was learning.

What I wasn't learning so well was how to stop thinking about Syd. I'd thought about going back on Match.com, but I wasn't interested in dating again at that time. If I went back on, it would only be to see if he was still on. *If only I could text him or email him or call him. If he could see me now.*

Unfortunately, all he was seeing, if anything, was Jada stalking him on my behalf on every social media platform available. She had done a cross-check of possible friends of friends and connected with them so she could get that much closer to Syd "electronically" and see what he was up to.

But despite all of this cyber-circling, she wasn't able to glean much. I appreciated her efforts though.

"That's what friends are for," she said. "If I needed you to connect with Mark's cousin's yoga teacher and then spend hours going through all of the photos she's liked or commented on to see if his cousin posted a picture from a family wedding and if it looked like he had a date, I know you'd do it in a heartbeat."

I had to laugh at the lengths she went to, all for me. "In a heartbeat," I said.

"Hi, I'm Veronica Buccino with NewYork3News. We are in Millersville, New York, about fifty miles outside the metropolitan area, but we've made the journey here for a very good cause. Trista's Treats, a traveling purveyor of baked goods that local workers in office parks all over the area run to like kids to an ice cream truck, will be honoring National Breast Cancer Awareness Month in a very special way. And we're here to find out how."

I stood in front of the pink truck, parked in the lot of a large office building, with Trista standing next to me in a pink apron, her hair in a ponytail. She stood tall and proud as if to say, "Look at me now."

That makes two of us. Who would've thought?

"Trista Hines, you are, of course, the Trista behind Trista's Treats. What can you tell us about how you'll be doing something a little different starting Saturday, October first?" I held the microphone out to her.

"Thanks. Sure. We're a cupcake truck. Like an ice cream truck, except we're cupcakes and some other baked goods. And we drive all around this area. There are a lot of office parks in this area, and we hit them all every day between ten and three. And you'd think we were giving something away most times. It's like all these workers, they're like little kids, they come running down when they see us pull up. It's really funny. And well, for the entire month of October, we're going to honor National Breast Cancer Awareness Month by giving away our pink vanilla cupcakes with a pink ribbon in exchange for a donation."

"So, you're giving away these cupcakes?" I looked toward her. "Why not just sell them and donate the profits?"

"Well, we feel—I feel—that I've been really blessed, really lucky. I'm so grateful. I want to show my gratitude to our customers. And if they feel they want to donate in return, that's great. And we'll send all of that money to a charity that helps the children of breast cancer patients."

"So, tell us, why this charity?"

"Because they helped me... and my kids... when I was sick. I'm a breast cancer survivor."

After Vince and I rode around town with Trista and her sister in the Trista's Treats van and sampled several cupcakes, I did the closing with a sugar rush.

"And that makes Trista Hines our very first NewYork3News Hero. Read the full story at NewYork3News.com. I'm Veronica Buccino."

"Is that a wrap?" Trista giggled.

"That's a wrap!"

As Vince was loading the camera back in the van, I thanked Trista again and let her know the story should be up on the site the next day or the day after.

We hugged before I got in the van—me hugging the woman that my former client was suing only months ago. Life was funny. That, I was learning.

Chapter 37

JUST AS JADA WAS ABOUT to close out of Facebook one day, she had a breakthrough. Syd's cousin's yoga teacher liked a photo of Syd's cousin that promoted an upcoming cancer charity bike ride. It wasn't clear if Syd would be participating, but he also liked the photo and commented with "Thanks for sharing."

"You're like a social media Sherlock Holmes," I said.

"You know it, my dear Watson," Jada replied.

"He wouldn't be thanking her if he didn't have some vested interest, right?"

"Right," Jada said. I could hear her sip her coffee on the other end of the line. "But who knows. He's either participating, or he's not. There's only one way to find out. We have to go."

"Just go and mill about? Hoping to run into him? I don't want to look pathetic. I mean, I am pathetic, but I don't want to actually look pathetic."

"We'll think of a cover story. I'll hop on a fucking bike if I have to."

A story? Yes! A story.

After I hung up with Jada, I walked toward Dave's office.

Initially, I was going to say that the spokesperson for the charity asked us to cover it, but as I placed my hand on the doorknob to his office, something occurred to me. *I'm sick of fibbing, no matter how small the fibs may be. It's time to cut that out.*

"I like a boy, and he's doing a bike ride on Saturday, and I want to cover it."

Okay, I have to work on making the truth sound a little more polished and mature. Practice'll make perfect, or better.

But Dave didn't miss a beat. "When is it? Saturday?" He threw the basketball toward the hoop and missed.

"Yeah, but it's in the city so we won't need the van. Just one cameraperson."

"Okay, check the schedule. If there's a free camera, I'll approve it." He tried the shot again and made it.

We both held our arms up in victory, for different reasons.

Game on.

On the morning of the charity bike ride, Jada arrived at the starting line in a trench coat and large sunglasses. "Do I look newsy?" she asked.

"More like a flasher," Chuck, the new cameraman, said.

"Perfect," Jada said.

"So, this is the plan." I tightened the top of the microphone to the base. "Jada, walk around, cover this whole area until you find Syd. When you do, text me his location and the color of his shirt. Do not lose him. If he's walking around, keep following him, but don't make it obvious. Chuck, we're going to stay put here, interviewing participants until I get the text from Jada."

Chuck had been fully briefed on my need to find Syd. I had to be able to speak freely with Jada about the mission, so Chuck soon became a participant. Luckily, he was a willing participant. "Let's find your dude," he said.

Unfortunately, my dude was nowhere to be found. The race started, and we waited until every last biker rode off. I stood there, microphone by my side, disappointed.

We had enough for a complete story by that point, since I'd interviewed several participants as well as one of the organizers. So I told Jada and Chuck that we could go home. After asking them to be up at seven in the morning on a Saturday, it didn't feel right to ask them to wait around for three more hours to see the finish on the slightest chance that Syd would come flying around the corner on a bike. Not to mention, I didn't know how good the chance was that he would even be receptive to seeing me.

But they insisted. "I'm scheduled to work anyway," Chuck said. "Don't make me go back to the office."

And Jada assured me she had nothing else to do on that Saturday, that Mark was in Miami for work. I knew there were better things she could be doing, but I was grateful for her dedication to the mission, particularly when Syd did, indeed, come flying around the corner on his bike.

"There he is! That has to be him!" I shouted.

He was wearing a helmet so I didn't recognize him from his clean-shaven head, but he was wearing a yellow shirt that read "Syd" in black letters under his number.

How many other Syds are there in this race who also spell it that way?

Jada, Chuck, and I jogged toward the maze of folding tables, which were filled with bananas and power drinks. And that was where I found him.

With a girl.

I didn't know if she was just a friend or another cousin—I hoped—but they hugged, and my heart fell. She had long, auburn hair and was pretty, I had to admit, even though she'd just ridden fifty miles and was all sweaty.

"Who's that bitch?" Jada asked.

"I don't know." I couldn't take my eyes off of them. "But let's interview him... I mean, them."

Please let her be his sister.

We followed them, and as the girl was chatting with another cyclist, I tapped Syd on the shoulder.

He turned, and when he realized it was me, he smiled. "Hey, Veronica." He leaned in for a hug. "I'm sweaty. Sorry."

"I don't mind." I beamed. "Congrats on the finish."

"What are you doing here?"

"Just—" I shrugged. "Oh. Um, covering this race for my new job at NewYork3News." I said that last part slowly and held up the microphone.

"Wow, congratulations!" He touched my shoulder.

And then the girl he'd been hugging walked over, holding a banana and a cup of water. She said, "I'm ready to wash this banana down with champagne. Brunch is at noon, right?"

"Yeah," Syd said. "Lisa, this is my friend Veronica. Veronica, this is Lisa."

My friend? I suddenly found it hard to swallow. I had to look away for a moment.

"Where are you going to brunch?" Jada asked.

"At a friend's house," Lisa replied sharply.

We all stood there silently for a moment.

"Can I interview you privately?" I asked Syd. "Over here." I pointed aimlessly to my left.

He got the hint. So did Chuck, who didn't follow us with the camera.

"You look great," I said, studying his face and the glistening sweat above his lip. *His perfect lips.*

"So do you. And congratulations on the job again. That's great. Really great, Veronica." He looked at my lips, and I thought for a second he was going to kiss me, right there, sweaty and only feet from Lisa with the auburn hair.

But then, he took a deep breath. "Wow. You know how to surprise me."

I glanced down, thinking of my last surprise appearance at his apartment. "Listen," I started to plead. "I know—"

He shook his head. "Stop."

"Just—" I didn't want to stop. I wanted to say something perfect that would fix it all, and I wanted us to ride away together even if I had to sit on the handlebars.

"Hey!" Lisa appeared. "We're going to be late, and we still have to shower."

I wanted to grab her bike helmet and slam it over her head.

"Well, it was good to see you." Syd patted my shoulder again as if I were an old friend from the neighborhood. "Thanks for covering this. I'll have to look it up on the site." He took a few steps backward as he spoke then turned and walked away with Lisa.

I sobbed in the cab on the way back to the NewYork3News offices.

"Lisa is a slut's name," Jada said.

Chuck agreed. "It is. I know at least three."

"I tried to get us an invite to brunch," Jada said.

"Thank you." I wiped my cheek. "It's all right. I guess that was closure."

"I hate closure," Jada said, looking out the window.

Chapter 38

I TURNED THIRTY ON A Saturday. The sky didn't fall. Time didn't stop. I wasn't as depressed as I'd thought I would be. Only when I thought about Syd.

Maybe I'll get a happy birthday text. Ha! It's been a month now since he rode off into the sunset with that redhead. But a girl can dream, can't I?

I didn't have to work that day. I didn't always get weekends off, but unlike at Ellis & Blackmoore, I didn't mind working weekends at NewYork3News. There was always something fun to cover.

But on that Saturday, my schedule was wide open. I woke up to an empty house. I checked my phone before getting out of bed and couldn't help but smile at some of the messages I had already received on Facebook—mostly from people I hadn't seen in more than a decade. I would sometimes forget about Facebook for weeks or months at a time, but it always made me feel like a rock star on my birthday.

I walked into the kitchen where my mother had placed thirty pink roses in a vase on the table with a card. She'd also left a note that read, "V – Happy Birthday! JAt the mechanic with Don. We should be back by 1:00 to take you to lunch."

I opened the card. The first thing I noticed was that it wasn't a birthday card. There was a drawing of a young ballerina, leaping through a star-filled black sky, and it read, "You inspire me."

Dear Veronica,

I know this year has been a roller coaster. But no matter

what, you always make me proud. And even though I love
my new roommate—haha—I know you won't be in your old
bedroom forever. I can't believe that it was thirty years ago
that I gave birth to such a brave girl who is now a brave
woman. All of your dreams are going to come true. Happy
Birthday, Veronica!

This made me choke back tears. I cleared my throat and made coffee.

While I was at lunch with my mother and Don, my father called. My mother insisted I pick up.

"Happy Birthday, Veronica. How's your new job? Been able to pay your school loans?"

"It's great. Yes, I have." I laughed a little. "I have to send you links to some of my stories. Are you dropping off the trays today?"

"Already done. They're on your mother's back porch."

I was impressed, and it must have shown in my face. My mother mouthed "What?"

"Thank you. I really appreciate it."

"You'll never guess who is at Bella right now, sitting twenty feet from me as we speak."

"I'm sorry. I'm at lunch with mom and Don. I have to go, but—"

"The governor of New Jersey's cousin," he whispered.

"Wow. That's really cool. Listen, I'm sorry. I should get off the phone. I feel rude. Say hi to Carla. And… I'll send you the links to my stories. And thanks again for the trays."

I caught my mother's eye, and her eyebrows rose. She looked away and asked Don something.

Say hi to Carla. I said it. To forgive is to forget. And no time like your thirtieth birthday to grow the fuck up.

I was the first to show up for my birthday dinner at El Cubano. The plan was for me to spend the night at Jada's since she spent almost every night at Mark's place. I lugged the box of aluminum trays on the bus from New Jersey and dropped them off at Jada's apartment for Dave to pick up later. Then, I changed and finished my hair and makeup in Jada's quiet apartment.

I checked in with the hostess at El Cubano and found a seat at the bar. In a few hours, the dining tables would be moved aside to make room for dancing, and the place would be packed and hot and even louder. The first-daters would probably be making out, the blind-daters would likely already be home, the second-daters might be at each other's apartments, and the old college friends would still be reminiscing or hugging goodbye. I was pretty sure my night would end long before any of theirs. Sometimes thirty was just a more easily tired twenty.

Jada arrived about fifteen minutes later, holding five pink balloons. *Balloons? At a bar?*

"The hostess is a bitch. Happy Birthday. Here."

"What am I going to do with these?" I looked up at the balloons.

"You better fucking rejoice over them is what you'll do," she said. "The hostess told me I couldn't bring them in here, and then I threatened her life, and then she said they better not pop or take out a light fixture, and I was like, 'She's not five years old, she's thirty, she'll hold on to them.' So don't get too drunk and let one go, please." She scanned the room. "Did anyone get here yet?"

"Nope." I shrugged. "Just me." Just single me at the bar. Thirty-year-old me, now holding balloons.

She called to the bartender. "Patrón, please. Two shots! Right here!" She pointed to me. "You're wearing blue." Jada looked me up and down.

"Oh, yeah. I wear color now. All-black doesn't always look good on camera."

"I like it. And tonight of all nights to make such a debut." She smiled widely. "It's perfect. To Veronica, now in living color." Jada toasted with our shots.

The rousing rendition of "Happy Birthday" came with a giant chocolate cupcake with vanilla frosting and a candle in the center.

"Are you happy, my little *brasciole?*" Jada put her arm around me and rested her head against mine. I imagined we looked like two drunk Precious Moments figurines.

All of our friends were here. Our friend Ross Davidson was ordering another shot, Lauren was laughing hysterically over something with our friend Nick James, and my new work friends were there—Dave, Mean Joe Dean, Vince the Prince, Doug the Intern, and even Sara, who'd gotten a babysitter that night just so she could come to my birthday party. Sebastian Gilbert "couldn't make it," but at least he RSVP'd. Even Asa, Elena, and Jo stopped by.

"I am," I said. "Thank you for coordinating this."

"Are you drunk?"

"I am."

"Well then, I believe my work is done here. Don't stay out too late, birthday girl."

"I would think you would say the opposite."

She shrugged. "I have to visit the ladies' room first."

"I'll come with you." I scooched over, checked that my balloons were still securely fastened to my chair, and excused myself from the table.

While Jada and I were in the bathroom applying lip gloss at the mirror, it happened. The door opened, and in walked a dark-haired woman dressed nicely in a royal-blue top and gray pants.

She said, "Hi, girls," as though she knew us and went into a stall.

I realized I was furrowing my brow. Jada's jaw dropped.

And then my jaw dropped. And my feet started doing a little dance.

That was when Jada covered my mouth with her hand. "Shhh," she whispered and mouthed, "I'm texting you." Jada reached for her phone and typed: *That's Rosanna fucking Zotto.*

Holy shit, what do I say?

Nothing! Do not make a fool of yourself. You're drunk. Do not say a fucking—

It was too late to finish. She—Rosanna Zotto—emerged from the stall. She rested her clutch on the sink and smiled politely as she noticed us staring at her in the mirror. She started to wash her hands.

"Hi," I said, not taking my eyes off her.

"Hi," Jada said confidently.

We stood there, watching her wash her hands until I said, "Um,

Ms. Zotto." I felt Jada pinch the back of my arm, but I continued. "My name is Veronica Buccino, and I'm a huge fan of yours. I'm such a huge fan that my handle on HumanInterestStories.net is RosannaZotto2.0."

Did she just laugh? Or was that a nervous laugh, like she's afraid I'm going to rip out a piece of her hair and seal it in a plastic bag?

"Well, I just have always identified with you. I'm Italian, and... um... well, I'm a lawyer, but I've made a career switch to journalism. Oh, I did a story recently. It was on the Dr. March trial. I interviewed the neighbor."

Rosanna had interviewed Filamina, who hadn't revealed much but kept repeatedly insisting that she'd never believed he would conspire to have her killed, and that she'd forgiven her husband for his infidelities, and that he'd forgiven her, that love prevailed.

"Yes, the elderly neighbor," Rosanna said as she dried her hands with a towel. "I saw that. I'm familiar with it. Good job."

"You're... you're familiar with it? You're familiar with my work?"

"Yes." She applied lip gloss and smacked her lips. "Good for you for transferring careers. That can't be easy. Are you a member of the Association of Women Journalists?"

"No... not yet." *Because I've never heard of it.*

"You should join. It could be a great resource for you."

"I will! I definitely will! Are you a member?"

"I am." She reached for something else in her bag. "What's your name again?"

"Veronica Buccino."

"Here's my card, Veronica. Email me if you ever have any questions. Nice to meet you."

After she left, Jada and I looked at each other.

"What are the fucking chances of that?" Jada asked. "And on your birthday?"

I couldn't stop smiling. But I did stop smiling as we walked out of the bathroom because it occurred to me—*Syd would love this.*

We told everyone at the table—Asa, Jo, and Elena appreciated it the most—then we moved the party to the bar. Jada yawned, and I thanked her again. She told me again not to stay out too late, then she and Mark strolled out of El Cubano, holding hands.

Shortly after Jada left, my guests started to leave one by one until it was just me, Dave, Nick, and Lauren. After another round, I put my glass on the bar and got up from the barstool.

"Where are you going, birthday girl?" Nick asked.

"I think it's time I call it a night." Lauren and Nick had been talking and laughing while Dave was chatting with the bartender. I suddenly felt as though it were New Year's Eve, and I had no one to kiss at midnight.

"Call it a night? You sound old."

"Nicholas"—I put my hand on his shoulder—"I'm afraid the birthday girl has had enough excitement for the night."

I tapped Dave on the shoulder. "So you'll come back to Jada's for the aluminum trays?"

"That was the plan." Dave finished the last sip of his drink. "Let's go."

I grabbed my bag and my balloons, thanked Lauren and Nick, and turned toward the door with Dave.

In the cab on the way to Jada's apartment, Dave was quiet, texting with his partner, who was visiting family in California. I stared out the window and thought of three things I was grateful for:

1. My new job. I glanced at Dave, pecking away.

2. My family, even my dad, who isn't perfect, but who is? And my mom, who isn't perfect, but I think she is.

3. My friends, especially Jada.

And of course, the birthday bonus:

4. I just met Rosanna Zotto in the bathroom at El Cubano. Did that really happen?

I thought that had made my birthday.

When Dave and I walked into Jada's apartment, it was dark. As I clawed at the air and walked down the hallway looking for the light, I felt a crunching under my feet. When I found the light and let my balloons fly up to the ceiling, I noticed the hallway was strewn with pennies.

Very funny, Jada. I wonder when she did that. After she left the bar?

They appeared to be forming a path to the living room.

"Does your friend make a lot of wishes?" Dave asked. "Shouldn't these be tossed in a fountain?"

"Long story," I said as I followed the pennies farther down the hall, past the bedroom, and into the living room, where the light was on. And that was when I saw Syd.

Chapter 39

HE WAS IN JEANS AND a black button-down shirt. His head was freshly shaven. I wanted to run up to him and kiss him. But the shock held me in place. I couldn't even speak, so he started to explain.

"Jada let me in. Actually, she knew. Well, she's known… for about a week. The doorman was in on it too," he said. Behind him, on the coffee table, was a bottle of champagne and a bouquet of wildflowers. "He let me know when you were coming up so I could turn off all the lights and then—"

Dave, who had been collecting the pennies in the hallway, walked in and said, "I think I got them all."

I wanted to say, "Syd, Dave. Dave, Syd. This is my journalism teacher who is now my boss. He's here to pick up aluminum trays. Yes, aluminum trays."

But I didn't have time.

I saw the shock on Syd's face. "Never mind," he said. "I see you've found someone to celebrate your birthday with." He quickly headed for the door, past me, past a confused Dave, to the elevator.

"Wait! Syd!" I ran after him but tripped over the cord of Jada's laptop charging on an end table.

The elevator door closed before I could reach him. I pressed the down button over and over.

"Oh, come on!" I panicked in Jada's hallway and all the way down until I finally reached the lobby, where the doorman pointed toward the front door as though he sensed my panic and knew I was about to hop in a cab and shout, "Follow that bald man!"

He was right, for the most part. As I ran out of the lobby onto the sidewalk, I saw Syd getting into a cab.

"Syd! Wait!"

But his cab took off down the street.

"No!" I called to no one in particular. "No, no, no," I muttered to myself as I flagged down every passing yellow cab until one screeched to a halt.

"How's your evening going?" the cab driver asked.

"Okay," I answered, craning my neck to see if I could spot Syd's head in the back of a cab. "Actually, not okay. I really need to—to—um, clear something up."

"Got his number?"

Yeah, I need to send him a text in all caps that says, "It's not what you think!"

That was when I realized I had nothing on me. No phone. No pocketbook. No wallet.

Noooo! Fuck.

I kept this to myself, but within seconds, it was as if the cab driver figured it out. He slowed down.

Please don't kick me out of this cab.

My heart was racing. My feet were tapping.

He made a turn down a side street. We were moving at a snail's pace, and I couldn't sit still.

"Can you maybe get back on Second Avenue?" I asked.

"Construction and traffic. Your worst nightmare."

You have no idea.

When we were back on a main avenue, heading downtown, the traffic sped up then slowed again.

I tapped my fingers on the seat as if that would somehow speed things up. Aside from needing to talk to Syd that very second and not knowing how I would pay the cab driver, I also realized that my new and currently perplexed boss was standing in my friend's apartment with a pile of pennies in his hand.

This can't be happening.

When we finally made it to Syd's apartment building, there was no sign of him out front.

"Can you hold on just one minute?" I asked the cab driver.

"How long?" he barked.

"One minute. Just one minute. Please." I raced into Syd's lobby and breathlessly asked his doorman if he was home. The doorman pointed behind me.

I turned to see Syd walking through the door.

"He's gay!" I shouted.

Syd's eyes darted from me to the doorman then back to me.

"That guy at Jada's apartment is Dave. Dave, my journalism teacher, who I now work for. He's my boss, and he's gay." I took a breath. "And I don't mean he's happy. I mean he's not interested in my lady parts. He's just picking up aluminum trays that my father donated for his partner's art project." I inhaled again. "Don't make me explain. It's not that interesting."

He walked toward me, looking me straight in the eye.

There was nothing more I could do. I'd told the truth.

And then, he kissed me. Right there in the lobby, right in front of the confused doorman.

My heart raced. Sweat dripped from my forehead. But I slowly exhaled then breathed in deeply, making sure to take in the delicious smell of Syd and the taste of his lips, making sure this was really happening, that it wasn't all some bizarre dream.

"I haven't been able to stop thinking about you," he said. "And I know this is going to sound crazy—well, maybe not to you—but one night, not long after I saw you at the bike ride, I had this dream about my grandmother. You know, the fly? I never dream about her. We were at Katz's Deli." He laughed, his arms still around me. "And she said, 'Find Veronica.' It sounds corny, I know. It sounds like a line, like I'm making this up, but I'm not. I swear."

I smiled. "I believe it."

We kissed again.

"Miss!" The cab driver was standing in the doorway. "Are ya gonna pay me?"

Chapter 40

TWO YEARS LATER

I WAS WEARING HOT-PINK SWEATPANTS and a pink tank top that said "Bride" in white rhinestones that Jada had given me for my bachelorette party. It was a stark contrast to the bridal suite, which was cream from floor to ceiling with cream-colored couches, carpet, and furnished benches.

As I hugged my grandmother, I squeezed tighter to take in her Nina Ricci perfume.

"You're going to be there, right?" I asked when we let go.

"Of course we are!" my grandfather answered.

It hadn't taken long for my grandparents to help Aunt Mary's grandson a couple of years before, and we returned to having our dream visits around the time I started dating Syd again.

"We wouldn't miss this day!" Grandma Ant said. She looked down at my hands. "Now you can really forget about my ring. Lose it for good if you want."

"No! I'll still wear it." I hadn't taken it off since I'd found it in my underwear drawer, but I did lose the habit of reaching for it with my thumb even before then. "On my right hand."

Grandpa Sal took both of my hands and kissed them. "Congratulations to our little *brasciole* and her wonderful husband." He winked.

"God bless ya both," Grandma Ant said as she pushed my hair behind my ear. I held her hand against my cheek for a second, feeling her soft skin against my face.

They were very simple earrings—pearls, hanging from a straight line of three small diamonds. I was as surprised as I was impressed and, of course, grateful. They were in a beautiful black velvet box.

"They're real," my father said.

"Thanks, Dad. Thank you, Carla. They're beautiful. Of course I'll wear them." They both smiled widely.

"Oh, they're gorgeous," my Aunt Marie said. "They'll look beautiful on you."

I looked in the mirror and put them on. "So Grandma and Grandpa came all the way from Florida? I'm so glad they could be here."

"Can you believe it?" my father asked. "But this is a big day."

I turned back to them. My father, Carla, Aunt Marie, and Uncle Al were all staring at me as I stood there in the bridal suite, completely dressed—a strapless trumpet gown with lace overlay—except for my veil.

"You look beautiful," my father said.

I got choked up at this and quickly turned back to the mirror. "Where's Mommy? I need help with my veil."

My mother walked in at that moment, and everyone else in the room made a polite exit. I took a deep breath, excited to marry the love of my life and nervous about the details of the day—the music, food, photos, everything I'd been planning in such detail since I'd pretended to be a bride at my grandparents' house.

My mother lifted my veil from the table in the corner. "All right, let's figure this thing out."

I watched as she gently pulled it out of the plastic wrapping. For the first and only time that day, we were alone.

"It's the strangest thing," I said. "I had a dream about Grandma and Grandpa last night. They were both in the dream, and we were in this room, the bridal suite. It seemed so real. I swear, I could touch them. I hugged them, and it felt so real, like it was really happening."

"It was a visit," my mother said as she concentrated on straightening the tulle of the veil. "It wasn't a dream. Dreams have that underwater feeling. It felt real and not like a dream, right?"

"Yeah." I secured the earrings on my ears. "They both kept hugging me, and I could really feel it. Don't laugh, but I swear I could smell them. I could smell Grandma's perfume." I laughed.

My mother grinned as she swept the veil forward and then backward on top of my head. She reached with her right hand for the bobby pins and started fastening the whole contraption to my head.

"I never experienced that before," I said.

"How do you know?" My mother walked in front of me to get a better look. "Just because you don't remember visits doesn't mean they don't happen." She pushed my hair back with one hand. "There's a reason things always seem better in the morning."

Our wedding album wasn't ready, but I had all of the pictures on my laptop as we sat at an outdoor café downtown. Grandma Ant was on my left and Grandpa Sal on my right.

"There ya are with your cupcake tower," Grandma Ant narrated as we went through each of the 777 photos. "There ya are, feeding one to Syd. How cute. Oh look, Syd looks like he's swatting a fly away in that picture. How funny."

It was a warm day, and my grandparents and I sat in front of the café's large picture window that, for the last two years, had displayed a local school's award-winning art project—a bunch of dioramas in aluminum catering trays, each one showing people of different backgrounds sharing a meal together. My favorite was the priest, rabbi, and some guy in a business suit eating Chinese food. The chopsticks were toothpicks.

"Why a cupcake tower?" Grandpa asked. "Did you ever think of getting a cannoli cake? They make those, ya know? They're all the rage, I hear."

"No, we like the red velvet cupcakes we had," I said without taking my eyes off the screen.

"They were out of this world. So delicious," Grandma said.

"Everything was delicious!" I heard a familiar voice behind me.

We all turned around and saw their friend Ruth Stein. She looked as if she were out for a walk, not in a hurry or on her way to a party as I'd always seen her before.

"Well, would ya look who it is?" Grandpa Sal asked. "The other cupid. Antoinette's co-conspirator. Where's your arrow?"

Ruth scooted in next to Grandma. "And there you are with my Sydney. Looking gawgous. So gawgous."

Huh?

"Stop furrowing your brow, Veronica," Grandma Ant said. "You've met Ruth before. Ruth is Syd's grandmother."

They both went back to poring over the wedding photos until Grandma eventually looked up at me.

"Close that mouth, Veronica. What are ya catching, flies?"

Epilogue

IT REALLY IS A BEAUTIFUL ring. But a beautiful ring, of course, does not a marriage make. Vanessa will realize this.

We sat on a bench in Central Park. Syd and I were on either side of Vanessa. She pulled her long, black hair to one side.

"The Skinny Vinnie wasn't good?" I asked. She had barely touched her pizza bagel.

"I'm not hungry," she said quietly.

"Veronica, do you like the Maui Howie? I didn't think I'd like a pizza bagel with ham and pineapple, but it's good," Syd said. We both appeared to be about the age we'd been when we passed to the other side, the way Vanessa would remember us. We were a little rounder around in the middle than we'd cared to be while on Earth and had several more creases around our eyes, but we looked happy and relaxed.

"It's delish," I said.

"Delish? You're so old, Gram," Vanessa said.

"Old? I'm dead. Who cares?"

Vanessa smiled. She held her left hand out and stared at it. "I like your ring better, Gram. I wear it all the time."

"I know. I see. And thank you. But really, it's just a thing."

"Not to me! If I ever lost it, I'd be devastated. It means the world to me."

"Ha! If you lost it, you'd go on just fine. Vanessa, these things are nice, but they're just things. What's more important is *who* you marry. Even if he presented you with a lollipop ring."

"I know." She sighed.

"Let me ask you a question. You're a doctor. You're a smart girl. But don't overthink this one. The question is: Do you want to spend the rest of your life with this man? If the answer is yes, then do it. If the answer is no, then don't. If the answer is I don't know, then don't."

"What if I never meet anyone else?" She looked me straight in the eye, her big brown eyes filled with worry.

"What if you do, but you're already married?" Syd asked.

"I'm scared to be alone."

"It would be scarier to be stuck in a mediocre marriage," I said. I wanted to shout "Merry Christmas," but it was not the time to explain all that. We just had to be there for her.

"How will I know when it's right?"

"You just do." I squeezed Syd's hand under the table.

"I'm sick of hearing that."

"The answer will come to you. Trust us," I said. "See how you feel in the morning."

Acknowledgments

To Howie, to put it simply, there'd be no book without you, my muse, my love, my everything.

To my mother, for always thinking I could do anything and somehow convincing me of the same. To my father, for being nothing like Veronica's father and making pizza whenever I'm home. To my brother, for always being so proud and supportive and for giving me three other family members to make proud too. To my in-laws, for being so damn funny, easy to be around and never wondering what I was doing with my life. To my brother's in-laws, for being my family too. To all of my aunts, uncles, and cousins, for being the most magnificent cheerleaders since day one. To my other squad, all of my amazing friends, you know who you are, and you know how grateful I am. Special megaphone shout-out to GJ, who has been rocking the pom-poms since we were in diapers.

To everyone at Red Adept Publishing. I'm still pinching myself that I was plucked from the slush pile and placed in your competent and knowledgeable hands. To Alyssa Hall, the best editor a girl ever could dream of, you helped me turn my ugly duckling manuscript into a swan. To Neila Forssberg, thank you for being an incredible line editor and for telling me in the kindest way possible to stop tinkering. To Streetlight Graphics, whose talent has given this story the most stylish and fitting overcoat.

To the person reading this right now, I always believed that every person who was meant to read this story would be led to it somehow. I am so happy you have found your way here & I really hope you enjoyed it.

About the Author

Fern Ronay was born and raised in Belleville, New Jersey. She is a lawyer and CPA as well as a writer, reporter, and blogger. After six years in Manhattan and six years in Chicago, she now lives in sunny Los Angeles with her husband.

In addition to writing novels, Fern authors the blog *Stop and Blog the Roses* and is a co-host on AfterBuzzTV. When she is not writing, reporting, or blogging, Fern can be found eating something, reading something, or running.

Made in the USA
Middletown, DE
21 May 2016